Praise for

The Lost Cities

"The Drift House books pick up the conversation where Madeleine L'Engle left off, and will inspire any reader to reflect on time and its spiraling possibilities." —*The New York Times Book Review*

"Wild inventiveness." —*Booklist*

"Thrilling. . . . Fans of *Drift House* will clamor for this second installment." —*SLJ*

"Fans of the first book will be mesmerized. . . . A series to place alongside His Dark Materials." —*VOYA*

Praise for

Drift House

A Book Sense Children's Pick
A Best Debut Series Book, KidsReads.com

★ "Thrilling. . . . Readers will flip madly through the many pages of this book to see how the siblings navigate the hazards on the Sea of Time." —*Publishers Weekly*, starred review

"Three plucky kids, a magical house that is also a ship, [and] an eccentric uncle named Farley. . . . In Peck's gifted hands they're so warmly and fully imagined that they seem brand-new." —*The New York Times Book Review*

"[A] spirited adventure." —*Time Out New York Kids*

THE DRIFT HOUSE VOYAGES

Drift House

The Lost Cities

The Lost Cities

A DRIFT HOUSE VOYAGE

DALE PECK

BLOOMSBURY
CHILDREN'S
BOOKS

For Joshua and Sarah,
and Vanessa, Stephen, and Alyssa—
and of course their parents too.

Published by Bloomsbury U.S.A. Children's Books
175 Fifth Avenue, New York, New York 10010
Distributed to the trade by Macmillan

The Library of Congress has cataloged the hardcover edition as follows:
Peck, Dale.
The lost cities: a Drift House voyage / by Dale Peck.—1st U.S. ed.
p.   cm.
Sequel to: Drift House.
Summary: Siblings Susan and Charles receive a mysterious book before leaving to
visit their uncle Farley at his time-traveling house, where they become separated
in the Sea of Time and struggle to find their way home.
ISBN-13: 978-1-58234-859-9 • ISBN-10: 1-58234-859-6 (hardcover)
[1. Time—Fiction. 2. Uncles—Fiction. 3. Brothers and sisters—Fiction.
4. Extinct cities—Fiction.] I. Title.
PZ7.P3338Lo 2007   [Fic]—dc22   2006016139

ISBN-13: 978-1-59990-226-5 • ISBN-10: 1-59990-226-5 (paperback)

Typeset by Westchester Book Composition
Printed in the U.S.A. by Quebecor World Fairfield
2 4 6 8 10 9 7 5 3 1

All papers used by Bloomsbury U.S.A. are natural, recyclable products
made from wood grown in well-managed forests. The manufacturing processes
conform to the environmental regulations of the country of origin.

"O Time your pyramids."
—*Jorge Luis Borges*

PART ONE

Return to Drift House

ONE

Via Messenger

"DID TOO!"

"Did not!"

"Did too!"

"Did not!"

Eduardo Ramirez was the senior doorman of the large apartment building on the corner of 81st Street and Park Avenue. He'd taken the position after returning from the Korean War and recently celebrated his fiftieth year on the job. This gave him leeway to prop the lobby doors open to let in the warm spring air, despite the fact that regulations said the front doors should be "kept closed at all times" so the building's climate-control system could work most efficiently.

Aside from the spring air, the open doors let in the combative voices of a pair of children whose squabbles were as well known to the elderly man as the squeals and honks of traffic.

"You did *too*," the male voice insisted now. "Don't tell me you didn't!"

"I *will* tell you I didn't," the female voice retorted, her voice tinged by a somewhat stilted British accent, "because I did, in fact, *not* do it. And don't tell me not to tell you I didn't!"

"I *can* tell you not to tell me you didn't," the boy shot back a little unsteadily. "And don't tell me not to tell you not to, to—whatever! You *didn't* do it!"

The children appeared in the doorway, a brown-haired, bespectacled boy, somewhat small for his age, and his darker-haired older sister, somewhat tall for hers (ten and almost thirteen, in case you're wondering). Both children wore bulging backpacks, and the girl carried a bag besides: it was the last day of school, and they were bringing their supplies home for the summer.

"I *did* too!" the girl maintained. "I've been telling you *all the way home* I did."

"Did what?" the doorman interjected.

"Did . . . What?" The girl looked up with a confused, slightly embarrassed expression. "Good afternoon, Mr. Ramirez," she said in the politest voice she could muster.

"Susan, Charles," the doorman responded, trying hard to

suppress a grin. "I was just wondering what it was you did—or didn't—do." He nodded at Charles.

Charles averted his eyes to the floor.

"Well, I, um, that is . . ."

"I'm sure it was nothing." The doorman reached beneath the counter where he sat. "A package came for you."

"A package!" Susan exclaimed. "For me?"

"Both of you's actually," the doorman said. He pointed to the handwritten label that had been affixed to the brown-paper bundle with a length of twine:

Susie and Charlie-o-o-Oakenfeld!

"Just in time for your big trip, yes?"

The moment Charles saw the package he couldn't take his eyes from it.

"See," he said, cutting in front of his sister. "It's for *both* of us."

As soon as the thick square object was in his hands, Charles knew there was something unusual about it. For one thing, it wasn't wrapped in paper at all, but in some kind of waxy fabric Charles had never felt before. But it was more than that. The package felt warm in Charles's hands, seemed almost to vibrate. It was as if there were a motor inside, or—well, Charles was going to say, as if it were alive, but he had never seen a living thing that was roughly the size and shape of a small pizza box. Maybe it *was* a pizza?

The coarse twine quartered the package like windowpanes, and Charles had the funny sensation that he wasn't looking at it but *into* it. "This wrapping isn't paper," he said without looking up. "It's sort of like leather."

The doorman watched Charles intently. "I believe it's called oilskin," he suggested quietly.

"And, Charles," Susan said, "there's no address. Just our names." She nudged the package up to look at the bottom. "No return address either." She turned back to the doorman. "Are you sure this came in the mail?"

"Never said it came in the mail. Hand-delivered, this was. By someone who looked enough like you"—he nodded at Charles—"to be your cousin. Dressed kind of funny, like Aladdin. You know, from the movie. Purple vest, funny slippers. Even had a little turban."

"A turban! Susan, do you think it could have been Mar—"

"Why, I'm sure it *was* M-M-Marco. He must have been coming from rehearsals for the summer play." Susan flashed Charles an older-sister look that could have only one meaning: *shut up!* "*Ali Baba and the Forty Thieves.*"

Now she nudged Charles down the carpeted lobby. Her younger brother let himself be pulled along like a puppy on a leash, his eyes transfixed on the package in his hands. When they were in the elevator, Susan stabbed the button for the

14th floor. "Do you know if Murray's home?" she called to the doorman, who stared at them with a placid, almost wistful expression on his face.

"Murray?" he said, as if the name were unfamiliar to him.

The doors slid closed.

If Susan had been less intent on escaping—or if Charles had been able to look up from the warm package he was clutching to his chest—one of them might have noticed the doorman rubbing a thin gold chain that hung around his neck. When the elevator was safely closed, he pulled on the chain, and a heart-shaped locket slid from beneath his vest. Sighing slightly, the old man snapped it open.

A pair of young, determined faces peered up at him, and the man in the doorman's uniform stared down at them for a long moment, then looked at the closed doors of the elevator. His wrinkled eyes were misty, his smile thin and pale.

"Goodbye, Susan," he said in a quiet voice. "Goodbye, Charles."

A half hour later, when Vera Abramowicz came in with her trio of Pekingeses—all four creatures white haired, lilac scented, and adorned with matching blue ribbons—she found the lobby strangely deserted for 4:30 in the afternoon. Following the sound of snores, she located Mr. Ramirez fast asleep in the mailroom, clad only in his socks, boxer shorts, and T-shirt. There was a wedding band on his left hand and a signet ring on his right, a knotted bracelet bearing the names of his three children on his left wrist and a matching watchband on his right. On his neck hung three thick chains, one of which supported an ornate cross. His doorman's uniform was neatly folded on a chair beside him. For weeks after the incident, Mr. Ramirez claimed not to know how he had come to be asleep in the mailroom, and a physical examination at his doctor's office confirmed he was as healthy as a horse. The doorman himself said his drowsiness must have been caused by the heavy lunch he'd eaten that day—*arroz con puerco y frijoles negros*—but for the next several weeks he added a scapular medal of Saint Francis di Girolamo to the assortment of necklaces around his throat. Proof against sorcery, he said to anyone who asked. Sorcery—and disguises.

TWO

Lost Cities

CHARLES HADN'T MANAGED TO UNDO the knot that bound the oilskin package by the time the elevator opened. As they walked down the hall, Susan hissed at him,

"I can*not* believe you, Charles Oakenfeld! You almost gave everything away!"

"Oh relax, Susan." Charles tugged at the string. "You don't think our hundred-year-old doorman is actually going to believe we discovered the Sea of—"

"Sshh!"

At just that moment, the door to their apartment swung halfway open. Charles's head snapped up. Some impulse made him want to hide the mysterious package, but there was neither place nor time.

"I thought I heard your precious voices," their mother said sarcastically. "My dears, if there were a medal for bickering, I would be the proudest parent in the whole building."

"Mum!" Susan said. "What are you doing home so early?"

Mrs. Oakenfeld smiled wanly.

"Brace yourselves. You're in for a bit of a shock." She pushed the door all the way open, revealing the diminutive form of Susan and Charles's younger brother. Murray's visible skin—his forearms and ankles and all of his face and neck—was spotted with angry pink dots.

"Murray!" Charles exclaimed. "Have you got chicken pox?"

"I'm afraid he has. He went for a play date with Davey Peterson on twelve. Apparently they don't vaccinate in South Africa, where he's from. And Murray was supposed to get his vaccination last year when you went up to your uncle's." Their mother shook her head. "Of course, Mrs. Peterson didn't let him stay, but I'm afraid opening the door was all it took—it's so contagious."

Susan looked curiously at her youngest brother. "Davey Peterson? Isn't he the first grader who spends all his time playing with that ant farm? I thought you didn't even *like* him."

Murray didn't meet his sister's gaze. He was too busy staring at the parcel in Charles's hands. Now Mrs. Oakenfeld noticed it too.

"My goodness, Charles, whatever is that enormous package? Is it some sort of end-of-school thing?"

"It *is* the end of school!" Susan said before Charles could answer. "And he *did* receive it today." She chose her words carefully so that, technically at least, she wasn't lying.

"It looks quite impressive. Let's see what it is."

Their mother ushered them into the living room, where she fetched a pair of scissors from the credenza. Before she could snip the twine around the oilskin, however, her phone rang. Frowning at the caller ID, Mrs. Oakenfeld said, "Can't those people get along without me for five minutes?" She handed the scissors to Susan and walked into the study.

Susan couldn't help gloating just the tiniest little bit that her mother had handed the scissors to her. When Charles reached for them, she eluded his hand and deftly slipped the blade under the string and snipped it.

"Voilá," she said. She had gotten an A on her French final that day, the fact of which she looked forward to announcing at dinner.

Charles was about to unfold the oilskin when Murray spoke for the first time.

"I won't be going to Drift House with you."

Susan and Charles looked up with horror.

"Murray, no!" Susan said.

"You *have* to go," Charles said.

"Mum says it's not safe for me to fly when I'm sick—and I could infect other people."

"We'll wait a week or two," Susan said. "It—it just wouldn't be the same without you."

With a gesture the two older Oakenfelds had become very familiar with over the course of the past nine months, Murray reached a hand to his throat and pulled a small golden locket from inside his shirt. He began rubbing it idly as he always did, but then his pockmarked hand strayed to his equally spotted neck and began scratching that instead.

"I'm sorry. I just don't think it's wise." Though he was only five, Murray sounded as though he were the eldest child explaining things to his much younger brother and sister— another circumstance the two older Oakenfeld children had grown used to in the eight months since their first trip to Drift House.

"Murray!" Susan exclaimed. "Did you—did you go to Davey Peterson's on purpose? To get chicken pox, so you wouldn't be able to go to Uncle Farley's?"

Murray half smiled, half shuddered. "That ant farm is the creepiest thing I've ever seen. Davey keeps it on his bedside table, right next to his jaw expander. It makes me have nightmares of ants crawling in and out of my mouth." Still rubbing the locket, he added, "Let's just call it intuition. I think I should stay off the Sea of Time—something I know the two of you will be unable to do."

At the mention of the Sea of Time, a thrill of anticipation ran down Charles's spine. But go without Murray? It just didn't seem right. "Do you—do you remember something?" he asked his little brother now. "A warning from the future?"

As a boy with a scientific bent, it was hard for Charles to make a statement that was so obviously contradictory. Yet as far as he and Susan knew, Murray had somehow journeyed into the future last fall, returning with the golden locket he never took off, along with a haze of memories of things that might—and then again, might not—come to pass. Charles had even crossed paths with an older version of his little brother, who had been sporting a purple vest and turban like the one Mr. Ramirez had described, not to mention a new name: Mario.

Which reminded Charles:

"Murray," he said as he unfolded layer upon layer of oilskin. "Mr. Ramirez said the person who gave this to him was wearing a purple vest and a turban. Do you think it was—"

"Me?" Murray said, as if he'd anticipated the question. "Mario, delivering a message from the future?" He shrugged. "It could have been. There's certainly something about this book that has me all jittery."

"Book!" Susan said. "How did you—oh!"

For Charles had pulled back the last flap of oilskin, revealing the elaborately tooled red leather cover of the biggest book either Oakenfeld had ever seen. Thirteen gold letters had been stamped into the cover:

THE LOST CITIES

"The . . . Lost . . . Cities."

The words came out in a whisper. Susan wasn't sure why she whispered. It just seemed like the kind of thing to say in a respectfully hushed voice. "And look," she went on. "There was some kind of seal or insignia here, but it's been pried off."

It was true: below the title, seven horizontal lines, each shorter than the one above it, had been scored deeply into the cover. They floated in the middle of a guitar pick–shaped patch of leather that was darker than the rest of the cover, as if it had been protected from the elements for many years.

Susan allowed her finger to trace the grooves. Charles almost jerked the book away before Susan could touch it, but he was curious to see how she'd react when she put her finger on it. He studied her face carefully, but she showed no signs of experiencing the warm pulse on his lap. The fact that Susan didn't seem to be feeling what he did filled him with elation, because he was convinced the book really *was* intended for him, no matter whose names had been on the label.

"Also?" Susan pointed out, since Charles was sitting there with a glazed look on his face. "There's a note." And she plucked a card from a fold of the oilskin.

This is all I can give you now.
I look forward to seeing you again.

Susan turned to Murray. He turned his palms up.

"I dunno. I *could* have sent it. I just don't remember."

Susan turned back to Charles, who stroked the book's cover as though it were a half-tame buffalo. "Well, what are you waiting for? Open it!"

Charles was torn. He was aching to see what lay beneath those strangely empty lines. But he also wanted to have that experience all to himself. *He* was the one who felt the tingling, after all. He was the one the book was calling. He should have the privilege of seeing what was inside first.

He reached for a corner, but just as he did Mrs. Oakenfeld walked out of the study. Charles quickly slapped the oilskin back over the book.

"Dr. Amy beeped in," Mrs. Oakenfeld said, sifting through a stack of mail. "She phoned in a prescription for an ointment to help the itching. I'm going to run out and get it—I'll only be a minute." As she picked up her purse, she added four words that struck a pit of terror in Charles's stomach.

"Susan," she said, "you're in charge."

An hour later, when Mrs. Oakenfeld returned, the book had disappeared, and Susan and Charles sat on opposite sides of the living room glaring at each other. Murray sat on a chair between them, playing Game Boy and scratching idly at his rash.

"You'll never guess what happened downstairs," Mrs. Oakenfeld said as she pulled a narrow white drugstore bag from her purse. "Apparently Mr. Ramirez took a nap in the mailroom. He got undressed and—" Mrs. Oakenfeld noticed her children's stony silence for the first time. "Oh dear. Dare I ask?"

"You said I was in charge—"

"Susan was being a bossy—"

Mrs. Oakenfeld held up a hand.

"I don't know what's gotten into you two. Lately you've done nothing but bicker and compete with each other. It's not too late to sign you up for camp, you know. Hiking and swimming and singalongs and all that."

It is a particular sort of child who finds the idea of hiking and swimming—and singalongs!—so unappealing that he or she wants to shriek in horror. As it happens, Susan and Charles were both that sort of child.

"No!" Susan exclaimed.

"Please!" Charles begged.

"We're sorry. We *promise* to get along better."

"Please please *please* let us go to Uncle Farley's for the summer."

"Children," Mrs. Oakenfeld sighed. "I do not want you to be good to avoid being punished. I do not want you to be good so that you can receive rewards. I want you to be good," she stressed, "because it is *the right thing to do*. You are very formidable adversaries. But don't you see that when you work against each other, you just cancel each other out?"

Mrs. Oakenfeld let her words sink in for a moment, then put a hand on Murray's shoulder. "Come along, dear, let's see if we can't do something about that rash. Don't you want to take off that necklace Farley gave you?" she added. "It must be itching your neck awfully."

But Murray, rubbing his locket with one hand and scratching his neck with the other, only said, "It's all right, Mum. I'll keep it on for a while longer."

THREE

The Caretaker

BECAUSE MURRAY WAS ILL AND likely to sleep fitfully, and because Susan and Charles were leaving the following day, Mrs. Oakenfeld put Murray in Susan's room and had Susan bunk with Charles. And because Susan and Charles had reached a stalemate, neither of them opened the book that had been delivered that afternoon—whenever either child approached the oilskin package, the other would glare over fearfully. The final hurdle was whose suitcase to put the book in. Susan finally agreed to let Charles stow it in his backpack, but after he had she took the small lock from her keepsake box and snapped it on the zipper. The key she put on a necklace, which she tucked inside her shirt as Murray did with his locket.

"Your bag, my lock. Now we're even."

The next day was filled with preparations and goodbyes, and before they knew it they were in a taxi. Mr. Ramirez had stowed their bags in the trunk, including Charles's backpack, so Susan and Charles couldn't even examine the mysterious book on the way to the airport.

"Mr. Ramirez," Susan said before they left, "I wonder if the boy who delivered that package yesterday said anything about it."

Mr. Ramirez looked at Susan blankly. "I was sleeping in the afternoon," he said, "but I think you're the one who's dreaming. You didn't have any deliveries yesterday."

Susan peered at Mr. Ramirez's face. He certainly didn't *look* like he was lying. But before she could quiz him further, Mrs. Oakenfeld ushered Susan and Charles into the taxi. She gave Susan money to pay the driver—she was staying home with Murray, and Mr. Oakenfeld had left much earlier on business. She complimented her children on their improved behavior and kissed them both one last time.

"Murray will be along in a week or two, when he's better. Now, you two keep up the good work, and give Farley a hug for me."

Three hours later, as the children's Air Canada flight banked left over Long Island Sound and the FASTEN SEAT-BELTS sign went off, Charles was finally able to pull his back-pack from the overhead compartment. Now the black nylon bag sat on his lap. Charles could feel a warmth on his thighs, a tingling from the object concealed within. All of a sudden he was nervous, so he said,

"I can't believe you made the taxi driver take that dumb detour."

"It wasn't dumb," Susan protested. "A little superstitious, maybe—"

"It was a *tree. Dumb.*"

Susan had to bite her lip to keep her mouth shut, because she didn't really know how to explain her odd sidetrack. Earlier in the spring, she had been shopping downtown with her friends Dehlia Mitchell and Courtney King when they happened upon a tiny garden on the corner of Houston and Bowery. The postage stamp–sized park was dominated by a single enormous tree with delicate needlelike leaves and reddish feathery bark that Susan (to the consternation of her shopping-minded friends) simply *had* to touch. Apparently she wasn't the only person to be lured in by the great tree: an informational placard mounted on a stake told her that the object of her fascination was a young redwood. While Dehlia and Courtney chatted about what they wanted at Urban Outfitters, Susan read that the trees were both the world's tallest *and* oldest living things, capable of reaching heights of more than 350 feet and ages exceeding three thousand years.

"Um, Earth to Susan," Charles said. "Sister Susan? Get your

head out of the trees." He tapped on the window. "It's already in the clouds."

Susan sniffed. "You should care about that tree more than I do. Its very existence is a *scientific* phenomenon."

"It's a *tree*."

"Redwoods couldn't grow in the Northeast until very recently. The winters were too long and harsh. But global warming has made it possible for them to survive here. Don't you think that's interesting?"

"What*ever*," Charles said. He pointed to the bag in his lap. "I'm much more interested in what's in here. Give me the key."

Susan returned Charles's stare with a thin-lipped smile. "Maybe we should wait till after lunch. We don't want to spill anything on Mario's book."

"I'm sure we can manage," Charles said dryly. "I was up all night wondering about it, and I heard you tossing and turning too. Come on, let's—"

Charles broke off. His eyes narrowed to slits.

"You . . . forgot . . . the . . . key." He said the words very slowly, as if willing Susan to contradict him. "Didn't . . . you?"

"I didn't *forget* it. I took it off when I was showering and—"

"YOU! FORGOT! THE! KEY!"

"Charles! Keep your voice down!"

"I will NOT keep my voice down! I am so tired of this, Susan Oakenfeld. Everyone thinks *you're* the responsible one, just because *you're* three years older and speak in a phony-baloney

English accent. Mum gives *you* the scissors to cut the string, Mum gives *you* the money to pay the cabdriver. But YOU! RUIN! EVERYTHING!"

Charles's voice was so loud that a flight attendant abandoned her trolley and marched toward them.

"Young man, I'm going to have to ask you to keep it down."

Charles was normally a quiet boy. Even in science, where he was the top student, he blushed and stammered if he was called to speak out loud. But now he seemed completely fearless. Clutching the bag in his lap, he exclaimed, "See! *Susan* messes up, and *I* get in trouble! Fine! I won't say anything else for the Whole! ENTIRE! FLIGHT!"

He was as good as his word. But the moment the two Oakenfeld children stepped onto the jetway in Quebec, his mouth flew open.

"So what are you going to do about this?"

Susan glanced to her left and right as theatrically as possible.

"Is someone speaking? I thought I heard a voice. Excuse me, sir," she said, tapping a man on the elbow. "Did you say something?"

"Be serious!" Charles said, even as the man murmured something about "*les Americaines*" and hurried away. "How do you plan on opening this lock?"

"I don't know why *I*—"

"Why?" Charles held up his backpack. "Because *you* were

the one who locked it, and *you* were the one who forgot to bring the key."

"I wouldn't have had to lock it," Susan said, "if I could trust you not to sneak a look at it and—and break it or something!"

"How do you *break* a book?"

"Well, you broke the lock on the drawing room door in Drift House last fall!"

"What does *that* have to do with anything?"

"I just thought that since you're so good with breaking locks you could find a way to pick it or—"

Susan's words—and her forward movement—were both halted abruptly when she ran into a pair of long, thin (and slightly smelly) legs. She looked up—and up, and up—to see a grizzled face glowering down at her.

"Picket what?" the incredibly distant face said. "Picket fences? Pick it up? Or pick-it a lock?"

"I'm s-s-sorry, sir. I didn't see you."

The man stared down at Susan for an uncomfortable moment, then nodded. He was bald on top but had long stringy gray hair fringing his ears and straggling past his shoulders.

"Yup. Too busy arguing with Charlie-o to see where you're going. That's Susan all right. Well, give it here." And the man held out a dirty hand capped by the longest, sharpest nails either child had ever seen.

Susan and Charles looked at each other hesitantly. Charles was the first to recover his manners.

"Ch-Ch-Charles Oakenfeld, sir," he said, shaking the man's hand.

The tall stranger took firm hold of Charles's right hand, and then, without letting go, bent over and snatched Charles's backpack with his left. But instead of running off with it, the man held the bag up to his eyes and squinted at the lock on the zipper. And then he did the strangest thing either child had ever seen (and these children had seen their fair share of strangeness). There, in the Quebec airport, surrounded by dozens of perfectly normal-looking people heading home or away on vacation or business, the tall dirty smelly stranger pulled his hand from Charles's and began biting his nails.

Just one nail, Charles realized after a moment: the one capping the longest finger on his right hand. He went at it intently, stopping to pull his finger from his mouth periodically to check his progress. Susan and Charles could only stare in fascinated horror.

" 'At should do it," the man said finally. And he spat a bit of nail onto the floor.

Susan and Charles looked at each other. Do what? they both wondered.

The answer wasn't long in coming. The man brought the jagged end of his bitten nail to the lock Susan had put on Charles's suitcase and deftly slipped it into the keyhole. He twisted his hand and the lock popped open with a thin *snap*.

"There you go," the man said, handing the open lock to Susan, the bag to Charles. "Problem solved."

Susan and Charles continued to stare at the man, dumbfounded. Finally Susan managed to swallow the lump out of her throat.

"Please, sir. Who—well, who *are* you?"

"Who *am* I?" The man sounded hurt that the children didn't know. "What, and after lighting your fires for three months you don't remember me? And doing the grocery shopping so's Applethwaite could fix you three squares a day plus snacks? Name's Zenubian, *of course*." And then, with a wink so tiny Charles thought he might have imagined it, the man— Mr. Zenubian—added, "What did you think, I was *invisible* or something?"

FOUR

The Charles Force

THE DRIVE FROM QUEBEC TOOK the rest of the afternoon, and after staring out the window for a while first Charles and then Susan fell asleep. The sound of crunching gravel woke Charles from disturbing visions of deserts and forests. On the opposite seat, Susan was stretched out. Judging from the expression on her face, her dreams were as tumultuous as Charles's. Her tongue filled up her cheek—a habit she had worked hard to break in the last nine months—and Charles smiled tenderly at this pre–Drift House innocence. He did love his older sister, even if she could be a bit bossy. He recalled all their recent quarrels with some anguish, as well as their promise to their mother to try to get along. If only older sisters didn't have to make everything so *hard*.

When he sat up he realized instantly they were on the last stretch of road before Drift House. A low stone wall ran on the left side of the road. Beyond the wall a wild forest sprawled up the side of a steep hill beyond which nothing was visible—just the sort of natural screen to hide a house that occasionally went for a trip out to sea. The coniferous fir and pine trees were dark and thick, but the deciduous oaks and maples were still thin leaved and delicate looking, their pale spring foliage only lightly tinted by chlorophyll. Charles was more interested in electronics than botany, but still, they were good, specific words, and, without thinking, he whispered them aloud.

"Chlorophyll. Deciduous. Coniferous."

On the other seat, Susan's eyes fluttered open. She peered at Charles blearily.

"What did you call me?"

Charles frowned, and used his tongue to stick out the side of his cheek. But even as he did so he wondered where all this antagonism came from. It seemed to get worse and worse the closer they got to—

"Drift House!" Susan said, sitting up.

It wasn't the house she'd seen, just the arched iron gate with its coat of arms at the crest. The crossed swords, and the Viking ship they now knew was the Captain Quoin and his

Time Pirates' *Chronos*, and the parrot on its sail: Xerxes, the great-grandfather of their very own parrot, President Wilson. A sense of boundless possibility fueled both children, but as they turned through the gates a harsh voice cut through their reverie.

"It's a foolish mind that confuses a thing with the sign for it. Drift House is still a mile behind these gates."

It seemed to Susan that Mr. Zenubian deliberately slowed to prolong the agony; on the other side of Charles's glasses, the tangle of trees and vines grew blurry, and he took off his lenses and cleaned them on his shirt. Bits of blue flashed between the branches. Pebbles snapped beneath the tires. And then:

"I see it!" both children exclaimed.

As the car descended the hill, the ancient ivy-covered structure shimmered into view. To Charles, it was bits and pieces: the cannons poking through the balustrade, the parrot-shaped weathervane atop the solarium, the window through which he had watched Susan vanish beneath the sea in the mermaids' golden bubble. To Susan, it was a hollow outline, flat decks, sharp prow, boat shaped. But to both children it felt magical: filled with mystery and adventure.

"Pshaw," came the jarring voice in the front seat. "Not a thread of smoke in sight. Can't the useless man even put a log on the grate?"

Well, that part didn't feel so magical.

Susan was out first and dashing up the gravel path, Charles

following quickly after. But halfway up the path he stopped. He'd suddenly remembered his backpack.

He'd remembered the book *inside* his backpack.

Mr. Zenubian had opened the trunk and the children's several bags stood on the driveway. Charles didn't want this unknown man to be handling a gift his time-traveling brother had gone to so much trouble to deliver. And so, glancing one more time at Drift House, he hurried back toward the driveway.

"I'll help," he said as he drew close to the tall, thin, smelly stranger.

"It's more than the other one offered. But that's girls for you, right, Charles?"

Just a few hours ago Charles had complained that Susan never let him do anything. But now he heard himself saying: "I hate girls!"

Mr. Zenubian handed Charles his backpack. "Older sisters is the worst kind of girls. Ain't that right, Charles?"

In his eagerness to reclaim his backpack Charles didn't notice that Mr. Zenubian had given Charles the one piece of luggage he wanted to carry. But as he did so, the caretaker looked Charles straight in the eye.

"Don't let her take it from you, Charles."

Charles stumbled backward a step. "Wh-what?"

"It's yours, Charles. Don't let her take it."

Mr. Zenubian didn't say what "it" was. He kept his eyes

fixed on Charles, and even though Charles found him creepy and mysterious, there was also something trustworthy in the directness of his stare. But to trust him more than Susan?

Just then Susan's voice echoed across the lawn.

"Uncle Farley!"

Charles turned and saw the figure of their uncle filling up the open doorway to Drift House. Miss Applethwaite's cooking had obviously added a few pounds to his already stout figure.

He glanced back at Mr. Zenubian, but the caretaker ignored Charles, as if the previous conversation had not taken place. And in Charles's head it already felt a little dreamy. Something about Susan? Taking something? Had he dreamed it in the car?

Mr. Zenubian had hoisted all the bags and now pushed past Charles, nearly knocking him down.

"Well? Is it helping, or is it just going to stand there all day?" And he stalked toward the house, his scarecrow form wavering beneath so much weight.

Charles shook his head to clear it. He turned, and there was Uncle Farley, his arms still clasped around Susan.

"Uncle Farley, Uncle Farley!" Charles shouted. And, strapping his backpack on, he ran across the lawn.

There were hugs and handshakes and more hugs and hot tea and still more hugs, and in the background the heavy tread of Mr. Zenubian's dirty boots as he carried the children's bags—all except Charles's backpack—up to the second floor. When he'd finished he appeared in the doorway to the music room, where the children and their uncle were enjoying fragrant pots of mint tea. The caretaker's lanky dark frame filled up the doorway like a tattered curtain.

"If that'll be all, I'll be catching up on my *regular* duties."

"Oh, ah, yes," Uncle Farley said. "Thank you so much for volunteering to pick up Susan and Charles. I'm not sure I could've even found the airport."

"Just follow the planes," Mr. Zenubian said. He vanished from view, a faint "Volunteering—hah!" lingering behind him, along with the manure-y odor of his shoes.

No one said anything until his heavy footsteps gave way to the slam of the front door. Then:

"Uncle Farley!" Susan practically yelled. "Who *is* he?"

Uncle Farley smiled weakly. "Mr. Zenubian, of course."

"We were here for more than three months last year," Charles said, "and we never saw him once. I thought he was like Miss Applethwaite. Did he just . . . appear?"

"That about sums it up. I looked out my window and there he was. Planting tulip bulbs."

"But, but," Susan stammered, "how can you know it's really him?"

Uncle Farley shrugged. "I can't see how it *couldn't* be him. He knows all there is to know about Drift House, and he seems to get an enormous amount of work done in no time at all, just like Miss Applethwaite—"

"Have you seen *her*?" Charles interrupted.

"No, no sign of her, though the dumbwaiter still works as splendidly as ever. Crumpet, Susan?"

Susan reached for the steaming buttered muffin.

Uncle Farley helped himself to a crumpet as well. "My guess is that taking Drift House onto the Sea of Time unleashed some sort of, I don't know, energy or force or something. This is obviously not standard physics we're talking about. It's more akin to—"

"Magic?" Charles suggested.

Uncle Farley nodded sheepishly at his nephew. "We're men of science, Charles. I prefer to think of it as something undiscovered, or unexplained. Perhaps they'll name it after you one day—the Charles Force."

Last fall Susan had grown used to the fact that Charles and Uncle Farley shared certain interests she did not. But still, she felt it best to nip this "men of science" and "Charles Force" stuff in the bud.

"Ahem. The important question is, does this mean Mr. Zenubian has to come with us when we go on"—she dropped her voice—"the Sea of Time?"

Uncle Farley tried to suppress a grin. "And what makes you think we'll be making any visits to the Sea of Time? Our last trip nearly ended in disaster."

"Uncle Farley!" Charles and Susan said at the same time.

Charles went on, "Why, if you try to stop us, I'll lock you in your bedroom and take the house out myself. I—I'll unleash the Charles Force on you!"

Charles's voice was so forceful that the conversation came to a brief, sharp stop. Stroking the bag in his lap, Charles tried to make a joke of it all.

"Avast ye maties," he said in his best imitation of a pirate accent. "I'll make ye walk the plank, I will."

Susan looked at Charles funny, then grabbed her uncle's knee.

"Where *should* we go, Uncle Farley?" Susan said.

"When?" Charles threw in. He felt a tingle on his legs from Mario's book and said, "Can we go—"

"Let's not get ahead of ourselves, children," Uncle Farley interrupted Charles. "It's very late, and here I am spoiling your dinner with savories. Let's get you settled and properly fed, and in the morning we can map out a few plans. Remember, we have all summer."

Susan, remembering a comment Pierre Marin had made when they left him on the Island of the Past, said, "We have all the time in the world."

Charles frowned. He'd remembered the same comment, and had wanted to say it himself.

Uncle Farley, seeing the charged look pass between brother and sister, stood up abruptly.

"All right then. What shall we have for dinner?"

"Spaghetti," Susan said immediately.

"Hamburgers," Charles said at exactly the same time.

Uncle Farley smiled wanly at his niece and nephew.

"I think we'd better have both."

FIVE

Caught in the Act

WHEN CHARLES AWAKENED THE FOLLOWING morning, he glanced over instinctively to see if Murray was still asleep. But the other bed was empty—Murray was still in New York. Charles wondered what had made his brother so afraid of Drift House that he'd deliberately given himself chicken pox. Suddenly it occurred to him that a clue leading to the answer might be contained in Mario's book. And Susan and Uncle Farley were in bed as well! This was his chance to look at it privately.

Jumping out of bed, he dashed toward his dresser. He stopped dead in his tracks after only two steps.

The backpack wasn't there.

"Noooooooooooo!"

Charles's cry of despair preceded him as he ran down the hall toward Susan's room. "You can't look at it without me! You can't! You can't!"

But instead of finding Susan curled up with the book, Charles found her still asleep. The most incriminating thing in her arms—Charles had to squint, because he'd forgotten his glasses—was her doll, Victor Win-Win.

Susan started upright. Then, seeing it was only Charles, she relaxed. As nonchalantly as she could, she slipped Victor Win-Win under the blanket.

"Whatever are you going on about, Charles?"

"The book! It's not in my room. I thought you must have taken it, but . . ."

As Charles's voice faded away, Susan's attention sharpened. The children looked at each other with the same thought in their heads.

"Mr. Zenubian!"

Charles dashed toward the stairs, Susan running after him. As he ran past Uncle Farley's bedroom, the door opened and the disheveled head of their uncle appeared.

"Here now. What's all the commo—"

"The book, the book!" was all Charles had time to say as he trampled down the stairs.

"He's taken the book!" Susan threw in, galloping after her brother.

"What book?" Uncle Farley said, knotting his robe and

looking about for his left slipper (which, as it happened, was on his right foot). "Who's taken it?"

The children were too preoccupied to answer. First Charles and then Susan bounded into the music room. Susan nearly knocked her brother down, because Charles had pulled up short at the sight of the tall, dirty (and slightly blurry) figure attempting to stuff the oilskin package into Charles's backpack.

From somewhere down in his belly, a deep voice rumbled out of Charles: "Drop it!"

His right hand had gone to his left hip, as if reaching for a sword, and somewhat sheepishly, he pretended to scratch an itch.

"Mr. Zenubian!" Susan said behind him. "What were you doing with Charles's bag?"

"Er, what?" Mr. Zenubian looked down at the backpack in his left hand, the package in his right, as if surprised to see them. "Why, I, uh, I was just unpacking it. Part of my duties."

It was true that someone (or, in Drift House's case, something) had unpacked the children's things yesterday, just as it— er, he, or she—had done last September. But Susan had always assumed Miss Applethwaite attended to those kinds of tasks.

Taking advantage of the children's momentary silence, Mr. Zenubian stood up straight. A note of wounded pride crept into his voice. Roughly shoving the oilskin package into the backpack, he said, "If you'll excuse me, I'll just be taking this up to your room now."

"No!" Charles said, and he leapt forward and took hold of the backpack. "I'll do it!"

Just then Uncle Farley shuffled into the room. His left slipper was on the proper foot, but his right foot was bare, and his toes curled away from the chilly floorboards.

"All right now. What could *possibly* be worth making so much noise over at this—" His voice broke off when he saw Charles and Mr. Zenubian holding opposite sides of Charles's backpack. Charles was blinking up at the caretaker with a frightened but determined look on his face, and Mr. Zenubian was looking down at Charles with something that was *not quite* a snarl curling up one side of his mouth.

Behind his glasses, Uncle Farley's sleepy eyes suddenly came into sharp focus. "What is going on here?"

For the first time in his life, Charles wished Susan could be her usual blabbermouth self and come up with a good explanation for what they were doing. But Susan was beginning to suspect she'd followed Charles under an incorrect assumption, and held her tongue.

"Well, ah," Charles said finally, "when I woke up my backpack wasn't in my room. And when I came down here I found Mr. Zenubian going through it, and—"

"Going *through* it?" The caretaker cut Charles off. "Putting away things you spoiled children is too lazy to put away yourself is more like it."

"Please, Mr. Zenubian," Uncle Farley said. "There's no

need to add insult to injury. Now then, Charles. Are you sure you brought your bag up to your room last night? I seem to recall you setting it on that table when you came in yesterday evening."

Charles racked his brain, but couldn't remember. But he would never have left something as valuable as Mario's book just lying around. Would he? *Did* he?

"Well, um, I think I, I mean, I'm not exactly sure—"

"I'm afraid it was here all night, Charles."

Everyone started at this new voice, whose minuscule speaker now stepped out from behind a chair.

"President Wilson!" Susan said—a little guiltily, because she was realizing she'd never asked after his whereabouts the night before.

The century-old parrot scratched the side of his red cheek with one foot, but before he could say something, Mr. Zenubian exclaimed,

"See! 'Twas here all night! And the boy's accusing me of thievery when all I was doing was trying to put it away!"

"Charles's bag *was* here all night," President Wilson said, "but you were hardly trying to put it away. You looked at that book for a good half hour, and when you heard Charles coming, you hastened to cover your tracks. That's not 'thievery.' But it *is* sneaky."

"Sneaky! This from a bird what was spying on *me*?"

"I won't apologize for it. Farley is a trusting man, but I find your sudden appearance perplexing, and your failure to offer a satisfactory explanation makes me suspicious."

"Please," Uncle Farley cut in. "It's very early. No one's even had breakfast yet. Why don't we have a bite to eat and then we can discuss this civilly?"

"Pah! You and your 'bites to eat.' I'll not be eating anything— or doing another stitch of work for that matter—until bird and boy both offer me apologies!"

"And I'll not apologize," President Wilson retorted, "until *you* can explain why you were poring over Charles's book with such interest."

Uncle Farley turned to Charles. "What book is this everyone keeps referring to?"

"Mar—" Charles began, but Susan cut him off.

"It's just some old book Charles got," she said, glowering at her brother.

Throughout this conversation Charles and Mr. Zenubian had been holding on to Charles's backpack, which contained the book in question. But now the bigger man suddenly pushed it away. Charles stumbled backward and nearly fell.

"And what would I be wanting with Mario's old book anyway?" Mr. Zenubian said. "I just noticed it had some pretty pictures in it is all."

At this comment, even a man as diplomatic as Uncle Farley looked at Mr. Zenubian a little skeptically. The latter man looked as though he was still wearing yesterday's clothes, and yesterday's dirt besides. He didn't give the impression of a man drawn to "pretty pictures" at all.

"I've offered you free rein of the library and my study, and you've never taken me up on it before. What was so interesting about this particular book?"

Mr. Zenubian looked at his audience like a cornered animal. He crouched down slightly, and began to back away. "I'll not be accused by the likes of you!"

"No one wants to accuse you of anything, Mr. Zenubian," Uncle Farley said. "But your actions are often mysterious. All we ask is that you tell us what's going on."

"I told you! It was just the pictures that caught my eye."

"Inside the backpack? Wrapped up in . . . is that oilskin?"

"It seemed to *me*," President Wilson added, "that you knew what you were looking for before you even opened Charles's bag."

"Enough! I tell you I won't be treated this way. I quit!"

The caretaker's words hung in the air for a moment. Then, pivoting on his heel, he marched heavily to the French windows and strode outside. He slammed the window so hard behind him that it bounced open again, rattling the glass. It was only after he was gone that Susan and Charles noticed the weather beyond the open door.

It was raining.

SIX

The Drawing Room

THE OPEN FRENCH WINDOW CREAKED on its hinges. A hint of breeze carried the smell of wet into the room. Outside, a steady rain was falling, and wisps of fog snaked over the great lawn down to the Bay of Eternity, pink hued in the light of the rising sun. For a long time no one moved.

The first time Susan and Charles had come to stay with their uncle, they had awakened to a blanketing fog and rain that swept Drift House onto the Sea of Time, an adventure from which they had narrowly escaped with their lives. During that first voyage, the Oakenfelds had defeated the mermaid Queen Octavia and, with the help of Pierre Marin, the man who had originally built Drift House, repaired the two radios that piloted the house through space and time. The children and their uncle had returned from that voyage with the assurance from Pierre Marin that Drift House could never again be taken onto the Sea of Time without its occupants' permission.

Right?

The sight of the rain held Charles and Susan transfixed. It was nothing like that first deluge, which was so thick not a glimpse of land had been visible. The children could see the patio wall, the lawn, scattered trees, the Bay of Eternity in the distance. But still . . . What if . . . ?

Uncle Farley cleared his throat. "What am I thinking? The damp is going to throw the harpsichord out of tune."

He hurried to the open window with a one-slippered shuffle. The latch settled into its groove with a definite click.

"Uncle Farley," Susan said when her uncle had turned back to the room. "You don't think . . ." She let her voice trail off, and nodded at the rain.

Uncle Farley laughed, the first easy moment since the ugly scene with Mr. Zenubian.

"It's just rain, dear Susan. I'm afraid it's been a wet spring up here. Nothing to worry about other than mud and mosquitoes. Now then, Charles. What is this book of yours that's causing so much commotion?"

"It's not Charles's!" Susan cut in before her brother could answer. "It's both of ours."

Charles glared at his sister—he'd been going to say the same thing, but Susan made it seem like he was some kind of hog, or even a thief.

"We think Mar—" Charles broke off, suddenly remembering that Uncle Farley didn't know about Murray's older version. "I mean, someone delivered it to our apartment in New York. Murray thinks it came from the Sea of Time." That seemed safe enough.

"Really?" Uncle Farley's eyes lit up. He joined Charles on the sofa. President Wilson hopped on the sofa's back, and Susan had to content herself with looking over the boys' shoulders.

Charles pulled back the oilskin. The book had a presence in the room like another person. It filled everyone's nose with the rich warm smell of leather, a drier tang of old paper. The gilt letters seemed to wink in the early-morning murk, whereas the deeply impressed grooves below the title seemed to suck up what little light there was.

"*The Lost Cities*," Uncle Farley read and, as Susan had done in New York, he ran his finger over the letters and the seven hollow lines beneath them. Charles watched his face closely, but Uncle Farley didn't give any sign that he felt the tingle Charles felt through his pajamas. The book was warm on his lap, like a baby or a puppy, but the feeling was more than physical. Charles knew—he just knew—the book was speaking to him alone.

Uncle Farley reached for the upper right corner of the cover.

"You know what, Uncle Farley?" Charles was startled by the sound of own voice. "Let's wait to look at this till we've gotten dressed and, um, had breakfast. I know it sounds funny, but I don't feel right looking at this in my pajamas. And, um"—he blinked rapidly, to draw attention to his eyes—"I need my glasses."

Never one to turn down a meal, Uncle Farley said, "Good point, Charles." He held up his one bare foot with a chuckle. "I commend your sense of decorum."

They left the book in the music room as they went upstairs. Charles didn't want to let it out of his sight, of course, but the look Susan flashed him said she wasn't going to let him alone with it. Uncle Farley asked President Wilson to "sit watch" over the book. The parrot seemed to take Uncle Farley's request literally. He hopped onto the oilskin as though it were a nest, and murmuring something about having been "up all night," promptly went to sleep.

Later, during breakfast, Uncle Farley seemed distracted, getting up from the table several times and walking to the windows. At first Susan and Charles wondered if he were worried about the weather, despite what he'd said earlier. But the rising sun burned away the clouds, and lent further proof that the rain was entirely normal. Then, before he'd cleaned his plate, Uncle Farley suddenly muttered, "Excuse me," and hurried out of the room. A moment later, a faint voice trickled into the room:

"Oh. My. Word."

The same lightbulb went off over Susan and Charles's heads.

"The drawing room!"

"What? What?" President Wilson started from sleep with a flurry of feathers. "Where is the scoundrel? I'll scratch his eyes out!"

"Guard the book!" Susan called to the parrot as she hurried out of the room.

"I am not a serv—" But the children were already gone.

From the hallway the children could see strange lights pulsing through the drawing room door. When they actually entered the room, they pulled up short. The room's walls were undulating in a way they'd never seen before: here an iceberg, there a wall of water, here a snowcapped mountain, there a massive sandy pyramid. It was like being in a movie theater with screens on all four walls. There were desert expanses on one side and solid clots of forest on another, wide stretches of dark open water over here and endless, empty expanses of blue sky over there. Strange houses with grass growing on their roofs alternated with cities of pale buildings that looked like they were made from dried mud. Something was on fire here, and clouds of smoke seemed to sting the children's eyes, while over there an almost perfectly circular island sank beneath the sea.

It was this last that caught Charles's eye. Perhaps jogged by the book in the music room, he said, "Is that . . . Atlantis?"

But even as he said it, the island was gone. Then, on the opposite wall, there was a burst of color so bright it painted everyone's face orange and red. A volcano was erupting in a wall of lava, and at its base rested a city of red brick and white pillars.

"Pompeii!" Susan exclaimed. But even as she said its name, the city was gone.

There was another city, this one surrounded by a wall, inside of which Charles spied an enormous horse, and then it too seemed to dissolve in flames.

"Troy!"

"Lost cities," Uncle Farley breathed quietly. "They're all lost cities. But why?"

There were other cities, some of which were no more than little camps, others that seemed so magical and splendid it was hard to believe they were of our world. Uncle Farley spotted the hard ones: Timbuktu, the ancient capital of West Africa, and the Arizona cliff dwellings of the Anasazi, and Tenochtitlán, the Aztec metropolis that now lies beneath Mexico City. Charles recognized Machu Picchu, the last home of the Incas. Susan guessed that a tiny stand of cabins was the lost colony of Roanoke. Everyone recognized the Easter Island statues, and the atomic bomb exploding over Hiroshima. And then there was another image that was even more familiar, though far, far more distressing.

"Uncle Farley!" Susan said. "It's the, it's the—" She couldn't say it.

"It's the twin towers," Charles said. His voice was cold and flat. It reminded Susan of Murray's voice, since he'd gone to the future and come back.

The horrific image grew and grew, until the two silver spires filled up opposite walls of the room. Smoke billowed from broken windows, shrouding the walls of the drawing room a uniform gray, and Susan actually coughed. The quality of the color thickened, seemed almost to dampen, and without quite knowing when it had happened the onlookers realized the smoke had turned to fog. And, also without understanding, the three people in the room sensed that the strange, overwhelming show was over.

"Uncle Farley," Susan said. "Do you think we'll go—we have to go—to all those places? Even—" She shuddered at the memory of the last image.

Uncle Farley didn't answer her. He walked over to a side table with a distracted expression on his face. There was a piece of pottery on a stand, into which the smooth contours of a woman's face had been impressed. The face was haunting—empty, blank eyed, yet searching for something.

"It's from Pompeii," Uncle Farley said quietly.

"Really!" Susan reached a hand toward the face, but Uncle Farley was still speaking.

"It's a death mask."

Susan jerked her finger back. "That was put on a dead person's face?"

"Not exactly. She was alive at first. It's lava. It vitrified around the woman instantly, preserving her face for eternity."

"Vitrified? That sounds like a word for"—she turned toward the door—"you, Charles. Charles?"

But she was speaking to empty air. Charles was gone.

SEVEN

Up a Tree (Without a Paddle)

CHARLES OAKENFELD WAS TWO MONTHS past his tenth birthday. Already in his short life he had been to Rome, London, and Austin, Texas, not to mention the Bay of Eternity, the Sea of Time, and the Island of the Past. He'd ridden the world's tallest Ferris wheel at the Millennium Fair, built homemade telephones and radios out of spare parts, and even figured out how to operate a flying carpet all by himself. But he had never climbed a tree.

He didn't know why climbing a tree was the first thing he thought of when he crept out of the house with the mysterious book in his backpack. The idea had come to him while he was watching the show on the drawing room walls, and as soon as

Uncle Farley and Susan got caught up with that creepy clay mask he had slipped out. It seemed to him Mario's book practically shivered with excitement as he stowed it in his backpack. He could feel it tingling against his shoulderblades as though wings were sprouting from his back. Maybe it was the image of wings, but Charles just *had* to get up high. If only he knew where Uncle Farley had stowed the flying carpet! But, in its absence, he settled for a tree.

Using the low garden wall for cover, he made his way toward the forested hills that ringed Drift House. Charles could see Mr. Zenubian's handiwork all over the place: tender green shoots stuck up out of a layer of thinly spread manure, which smelled almost sweet in the open air. He wondered who would manage the grounds now that the caretaker was gone. And where had the caretaker come from anyway? A vague feeling tickled the back of his brain, as though he had unfinished business with the strange, creepy, but compelling old man. But what? Charles couldn't remember.

Using a budding maple as cover, he turned back toward the house. It looked quiet, almost lonely. The cannons gleamed on the upper deck, and on either side of the building the calm waters of the Bay of Eternity glittered like diamond paste.

In the back of his head, Charles heard a voice. *Don't let her take it.* Charles didn't like this voice, yet he couldn't ignore it. And Susan *was* always taking things from him—taking all the credit for things they'd done together. If he opened Mario's book in front of her, she was sure to say *she* had figured it out, and since she was oldest and spoke in that hoity-toity accent, everyone would believe *her* version of things. They *always* did. Well, Charles was tired of coming in second place. It was his turn. And, squashing any further doubts, he turned and climbed higher uphill.

Fallen needles muffled his footsteps. The forest was eerily silent—no birds singing, none of the deer the children had seen so often last fall. Charles felt terribly alone, but excited too. He *was* equal to this challenge. He *would* do it on his own.

A thick branch barred his path. He was about to clamber over, when he glanced at the tree it was connected to. The branch sloped gently upward to a thick trunk about fifteen feet above his head: it couldn't have looked any more like a staircase unless it had had a banister and a sign: *climb here.*

The branch swayed lightly beneath his weight. As if he'd been doing it all his life, Charles shuffled up on his hands and feet. The tree's bark was deeply scored, offering plenty of hand- and toeholds. In a moment he was at the trunk. It reared up like a blank wall, blocking his way. It was so wide he couldn't see around it on either side.

"Well, now what?"

Since he couldn't go left or right, Charles looked up. There was a branch a few feet above his head. His fingers grazed the bottom of it if he stood on tiptoe. He could jump and grab it easily—if his fingers slipped, however, it was a long way down. But Charles didn't feel he was high enough yet, and so, tucking his glasses in his pocket, he took a deep breath and jumped. His fingers curled around the branch, and his feet walked up the trunk and he hooked his right ankle over the branch, then his left. For a moment he hung upside down like a giant sloth. He looked at the ground far below him, but didn't feel afraid. (The blurriness caused by his lack of glasses might have helped with that.) The truth was he felt like laughing—it was so *good* to be up so high, alone with his book. He wanted to go even higher.

It took a little shimmying to twist on top of the branch, but soon enough he'd done it. After that it was easy: branches poked from the trunk with ladderlike regularity. Charles climbed higher and higher. When he felt he'd reached the last branch that could safely support his weight, he turned and sat with his legs straddling the limb beneath him. His back was against the trunk, which, even at this great height, was still wider than his body. About twelve inches in front of him was a convenient fork that made a perfect strut to rest his bag on.

Charles felt a tickle of excitement when he thought what his parents would say if they knew how high he'd climbed. Still, no matter how many unspoken rules he'd broken, he was a prudent boy, and he tied the straps of his backpack to the two forks of the branch. Only when he was sure he'd made a secure resting place did he unzip the bag and pull out Mario's book.

For the first time he traced the edges of the golden letters, let his fingers trail over the ridges of the seven scored lines beneath the title. An electric buzz tingled beneath his fingertips. It was just strong enough that Charles instinctively pulled his hand back. He was sure Susan and Uncle Farley couldn't have felt such a charge without showing it, and this made him even more certain he really did have a special relationship with Mario's book. That his brother had sent it from the future with a special message for him alone.

Charles reached for the cover. He half expected something to stop him, as something had stopped him every other time he'd tried to open it. But the forest remained silent, as if it too was waiting to see what lay beneath those seven empty lines. Sucking in a breath and holding it, Charles lifted the thick piece of tooled leather . . .

. . . and immediately let his breath out in a gasp. Charles didn't know what he'd expected to see, but he was completely mystified by what appeared: a double spread of swirly muted pastels, pinks, greens, pale browns. Charles stared at the pages for a long time, trying to decipher a pattern in the swirls, and then, with a sheepish start, realized he was just looking at the book's marbled endpapers. Laughing at himself, he turned to the next page . . .

. . . and gasped again. But this time there was a real picture before his eyes. It seemed to be painted, yet it was more vivid than any photograph Charles had ever seen. The two pages depicted nothing more than a large field of grass, but each blade was so distinctly realized the image seemed almost miraculous. Charles could see the seams running down the center of each stalk, could make out bug bites and bits of brown and even the infinitesimally small hairs that lined their edges. Only after he'd marveled at the technical skill that had gone into the painting did Charles notice that the field wasn't completely smooth. A series of low oblong mounds jutted from the ground in a regular pattern, and as Charles looked at them, the answer to what the mounds were seemed to pop into his head.

They were graves.

Charles was surprised at his reaction to this realization. He wasn't scared, or sad, or grossed out. Instead he felt a stillness, a cool spot in his stomach that acknowledged what he was seeing but didn't get overwhelmed by it. He looked at the picture one last time, then turned the page.

And gasped a third time.

For a walled garden filled the pages before him. No tree or flower was the same as any other, nor were any of them recognizable to Charles. Each and every one was lush and green and perfect—not a bit of rust marred a single leaf in the entire picture. The plants were blooming if they bore flowers and heavy laden with red or yellow or purple orbs if they bore fruit. At the center of the image was one tree, smaller than many of the others, but irresistibly luminous. As Charles stared into its dense foliage he could see each leaf, each twig, the flakings of bark and the little holes insects had drilled in search of food and birds had widened in search of insects. But what he couldn't quite make out was the scattered fruit that hung from the tree. Every one was partially hidden by leaves and branches, as if the fruit itself—gold, not red, and egg shaped, with a pink blush on the sunny side—were shy, or coy. Tempting. Yes, that was the word. Tempting. Charles put his finger on the page and stroked the curved skin of one of them. Though the picture itself was smaller than his fingertip, he could feel the heft of the fruit, its weight, its shape, as if he'd already pulled it off the branch and was bringing it to his mouth.

With a start, Charles jerked his finger back. The sound of his own nervous laughter made him start again. The Oakenfelds weren't a religious family, but still, this image, this tree, the act he was contemplating . . . they sounded a chord deep within him.

"*Wow.*"

Charles shook his head in wonder. The drawing room's walls produced uncannily detailed images, but the pictures in this book seemed to be able to put thoughts in your head that weren't actually on the page. Charles felt as though he could look at this single scene forever and still not take in everything it was trying to tell him. But the sun was high in the sky now, and he'd looked at only two pictures. Sooner or later Uncle Farley or Susan was going to come looking for him.

He began turning pages faster. He found it didn't matter how quickly the pictures whizzed by—each was fully present to him, whether he glanced at it or stared for several minutes. Many of the places the book showed had also appeared in the drawing room's mural, like Tenochtitlán, the Aztec capital, and the statues on Easter Island's grassy hills. But these images came with so much more information. As Charles glanced at the solemn statues on Easter Island—they were called moai, he knew, and the people who had built them were the Rapu Nui— he saw the trees that had once covered the bare hills, and the villages full of warriors and farmers and sculptors, and he saw them slowly starving to death after they'd cut down every tree and eaten every animal on their isolated island home. He saw the first Aztecs ascending to a high plain on which sat a wide, flat lake, and in the center of the lake he saw an eagle perched on a cactus with a live snake in its beak, and he knew that this was the sign that told them to build there. As a tiny, ice-bound village passed before his eyes, Charles could see the paths leading to hilltop pastures and fjords that seamed between mountainous glaciers. Charles knew "fjord" was the right word, rather than "valley," just as he knew the village's name was Osterbygd, and he knew that Osterbygd meant "Western Settlement." As the Tower of Babel flashed by Charles could see every route through the city that led to the great blue ziggurat. He knew the building was called a ziggurat, not a pyramid, knew that it was built out of mud bricks covered in kiln-fired tiles, knew that there were 999 steps in the stairway that scaled the building's seven tiers, and that the small columned temple at the top housed animal sacrifices (unlike the Aztec temples, where human blood was spilled). He even saw a second, larger temple buried deep beneath the tower—could hear the thudding of footsteps as soldiers marched into the subterranean chamber, almost smelled the smoke of the burning city as he ran through its narrow streets in search of—

"Quite impressive, isn't it?"

Charles had taken great pains to make sure Mario's book was safe from falling, but had not been so diligent about his person. At the sound of the voice he jerked in surprise and racked back and forth on his branch. A dizzying blur of the ground far below wavered in front of his eyes, but Charles's first thoughts were of the book, which he slammed closed. Even as he regained his balance, however, he continued to shake a little, because when he glimpsed the ground he realized he didn't have his glasses on. He'd been examining Mario's book unaided, yet all its images had been crystal clear.

As he fumbled in his pocket, he noticed a green and red blur perched on a branch about five feet above him, and when his glasses were on his face, this blur resolved itself (not unexpectedly) into the shape of President Wilson. The parrot seemed unconcerned that he'd nearly caused Charles to plummet to his death.

"I couldn't see what Mr. Zenubian found so remarkable earlier. But now I'm beginning to understand. There is something extraordinarily . . . *compelling* about this book."

Charles only glared at the parrot. "Did Susan send you to spy on me?"

President Wilson did something that on a human would be a shrug. "'Spy' is a strong word, Charles—as is 'send' for that matter. I came to see if you were all right. Mr. Zenubian is still unaccounted for, after all."

Charles dismissed the idea that anyone, even Mr. Zenubian, could take Mario's book from him. He was more convinced than ever that it had chosen him, and that only it could decide when to leave.

"Of course I'm okay. I'm not a baby."

"You've certainly been acting like one. Throwing temper tantrums and sneaking off when people's backs are turned."

"It's not my fault! Susan gets to do everything because she's oldest. Everyone says wait till you're as old as Susan, but she'll *always* be older than me. I want to be in charge for once."

President Wilson let Charles finish, then hopped down to a lower branch.

"Do you know how old *I* am, Charles?"

Charles pulled up short. It's not like parrots got gray hairs—or, he supposed, gray feathers. President Wilson's plumage seemed as bright as a baby parrot's.

"One hundred and three. Yes, Charles, I was born in the last year of the nineteenth century, lived through the entirety of the twentieth, and am now making my way into the twenty-first. And if I have learned one thing during all that time, it's that there is always someone higher up the ladder who will tell you what to do. The key is not to worry about what other people are about, but what you need to do yourself. Charles, are you hearing a word I'm saying?"

A faraway look had taken over Charles's face. President Wilson glanced at the backpack at first, as if the book inside might be distracting the boy, then turned and looked over his shoulder in the direction of the bay. What he saw nearly knocked *him* from his branch.

Far out on the Bay of Eternity, a wall of water was catapulting toward Drift House. It was shimmering and soundless and huge—less a wall than a gauzy, delicate curtain.

But when the wave reached the beach and tore up the lawn, it was no longer silent. It roared with a sound like a hundred jets taking off at once. It frothed and churned and swallowed everything in its path. Drift House disappeared beneath—inside—it, as did even the highest trees on the lawn. And still the wave continued to advance, smashing into the hillside and climbing with terrifying speed. Charles and President Wilson could only stare, transfixed, as the water rose higher and higher. It slowed a little as it stretched farther from the bay, but still the ease with which it surged forward looked less like water than like a shadow thrown across a wall by a moving car. When it was a few feet below them Charles pulled his legs onto the branch. He turned to President Wilson.

"You should save yourself. Fly."

But President Wilson had recovered from the first shock, and now he hopped down to the very branch on which Charles sat.

"I'll take my chances with you, Charles." He glanced at the closed backpack. "Something tells me we'll be fine."

The water rose right up to the bottom of the branch the two were sitting on—and there it stopped. Charles could hear the tiniest gurgle as it lapped against the bark. The water's surface was eerily calm, no more disturbed than a bath after you've slipped in. And clean too. Charles could look down and see the branches of the tree beneath him, swaying lightly in the current. They swayed toward the hillcrest, then swayed back toward the bay.

"President Wilson! The water's reversing direction!"

"Hmph." The bird did not seem surprised.

The water receded almost as rapidly as it had come, as if some enormous—great—drain had been opened. The trees emerged, then the hillside and the garden. Not a single branch seemed to have been broken, not one of Mr. Zenubian's tender shoots uprooted. Aside from the puddles and rivulets that stood everywhere, everything was exactly as it had been before the wave washed over the land.

Except one thing, that is.

Drift House was gone.

PART TWO

Separated at Birth

EIGHT

Into the Woods, or the Second Solo Expedition of Charles Oakenfeld, Esq.

"PATIENCE, CHARLES OAKENFELD," PRESIDENT WILSON panted, hopping from branch to branch as his human charge scrambled down the hillside toward the Bay of Eternity. The backpack containing the mysterious book bounced from one of the boy's shoulders to the other.

"Patience? Did you *see* that wave? That was no *ordinary* wave. That wave came from the Sea of Time!"

"Undoubtedly," President Wilson agreed. "From the Sea of Time it came, and from the Sea of Time it is likely to return, bearing Drift House with it. And you do not want to be standing in the foundation when that happens."

"Oh, uh, right." Charles looked down at his feet, even

though the foundation was still some distance away. "You think it'll just come back? To, like, the very moment it left?"

"It always has before."

"It didn't that once," Charles said, almost as if he hoped his sister and uncle wouldn't come back. "When you and Uncle Farley went out the first time, and Frejo had to push you back. You were gone for a whole week."

"That was before Pierre Marin fixed the antenna. Now I suggest we find a shady spot and sit down. Perhaps we could continue inspecting your book."

"Yeah!" But even as Charles reached for his backpack, the images came flooding back to his mind's eye, as clear as if they were laid out before him like a deck of cards. He glanced suspiciously at President Wilson. Clearly, Mario's book hadn't made quite the same impression on the parrot, or he wouldn't have requested to see it again. "You know, I think I'll wait. Till, um, Susan and Uncle Farley get back."

"Suit yourself." The parrot settled atop a low wall built of gray stone, eyes already closed.

Some minutes passed.

"It's not back yet," Charles announced.

"Hmmm? What?"

"The house isn't back yet." And, shouldering his backpack, Charles set off across the lawn.

President Wilson scrambled and hopped along the wall, feeling like a peewit or sandpiper, or some equally common bird.

"Really, Charles, I see no need to get agitated—"

"There are puddles and pools all over the place. They've got to be from the wave."

"That would be the, ah, logical conclusion," President Wilson panted.

"And there's that," Charles said.

"What are you—oh."

A thin silver stream flowed into the lawn, flooding the flower bed that Mr. Zenubian had worked yesterday. The rivulet was only a few feet wide and a few inches deep, but it caught the rising sun and sparkled all the way up the hillside.

"That wasn't there before, was it?" Charles said.

"I don't believe it was," President Wilson said quietly. Despite its tininess, there was something eerie about the stream, like a great silver snake lying in ambush.

"Well, if the wave really *was* made of water from the Sea of Time, then this stream probably is too."

"What's your point, Charles?"

"I'm going to follow it."

"Really? And where do you expect it to lead you?"

"If my theory is correct, to Susan and Uncle Farley."

By now Charles had come to the edge of the stream. It flowed smoothly, without a sound.

"Really, Charles," President Wilson said. "Your 'theory,' such as it is, relies on so many guesses I hardly know where to begin."

"How about"—there was a lurch and a splash—"here."
Charles had jumped into the stream.

"President Wilson—look!"

"At?"

"My feet! My feet!" Charles's voice was filled with excitement. President Wilson had to hop to the right to see the boy's feet. Or, rather, *not* see them, for they weren't there. Charles's thin legs and even thinner ankles descended straight into the shallow water, but beneath them there was just grass, drifting ever so slightly in the clear water's current.

Suddenly Charles started running. President Wilson launched himself into the sky. It is very hard for a parrot to keep pace with running humans—not because they're too fast, but because they're too slow. The parrot had to fly rather wobbly loops around Charles to keep his charge in earshot.

"Really, Charles, if you would just—"

"How do you think it works? Do you think there'll be like a poof! and then suddenly we'll be somewhere else?"

Charles's voice was broken up with pants and then gasps for air. He was running uphill, after all, and in four inches of water, and he couldn't see his feet besides. Finally he had to catch his breath. The stream was more or less gone now, but everything was pretty much as it had been: trees all around, blue sky above.

"Nothing . . . happened?" he panted. "But . . . I was . . . so sure!"

"Hmph," President Wilson snorted. As the trees had thickened he had been forced to weave in and out of branches, and then finally to alight and hop from one to another. He took a moment (well, several moments actually) to catch his breath, then said, "I tried to tell you: there were any number of unsound points to your theory."

"I guess you're right." Charles peered at the trees, half hoping they might start talking and moving like the trees in *The Wizard of Oz* (or *The Lord of the Rings*, which was way cooler). But all they did was rustle in a breeze that was cold against Charles's wet legs. "Well, I guess we'd better head back and wait for Susan and Uncle Farley." His head hung from his neck like a half-deflated balloon, and he stared at his sneakers, which were depressingly visible now, not to mention caked with mud.

"Ahem, Charles."

"Look, I said I was going back, okay?"

"I think you'd better look where you're going."

"What do you—oh."

Charles looked up, expecting to see Drift House's broad lawns and the Bay of Eternity beyond. But all he saw was an incredibly thick knot of tree trunks. The trunks were fat and dark and piled one on top of each other, and Charles could see nothing through them.

"President Wilson?"

President Wilson's voice sounded remarkably droll. "Yes, Charles?"

"What just happened?"

"What do you mean? You wanted to go back in time. It would seem your wish came true."

"But . . . *how?*" Charles turned away from the place Drift House was supposed to be. Everywhere he looked he could see nothing but trees.

"Not everything is dramatic, Charles. There don't have to be sparks or smoke for something astounding to happen. You just have to pay attention."

Charles wanted to point out that President Wilson hadn't believed they would go back in time at all. But, unlike the parrot, he didn't feel the need to gloat. And besides, there were bigger questions now. Like, where was he? *When* was he? And most important: how was he going to get back?

With sudden resolve, Charles reached for a limb of the nearest tree. It was a pine tree, and his hand was immediately covered in sticky pitch, but he pulled himself up anyway.

President Wilson flapped to a nearby branch. "Charles? What *are* you doing?"

"I need to take a look around," Charles grunted, pulling himself to the next limb.

The parrot flapped to a limb a few feet higher than Charles. "Er, Charles? I *am* a bird?"

"Yes, well, I'm a boy. And I need to look around myself."

"This is silly," President Wilson said, following Charles up the tree. "You're endangering yourself needlessly."

"It was you who said I needed to pay attention."

"I didn't say you had to risk your life doing it."

"Pshaw," Charles said, using one of President Wilson's favorite expressions. "Climbing trees is perfectly safe. I can't believe I never did it before today."

President Wilson followed Charles ever higher up the pine tree. It was slow going, but eventually they emerged above the canopy of the shorter deciduous trees. Charles didn't sit down as he had before, but stood, holding on to a thin branch for balance.

"Well, let's see what we can see."

He turned toward where he thought the water should be. An uninterrupted growth of trees ran all the way down the hill, but beyond that Charles could just make out a glittering rim.

"I see the bay!" he said excitedly.

President Wilson hopped up four feet higher than Charles could go. "Yes, I do think that's it."

"Do you think we're in the same place? Just farther back in time?"

"It seems logical," President Wilson said, although his voice sounded unsure. "There's no reason to assume we shifted position—the stream wasn't big enough to move us, as the wave appeared to do with Drift House."

At the mention of Drift House, Charles grew silent. Then: "How are we ever going to find them, President Wilson? How are they going to find us?"

President Wilson had turned to survey the opposite direction. Now he pointed with his wing. "Well, we might want to start there."

At first all Charles saw was an expanse of rolling forest capped by a cloudless blue sky. Then, finally, a single thin column of black became visible. It seamed the horizon into left and right halves, as if the sky were an open book with pages that could be turned forward and back. At the thought of that image, Charles checked the security of Mario's book in his backpack. He had the sneaking suspicion that the book had gotten him into this situation, and he figured it was probably the only thing that would get him out.

He cleared his throat. "Is that . . . smoke?"

"I believe it is," President Wilson answered. "And where there's smoke, there's fire."

"And where there's fire?" Charles said. He looked at President Wilson.

President Wilson looked very thoughtful.

"That," he said finally, "is a very good question."

NINE

Say Hello to Bjarki

AT FIRST IT SEEMED LIKE Drift House turned upside down.

Then it seemed like Drift House turned inside out.

And then everything seemed to straighten out, save that Susan felt the familiar sensation of rocking floorboards beneath her feet.

Drift House was afloat.

"Um, Uncle Farley?"

"I don't know, Susan."

"I didn't ask a question yet, Uncle Farley."

Uncle Farley sighed. "Ask away."

"Um . . . what just happened?"

"I don't know, Susan."

"Oh. Okay."

There was another long silence. Susan looked around the room. Though it had felt like an angry giant had picked up the house and shaken it, nothing was out of place. There was a teacup in its saucer on the table. The metronome on the harpsichord was as still as it had been a moment ago. Uncle Farley had been standing; now he sat in a chair, but Susan didn't think he'd been knocked down.

"Do you," Susan began quietly, not wanting to startle her glazed-looking uncle, "do you think Mr. Zenubian had something to do with this?"

Uncle Farley sighed heavily. "Mr. Zenubian took the little radio."

Susan was confused for a moment. "Mr. Zenubian took the—" Suddenly she got it. "He took the little *tombstone* radio?"

The last time she had been here, Susan—along with her uncle and everyone else in Drift House—had learned that the house's time-traveling abilities were controlled by a pair of radios, which, because of their arched shape, were referred to as tombstones: a large one in the drawing room, and a smaller one Uncle Farley kept in his bedroom. But:

"Once I figured out how to work the radios," Uncle Farley said, "I moved the smaller one to my study. After Mr. Zenubian stormed off, it occurred to me that I should make the rounds to see if he'd taken anything. As far as I could tell, the radio was the only thing missing."

"But could he . . . I mean, can the radios control Drift House if they're not in it?"

"I keep meaning to ask Bjarki that very question, but always forget."

"Bjarki?"

"Bjarki Skaldisson. You heard his voice once, on the big radio. 'Echo Island to Drift House . . . '"

"You've *talked* to him?"

A slightly mischievous smile crept onto Uncle Farley's face. "A few times, yes."

Susan was a respectful preteen, but she felt herself get the *teensiest* bit impatient with her uncle. "Do you think perhaps we could talk to him *now?*"

Uncle Farley bopped himself on the forehead. Springing from the chair, he grabbed his niece's arm and headed toward the hall.

"Susan, my dear, you are ten times the tactician I will ever be. Sometimes I think I would lose my beard if it weren't attached to my cheeks."

The drawing room walls were still dark, and Uncle Farley had to throw the curtains wide to let in light. Susan glanced at the expanse of blue beyond the glass, then followed her uncle to the cabinet-sized radio on the opposite side of the room. The peak of the radio's arch was a few inches taller than she was, but its knobs were situated close to the base, just above the fretwork that covered its single large speaker. Uncle Farley squatted down and turned the left knob, and immediately a voice barked into the room.

"—land broadcast, to any and all transtemporal vessels within range. I repeat, this is Echo Island. Drift House, *Chronos*, *Equus*, do you copy, over."

"Uncle Farley, it's working!"

Before her uncle could answer, the voice on the radio said, "Farley, is that you? Confirm receipt of signal, over."

"Bjarki, it's me. I'm here with my niece, Susan Oakenfeld, over. Er, Susan, say hello to Bjarki."

"Hello, Bjarki!" Susan said, in the kind of voice you use to talk to deaf people. "This is Susan, over!"

Bjarki's wince was almost audible. "No need to shout, Ms. Oakenfeld. I can hear you just fine. Confirm Drift House on Sea of Time with two passengers aboard, over. Hello, ma'am," Bjarki added, then paused. "Where's . . . the bird?"

Uncle Farley chuckled at what was apparently a private joke between him and the voice in the radio. "President Wilson and my nephew Charles weren't in the house when we, that is, well, what *did* happen?"

"Something extraordinary, Farley. A temporal squall of a magnitude I've never seen."

"What's a temporal squall?" Susan said.

"Well now, ma'am." Susan heard a squeak, and had a vision of a bearish man settling back in a reclining chair. " 'Squall' is a convenient term we use to describe certain events on and

around the Sea of Time. It's a disruption in the regular temporal flow, a bit like a storm breaks up the normal weather."

It made sense that if there was a Sea of Time there should
be storms on it. Still, Susan wondered: "Do you know what
caused this squall, Bjarki?"

"Well, now, I'll come clean and tell you, ma'am: no I don't.
This storm is like nothing I've ever seen before. It's a regular
temporal hurricane."

"Bjarki," Uncle Farley cut in, "are you saying it's still going
on?"

"Raging from the conquest of Egypt in the eighth century
right up to the Gulf War in 1990. And spreading."

Susan, who had never thought to measure the weather—
even temporal weather—concentrated on the obvious.

"But it's quite calm where we are."

"I assumed as much. You're in the eye. We both are, or else
I doubt you'd be receiving this transmission."

"Bjarki," Uncle Farley interjected, "I'm quite concerned
about my nephew. How exactly do we get out of the, um, eye?"

"There'll be no sailing through *this* squall. There are warps
in time and space. You're as likely to end up green as end up
on the Bay of Eternity."

Uncle Farley glanced at Susan. "We're stuck here?"

"For the duration. And there's no telling how long that'll
last."

"Isn't there anything we can do?" Susan said.

"Actually," Bjarki said, then hesitated. "Pardon my forwardness, ma'am, but you're just a girl, yes?"

Despite the fact that Bjarki couldn't see her (well, she assumed he couldn't see her) Susan stood up straight.

"I'll be thirteen in August."

"Mmmm, yes, Farley told me you were young."

"Mr. Skaldisson," Susan said in the sternest British accent she could muster, "if you are refraining from saying something because you think I am too inexperienced or delicate to handle it, I should inform you that I am *quite* capable of taking care of myself."

"Susan," Uncle Farley said, "it would be remiss of me to put you in danger. After what happened last time—"

"Last time? You mean the time I successfully impersonated a pirate, defeated Queen Octavia, became the first person to return from the Great Drain, and saved the flow of time?"

A chuckle came through the speaker. "She's got a point, Farley."

Uncle Farley sighed. "Well, what were you going to say, Bjarki?"

"Just this. The squall seems to be centered somewhere around 1500 or so, just off the northeast coast of Canada. If I had to guess, I'd suggest the southern tip of Greenland."

"Greenland," Uncle Farley said. "Isn't that where the Vikings had their New World colony? Their own"—he paused, glancing at Susan—"lost city?"

Susan had a vague memory of this—something about Erik the Red, maybe? But Uncle Farley was still speaking

"But, Bjarki," he said, "it was my impression that the Viking settlement had died—er, disappeared by 1500. And at any rate, are you actually suggesting someone in a medieval Viking colony might have caused this squall?"

"Well, now, history's your department, not mine. But near as I can recollect, the Vikings hung on till right around the time we're talking about. As for them causing the squall, well, I wouldn't go that far, but only because I don't know how *anyone* could cause a disturbance like we've got here. Still, time's a pretty even-tempered entity. It's only your kind that tend to stir it up."

At this "your kind," Susan caught her breath, suddenly realizing Bjarki might not be human. But she was too caught up in another possibility to give this idea much thought.

"You want us to investigate?" she said, doing a poor job of keeping the excitement out of her voice.

"Susan, please—" Uncle Farley began, but the voice on the radio spoke over him.

"I've tried hallooing the *Chronos*, but they're not responding. My guess is Captain Quoin had them out beyond the squall's perimeter on one of his missions or other. Ditto the Island of the Past. You're the only contact I've been able to make."

"You must understand, Bjarki. It's not that I don't want to help. But Susan is my niece. My sister sent her to me for a summer of diversion and esoteric study, not to remedy anomalies in the temporal flow. I can hardly risk her well-being by dragging her into this"—he glanced at Susan—" 'investigation.' "

"I hate to belabor the obvious," Bjarki said in a gentle voice. "But she's already in it. The question seems to be, how are you going to get her out?"

Susan was wise enough to bite her tongue here and let the truth of Bjarki's words sink in.

At length Uncle Farley sighed and, in a resigned voice, uttered two words.

"Where?" he said. And then the magical addendum: "When?"

TEN

Stealing Fire

"REALLY, CHARLES," PRESIDENT WILSON'S SLIGHTLY wheezy voice floated down from the trees. "There is no need to run."

"Whatsamatter?" Charles said. "Too old to keep up?"

Ever since he'd realized he'd gone back in time, Charles had been filled with exhilaration. He, Charlie-o-o-Oakenfeld, was on his own in North America's preindustrial past! Here was his chance to prove his resourcefulness and bravery! He would make his own way back to Drift House, and never have to stand in Susan's shadow again!

"Need I remind you that I am, at the present moment, your only ally?"

"We don't even know when the present moment *is*,"

Charles said. "And what good's an ally if he can't—keep—*up*?" Charles had picked up a stout limb to use as a walking stick, and his last words were punctuated by crashing sounds as he mauled some hapless bush to the ground.

"I assure you, Charles Oakenfeld, I am perfectly capable of outpacing you and any other two-legged creature. But these branches are so infernally thick I can't fly more than five feet at a time."

"Well, ride on my shoulder then."

President Wilson blinked in the bright light. He was above all else a prudent bird (and, at 103, he was, if you will pardon the expression, no spring chicken). Nor was he a hummingbird or a roadrunner, and so, as Charles plunged into the underbrush, the parrot launched himself at the boy's left shoulder, digging his claws somewhat more aggressively than necessary into the straps of Charles's backpack. Fortunately the wide, padded straps blunted the edge. There was a moment of silence (if you don't count Charles's smashing stick and the crack of dead limbs underfoot), and then President Wilson chuckled slightly.

"We are an unlikely pair, no?"

Charles laughed. "I can't say I ever imagined I'd be spending *this* much time with you."

"I remember when you were afraid of me. Life was simpler then. Tell me, though: why didn't Murray accompany you and your sister on this trip? Of all of us, he has the largest investment in Drift House."

"He was vague about it. I dunno if he just didn't remember, or if there were things he couldn't tell us. He just thought he shouldn't be on the Sea of Time."

"Did he think it was dangerous?"

Charles whacked a branch out of his way, wishing he could clear up Murray's story as easily.

"I think maybe it had more to do with Mario."

"Mario?"

Charles remembered that President Wilson didn't know about Murray's alter ego. Realizing there was no need for secrecy anymore, he told the parrot about the older version of his brother, who had adopted the name Mario during a stint with Captain Quoin and the Time Pirates.

"Fascinating," President Wilson said when Charles had finished. "A second Murray. Do you think there's a second President Wilson out there, or another Charles Oakenfeld?"

"Wouldn't we have to be Accursed Returners for that to happen?"

"Hmmm, good point. In any case, we should keep an eye out for this Mario."

"Why?"

"Well, we know Murray has been to the future and back, and that he retains some shadowy memories of what happened there. It stands to reason that if he's worried about meeting Mario, then he must have a strong sense Mario's path will cross ours at some point."

"Duh," Charles said. "I can't believe I didn't figure that out."

"That's what teamwork is for, Charles. What one comrade misses, the other catches."

After what felt like hours, the two hikers (or, more accurately, the hiker and his passenger, who had been snoring lightly in Charles's ear for some time) came to a place where the trees were a bit thinner. President Wilson roused himself and suggested he fly up and check their bearings. After the parrot had launched into the air, Charles made his way to the nearest tree and sat down against it. The tree had thick exposed roots and he settled himself comfortably between two of them. His feet were hot, so he took off his shoes and socks to let them breathe. Leaves rustled, the occasional bird called. In every direction, no matter how far he looked, Charles could see nothing but tree trunks and underbrush, blurring in the distance into a brownish greenish wall. It was a big world, he thought. A big empty world. At least it had been, before it filled up with people.

He noticed a cluster of mushrooms growing on one of the exposed roots of his tree. They were pretty mushroomy-looking mushrooms: tan, with thick, slightly wrinkled stems and rounded tops shaped like the dome of a sports arena. Charles wondered if they were edible. You were always reading about people being poisoned by toadstools, but he'd never heard of it happening in real life. Of course, he'd never heard of anyone eating a wild mushroom either. Mushrooms—like all food—were something you bought in a store, or maybe at a farm stand when you went to the country.

Charles's stomach rumbled loudly. He was suddenly very hungry, and there were no grocery stores around. No farm stands either, despite the fact that he was surrounded by the countriest-looking country he'd ever seen.

The fact of the matter was, Charles didn't particularly care for mushrooms. Mushrooms seemed to him one of those extra things you put on food to make you appreciate the main part— the tomatoes if you were eating salad, or the steak if you were eating steak. But these mushrooms were starting to look like the tastiest thing he'd ever seen in his life. Charles picked one and brought it to his nose. He sniffed. The fungus smelled like wet mud, and as bland as that might sound Charles's mouth still watered at the scent. If you cooked one, he reasoned, wouldn't that neutralize any poison? Or would it activate it? Which raised another question: how to start a fire?

Just then President Wilson landed on the exposed roots of Charles's tree. Despite the fact that he had no lips, the parrot still had the uncanny ability to look as though he were frowning.

"Is there something wrong, President Wilson?"

The bird shook his head. "Not exactly."

"We're still on course?" Charles had heard of people walking in circles in the forest. Maybe that had happened to them?

Now President Wilson nodded. "As nearly as I can tell. But the column of smoke doesn't seem to be any closer at all."

"Do you think we walked in circles?"

"I doubt it. The ocean has quite disappeared from view, so we must have made some progress. That said, however, I think we ought to consider the possibility of stopping for the night."

"But isn't it, like, only the middle of the afternoon?"

"I imagine making camp will take a bit of time. There's shelter to be built, and food to be gathered"—President Wilson nodded at the mushroom in Charles's hand—"and it would be nice if we could get some sort of fire going. I imagine nights are quite cool in the open."

"I've got an idea about that," Charles said. He took off his glasses and looked at them.

"Er, Charles? Aren't you supposed to look through them? Not at them?"

"Cute," Charles said. He rolled into a patch of sunlight, then moved his glasses around until the lens caught the sun and focused it into a bright spot of light on the ground. "I think," he said, reaching for a bit of dry grass, "I can use them to start a fire."

A breeze stirred the leaves and Charles lost his patch of sunlight. He rolled over and sat up.

"We're going to have to find a place where the trees aren't so thick."

"I spotted a clearing about half a mile that way." President

Wilson pointed with his wing. "And I think there was a stream nearby."

"Water!" Charles said, suddenly realizing he was as thirsty as he was hungry.

Before they set off, Charles gathered all the mushrooms from the tree roots and put them in his bag (except for one that had some white fuzzy stuff growing on it, and smelled gross). President Wilson led the way. Charles kept a careful eye on his companion. Maybe it was because President Wilson had told him how old he was, but Charles couldn't help thinking that the bird looked exhausted. He barely flapped his wings as he moved from one branch to the next, and panted heavily between the short flights.

Suddenly the oaks and maples gave way to a thinner stand of white birch. Toward the bottom of the hill, where the ground was significantly damper, dark green fern grew in dense clumps. A sound he realized he'd been hearing for a while resolved itself into the gurgle of running water—only to be drowned out by the crash of his footsteps as he hurtled toward the stream.

"Careful, careful," President Wilson called in a breathless voice. "The last thing we need is for you to sprain your ankle."

Charles ran on, but when he reached the stream his fastidious side reasserted itself: instead of throwing himself on the muddy ground, he stretched out on a large brown rock, then scooped up handful after handful of water and sucked it into his mouth. It was as cold as ice cream, and had a slight vegetable taste. Charles thought he had never drunk anything so refreshing in his life.

At length he looked up to see President Wilson a few feet away. The parrot had made his way to the water's edge, and sipped at it demurely. For some reason the sight of the bird—the lone spot of red amidst the endless brown and green—unnerved Charles, as he realized not only how alone they were, but how far from everything he knew.

Boy and bird looked at each other. From the expression on President Wilson's face, Charles thought he might be having the same thought.

President Wilson spoke first. "Right then. Camp. I'm afraid I'm not going to be much help with the construction"—the bird flexed his wings as if to show their tininess, or lack of fingers—"but perhaps I can spy something to eat."

Charles nodded. "I'll try to build a fire first, while the sun's still strong."

"Right then. Onward and upwards."

The parrot flapped into the air, leaving Charles to trek uphill in search of drier ground. From a fallen birch, he pulled several sheets of bark, as well as twigs and tiny branches. The branches were brittle and snapped sharply when he broke them off, and Charles knew this meant they were dry, and would burn easily.

Kindling at hand, he cleared the ferns from a large area

open to the sun, then scooped out the earth to form a hollow firepit. As he pulled the ferns he noticed that they were soft and springy, and he figured a thick pile of them would make a nice mattress. He shook the dirt from their stems and set them aside, then lined his firepit with good-sized round stones. Even as he wondered why he did this, the answer came to him: the stones would capture the heat and reflect it upward, rather than letting it be absorbed by the porous soil. He was deeply impressed with himself for sussing this out, though some part of him was a little troubled by *how* he knew it, just as a part of him wondered how he knew to shred the papery bark into bits and stack them in a small, airy pile atop the stones. He knew why he stacked the bark so: the fire would need the air to burn more freely. He just wasn't sure how this factoid had entered his brain. But he was too nervous about the next step to give it much thought. The moment of truth had arrived.

Charles sat down next to his pile of shavings and pulled off his glasses. He had scorched paper with them before, but no matter how much the bark looked like paper, Charles knew it was thicker and less combustible.

"Com*bust*ible," he said aloud, taking strength from the word. But all he succeeded in doing was blowing his stack of bark apart. He built it again, then held his glasses over the tiny, shredded pile. He had to adjust the angle to get the light to focus, but soon enough a bright yellow dot was aimed at the pile. The dot was watery, like a spilled drop of food coloring, and Charles found himself doubting it could ignite anything. But after an endless moment the bark began to darken. And darken.

And darken. And . . .

. . . darken.

Charles's arm started to ache. He had no idea how long he'd been holding his glasses in the air. They weighed only a few ounces, yet the boy felt as though he were holding back a lunging German shepherd by its leash.

He sat up. This wasn't working. He had felt so sure it would. Not scientifically sure. He just *knew* it was going to work. There must be something he was missing.

He held his glasses in front of his face. Two lenses connected by a thin bit of metal, two spokes shooting off either side. The glasses were too small to conceal any secrets, and yet he just *knew* there was something he wasn't getting.

Suddenly he saw it. Putting aside thoughts of how much his parents had paid for them, Charles twisted his glasses at the nosepiece so the lenses were stacked one on top of the other. He replaced them in the sun and fiddled with the angle until a new spot of light shone on his little stack of bark. This spot, focused through the pair of lenses, was noticeably thicker than the previous one, more golden in hue. "Come on," Charles muttered out loud, "you can do it. Come . . . *on*!"

As if responding to his words, the pale bit of bark turned

brown, then black. Sooner than he would have expected, it began to smoke. And smoke.

And smoke. And . . .

. . . smoke.

Charles's arm was aching again. But he *knew* this would work. Worming closer, he blew as softly as he could on the delicate pile. Immediately he was rewarded by an orange glow on the edge of a shaving. He blew again, and again, the littlest puffs. The glow thickened; so did the smoke. Charles could smell it faintly. He felt an urge to sneeze. *Light*, he told himself. *Burn.*

He puffed again. And again. And again.

His *arm* burned. That was for sure. His hand jiggled, and the dot of light disappeared for a moment. Almost panicking, Charles focused it again as quickly as he could.

Puff. And glow. And puff. And smoke.

Charles blinked. His instinct was to put his glasses on, but he held steady. Could it be? Was it?

The tiniest lick of flame had appeared. Charles was too afraid to blow on it. He simply breathed, offering the little flame the oxygen in his lungs as though he were resuscitating someone.

The flame sputtered, seemed to go out, then—no!—it was back again, bigger. A second shaving of bark was alight! A third!

Charles dropped his glasses in the dirt, reached for a larger piece of bark. He fed it edge-first into the fire until it too was burning. Soon he had a tiny but genuine blaze—no bigger than the five candles on Murray's last birthday cake, but no smaller either. Onto this he placed a couple of twigs. The fire seemed reluctant at first. It oozed a thicker, grayer smoke, but the flames were hungry: in another moment the twigs had given in. More twigs; then tiny branches. Now the fire was eager. Whatever went on it was alight almost instantly. Soon enough Charles was putting branches on it that were as thick as his wrists. His wrists were, admittedly, tiny, but to see the branches burn made Charles feel as though he were lighting a Yule log (whatever *that* was).

He had to run around then to gather more firewood. As he ran he sang out, "Ha ha ha! I, Charles Oakenfeld, have stolen fire from the gods! I am the mightiest of them all! Look upon my fearsome blaze and tremble!" At the moment, his fearsome blaze wouldn't've cooked much more than a marshmallow, but Charles didn't care. He had turned sunlight into flame! He had never felt more powerful in his life.

Nor, for that matter, more blind. After tripping and falling on his face, the mighty Charles Oakenfeld had to return to his firepit and feel around in the dirt until he found his glasses. He untwisted them as best he could and put them on. The left lens sat distinctly higher on his face than the right, but he'd think of a good explanation before he saw his parents. He figured he had at least a few hundred years to come up with one.

Charles fed his fire until it was as high as his waist and its crackle drowned out the stream's gurgle. He made a stack of firewood as tall as he was, then headed to the stream for another drink. The work of gathering the wood had made him thirsty (and hungry, though he didn't want to dwell on that). He drank his fill, and when he was finished he continued to lie on the rock, his eyes unfocused, the smell of water filling his nostrils.

A flicker caught his eye. Charles pushed his sliding glasses up his nose and saw a blue speckled fish floating in the pool beneath him. It was hard to tell, but the fish looked to be about eight or ten inches long. Thin but tall, an elongated silver oval suspended in the water.

Another flicker, and then another. With a mental *duh*, Charles realized the stream was full of fish. After his success with the fire, he felt there was nothing he couldn't accomplish. He kicked off his shoes and began rolling up his pants.

The shadows had lengthened considerably by the time President Wilson returned. Charles sat in front of the roaring fire. He had made a crude strut by driving two forked branches into the ground, and a pair of fish lay spitted between them on a thin stick. When drops of liquid dripped from the fish, the fire hissed and snapped as though it was as hungry as the boy. Charles turned his spit with a nonchalant expression on his face, but it was obvious from his quivering lips he was bursting to talk of his accomplishments.

President Wilson dropped a small branch in front of the

fire, on which dangled a dozen dark, limp-looking berries. The parrot's beak was stained purple, suggesting he had not waited to eat as Charles had done. Eyeing Charles's face for a moment, the parrot said, "Did you fall?"

Charles pushed his twisted glasses up his nose. "Er, no. I just had to make a little, um, adjustment."

President Wilson shrugged. He nodded at the branch he'd brought. "Blackberries, I think. Past their prime, I'm afraid. There might be more if you want to go back, but it's quite a—oh!"

For Charles had grabbed the branch and devoured the berries in an instant. His lips puckered from the tart taste, but they were still just about the sweetest thing he'd ever eaten.

"I see you've been busy," President Wilson said as Charles plucked the last shriveled berry from the branch. "A fire, and fish even."

"I built a lean-to too. A lean-to *also*," Charles said, jerking his thumb behind him at what President Wilson had at first taken to be a thicket. Now he saw that Charles had laid leafy boughs across a tree that had fallen at a sharp angle over the ground. The lean-to was about six feet long and four feet high, and carpeted with a tufted layer of fern.

President Wilson was—he had to stretch his brain for the word, since it was not one he used often—impressed. Astonished even.

"My word, Charles. How did you learn how to do all this?"

Before he answered, Charles used a stick to prod a flat rock out from the edge of the fire. On the rock were the mushrooms Charles had gathered earlier, sliced and sizzling.

"I think it was Mario's book," Charles said now. He speared the cooked mushrooms and transferred them to another flat rock to cool. "I think it taught me things."

"But there were no words," the parrot said, eyeing the mushrooms with a half-open beak.

"I know. I think it's, like, subliminal."

"Subliminal?" The parrot hopped closer to the mushrooms.

"Yeah, that's the word. Subliminal." Charles speared a mushroom and held it up for the parrot. "When I looked at the pictures, I kept getting all these flashes of other things. Stuff that wasn't on the page. And I knew it wasn't just my imagination, because the pictures in my head were so specific, and sometimes they even came with words and names and, I dunno, *history*. And then, when I was building the fire, it was like I knew *exactly* what to do before I did it. The fish too."

Charles turned his fish. He felt a slight tug on the stick in his hand, and when he looked back the mushroom was gone.

"How, um"—swallow—"how *did* you catch the fish?"

Charles's face beamed. He reached to his right and grabbed a branch behind him. One end of it was as plain as a broom handle, but the other end broke into a particularly tangled mass of branches from which all the leaves had been stripped, leaving a sort of jagged ball about two feet in diameter.

"It's like a cage," Charles said, standing up and holding the branch with the tangled branches facing downward. "I just stood on a rock in the water until a fish swam in front of me, and then—bam!" Charles smashed the jagged ball into the ground so forcefully that President Wilson jumped back. Charles laughed, and tossed the branch aside.

President Wilson's beak dropped. "Ingenious!" he said. And burped.

Charles's grin split his face from ear to ear, but he was also shaking his head. "I wish I could say I was that smart. But honestly, I didn't figure it out. I just did it. It was like I'd learned how a long time ago, and all I had to do was remember."

"That sounds a lot like the way Murray describes his premonitions."

"I know. At first I thought maybe I was like Murray. It's like you were saying before: how do we know we're not all Accursed Returners and just haven't figured it out yet? But Murray always had specific memories of things. And this, I dunno how to describe it, this is like knowledge. Like $A^2 + B^2 = C^2$, or never crossing the positive and negative wires in a circuit. Notice which way the wind's blowing?"

"Er, what?" President Wilson looked around. There was a slight breeze, gusting . . . the parrot didn't know his deep south from north-by-northwest. "It's blowing that way." He pointed with a wing.

"Yup. Taking the smoke *away* from the lean-to. That's the

kind of thing I'm talking about. I didn't consciously build the lean-to upwind. It just worked out that way."

President Wilson nodded. Then a thought occurred to him. "But I looked at the book too—twice in fact. Once with you, and once with that hateful Zenubian. And I've had no special insight."

"Maybe it was the angle—you were kind of looking at it upside down both times, weren't you? Or, I dunno, maybe . . ."

"Yes?"

"Well, maybe you're too old. Your mind is too . . . full. Or something."

President Wilson made a dour expression.

"I think the fish is done," Charles said to change the subject. As he took the spit off its struts he said, "I was torn. I had this idea of baking it on a rock like the mushrooms. Maybe wrap it in leaves to hold the moisture in? But the spit looked cooler, don't you think?"

"If only we'd brought a camera." President Wilson laughed. "No one will ever believe us when we tell this story."

Charles pulled over a pair of wide flat rocks and slid the fish off the stick, one to each rock. He divvied the mushrooms between the two plates, then added a few spiraling green things.

"Fiddleheads. They grow by our country house upstate, so I know they're good, although Mum always serves them with a vinaigrette."

President Wilson eyed the two plates. Wild trout, served

with sautéed mushrooms and a salad of fiddlehead ferns. The meal looked more like something you'd see pictured in a food magazine than the scrounged-up fare of a city slicker and a housebound parrot. The dark eye of the fish stared up at the parrot accusingly.

"Er, I think I'll stick with the vegetables. Please, eat my fish. You need the protein more than I do."

"Suit yourself." Charles was too hungry to protest for the sake of good manners. He had filed a stick as flat as he could on a rock, and with another whose prongs he'd sharpened into a fork, he sliced his fish open and tried to debone it the way he'd seen waiters in restaurants do. By the time he finished, the two fish were pretty much mangled to a pulp, but they smelled delectable.

He speared a morsel of white flesh and brought it toward his mouth. The cold water had been delicious, the tart berries had been extraordinary, but this . . . this was *heaven*.

A few moments later all that was left of the meal were two fish skeletons, tails at one end, heads at the other. Charles crunched the tart fiddleheads slowly, a sleepy, satisfied smile on his glistening lips. His twisted glasses slipped down his nose, and he made no move to push them back up.

"It's getting dark out."

President Wilson nodded. His own eyes were already closed. "Are you worried?"

"Too tired to worry. If a bear came, I'd just stare at him like old fish-eye here." He jabbed a finger at his plate.

The parrot's eyes snapped open. "Bear?"

Charles laughed sleepily. "I'll put a few more logs on the fire. That should keep them away." A thoughtful expression crossed his face. "We should bury the fish skeletons though. They're attracted to the smell."

"How do you know—oh right. The book."

Charles smiled and patted his backpack, inside which Mario's book rested securely. Now he stood wearily and placed several branches on the fire, then scooped out a shallow hole and buried the fish skeletons. When he'd finished he stretched and let out a sound that was half yawn, half yawp. The sound echoed through the otherwise silent forest, and President Wilson looked around nervously.

"Coming to bed?" Charles said.

"In a moment. I have to do my, um, birdlike things." The parrot ran his beak through his feathers.

"Suit yourself. See you in the morning." Charles crawled into the lean-to and rooted around the thick bed of fern like a dog, making a deep nest. He used his backpack as a pillow, felt the book's familiar tingling sensation on his cheek. "G'night, President Wilson," he called, half asleep already. He took his twisted glasses off and hung them on a twig poking from the wall of his shelter.

"Good night, Charles."

The parrot waited until the boy's breathing came evenly, then flew to a thin branch about ten feet off the ground. He could still see Charles from his perch, but he was pretty sure no bears could reach this high.

The branch swayed slightly in his grip, the way his roost did when Drift House was on the Sea of Time. The parrot wondered how the house was doing, and Farley, and Susan.

"Don't worry, Farley," he whispered, his own eyes closing. "We'll rescue you."

A moment later, the thousand thousand trees with their million million leaves heard something they'd never heard before: a parrot's snore.

ELEVEN

The Tempest

"OH, THIS IS GRAND!" SUSAN said as Uncle Farley knelt in front of the radio dials. "We're finally going back in time!" Without realizing it, she sucked in a deep breath and held it.

"Latitude . . . seventy degrees . . . thirty minutes . . . north. Longitude . . . twenty-two degrees . . . zero minutes . . . west."

Susan felt her cheeks burning, but continued holding her breath.

"Temporality . . ." Uncle Farley flipped the dial. "August . . ." Another flip. "Second . . ." Flip. "One . . ." *flip* "four . . ." *flip* "eight . . ." *flip* . . .

Popping noises in her ears, stars in front of her eyes.

"... three," Uncle Farley said finally. *Flip.*

The breath burst from Susan's mouth so loudly Uncle Farley jumped.

"August 2, 1483! I mean ... I mean. ..." Susan wasn't sure what she meant, really, besides: "Wow!"

The fifteenth century! It was just ... so ... before ... *everything.*

Bjarki's voice came from the radio.

"I'm afraid I can't get you right on the coast because of the squall. This'll put you a few miles offshore. Now, before you sluice, I want you to—"

"Sloosh?" Susan interrupted.

"Sluice," Uncle Farley whispered. "Travel back in time."

"—fill a few vials with water from the Sea of Time. Once you make land, you can use them to help you communicate. Simply put a drop in each ear and you'll be able to understand anything that's said to you, and a drop on your tongue to speak any language."

Susan was shocked. "But won't that turn us into Ac-ac-ac— Returners?"

Bjarki's chuckle had a faintly tinny sound. "Water from the Sea of Time deintensifies the moment it enters the temporal universe. Within a few days, it's indistinguishable from good ol' H-two-of-O. Now, bon voyage!"

For vials, Uncle Farley supplied a pair of test tubes from his study. Susan opened the front door and dunked them into the warm water of the Sea of Time. The tiny tubes filled instantly, but Susan lingered a moment, glancing over the wide blue expanse as if Diaphone's head just might poke above the gently rolling surface. But the sea was empty, and Susan wedged corks in the test tubes and closed the door between her and the loneliness of eternity, and hurried back to the drawing room. Its walls were blank now—a probable effect, Bjarki had said, of the squall's interference.

"Right then," Uncle Farley said when he saw her in the doorway. "Let's be off." And he reached to push a button on the radio.

"Do I need to sit"—Susan began, even as her uncle's finger depressed the button—"down or anything?"

Uncle Farley looked at her with a mischievous smile on his face. "Why would you?"

"Well, is it, I don't know, bumpy?" Susan was recalling her ride to the bottom of the Great Drain in Frejo's mouth, which had been quite bumpy.

"You tell me. Did it feel bumpy?"

"What? Was that it? Are we there?" But even as she spoke she caught a glimpse of her shadow on the floor, and realized they were indeed back in the temporal world. The rocking of the house had increased as well, indicating a less calm body of water than the Sea of Time.

"I'm afraid it's not very dramatic, is it? No flashing lights or fading in and out."

"Well, it's not the transporter on the *Enterprise*, that's for sure."

Susan wasn't sure if she was let down or relieved. Before she could decide, Drift House pitched dramatically to the right, and she had to grab on to the back of a chair to keep from falling over, nearly dropping her test tubes. A loud crash emanated from the other side of the room, echoed by several smaller crashes through the house.

"What was—"

Susan was cut off by a squelchy voice from the radio.

"—North Atlantic is famous for its own squalls." Bjarki's voice pitched and rolled like the house. "Nothing to worry about but your stomachs." The transmission was swallowed by a wave of static. "Lose radio contact soon" was the next thing Susan heard. "Interference . . . temporal squall." A longer wave of static, and then: "Remember," Bjarki's voice said with undeniable urgency, "watch for"—static—"babble."

And then: nothing.

Uncle Farley was still sitting on the pitching floor. With his soft belly and splayed legs, he looked a bit like a big bearded baby. He leaned close to the radio, speaking directly into the grille. "Bjarki, are you there?"

The house was rocking wildly from prow to stern, but Susan could feel its rhythm in the soles of her feet and her stomach. Anything that has a rhythm has some element of control also, so Susan wasn't too alarmed. If the house had been shaking erratically, she would have been more scared.

"I think we've lost contact," she said now. "Did you hear him say something about babbling?"

"I think he said Babel."

"Babel?" Susan glanced at the drawing room walls, which were still blank. "We saw the Tower of Babel there. But that's not in Greenland? I mean, right?"

Uncle Farley laughed. "No, ancient Mesopotamia. Er, modern Iraq," he clarified. "About seven or eight thousand miles apart, not to mention a few thousand years." He frowned now, not in displeasure, but as if he'd suddenly remembered something.

"What is it, Uncle Farley?"

"Oh, nothing, I'm sure. It's just the ancient Babylonians—"

"I thought we were talking about the, um, Babel people."

"Babel, Babylon, Babylonians, same people, same place. Anyway, there are legends that they made some extraordinary breakthroughs in temperology."

Susan's legs—and her stomach, fortunately—were getting used to the rolling ocean, and she stood up carefully and went to a window. "I'm not sure I understand, Uncle Farley." She looked out at a wide gray expanse whose dips and swells reminded her of pictures of the moon. "How does this affect us?"

"Well, I don't know that it does. I just wonder if perhaps

some artifact might have made its way from Babel to the New World."

"All the way to Greenland?" Susan said, still staring at the empty ocean. It was so big and empty that she could hardly imagine getting across it herself, let alone a civilization that had lived before steam engines and motors and airplanes.

Uncle Farley stood up somewhat less steadily than Susan. "Well, take that mask I showed you earlier. It originated in Pompeii, on the Italian peninsula, but I bought it in a market square in Buenos Aires. Things do get around, given enough time, and—oh. Oh, that's too bad."

"What is it, Uncle Farley?" Susan said, leaving the chilly window and wobbling in his direction.

"The mask. It's—"

"Broken!" Susan exclaimed. It was true: the beautiful, eerie, two-thousand-year-old death mask had fallen to the floor and broken into three pieces.

The fractured face sobered Uncle Farley. "No use crying over spilt milk and, um, broken masks. We obviously need to make our vessel shipshape. I'm afraid I've let it get much too domestic." He chuckled ruefully. "Where's Mr. Zenubian when you need him?"

The first thing he did was pull open a drawer and take out a package of bootstrings—black, Susan saw, and indicated for twenty-hole boots. He used them to make necklaces for each of the test tubes. He worked quickly and efficiently—rather like Charles, Susan thought, who never blinked when he'd set himself a task.

"I hope Charles is okay," she said as Uncle Farley slipped the vial over her neck.

Uncle Farley's face tightened as he slipped his own vial on and tucked it inside his shirt as Murray did with his golden locket. It seemed that the gesture reminded him of Murray just as it did Susan, because the next thing Uncle Farley said was, "We'll get back to Charles *and* Murray as quickly as we can. Until then, we shall have to trust in President Wilson's ability to lead your brother safely."

Susan and Uncle Farley looked at each other for a moment, and then the two of them burst out laughing.

"Can you imagine!" Uncle Farley guffawed. "Charles! Charles! Slow down, Charles!"

"Charles!" Susan echoed, doing her best imitation of President Wilson's panting. "You wouldn't happen to have any peanuts in your bag, would you, Charles?"

"I'm willing to bet five American dollars he's riding on Charles's shoulder at this very moment—and giving orders every step of the way!"

"Orders that I'm *sure* Charles is ignoring."

"Oh dear," Uncle Farley said, "we'd really better hurry back, hadn't we? They're probably a greater threat to each other than anything else."

Before Susan could answer, a faint "Rak!" echoed through-out the house.

"Was that—?" Susan began. "But I thought he was with Charles!"

Uncle Farley smacked his forehead.

"That wasn't President Wilson," he said, heading rapidly, if unsteadily, toward the door.

"What? Who—you mean Marie-Antoinette?"

"She spends most of her time in the solarium," Uncle Far-ley said as they made their way through the library. "She hides in here when President Wilson's wooing gets too much for her."

"Rak! Rak!" came from the far side of the closed doors, louder now, and distinctly angry.

Uncle Farley threw open the doors. Susan barely had time to register the splendor of the solarium's great banyan before a red and blue blur flashed into the passage and swooped around the two humans.

"Rak! Rak, rak!"

"She doesn't sound happy *at all*," Susan said, dodging the flashing wings until she realized Marie-Antoinette was actu-ally aiming for her shoulder. The parrot settled on Susan's up-per arm unsteadily, her claws digging into the girl's skin as she dragged herself upward. "Ow! Marie-Antoinette, please—"

"Rak!"

Uncle Farley smiled weakly at Susan. "We must remember

that Marie-Antoinette doesn't understand us like President Wilson—"

"RAK!"

Between the pitching floorboards and the screeching parrot in her ear, Susan felt ready to fall over. She was looking outside the solarium now, at the gray water and whitecapped waves and bullet-shaped clouds whipping through the air. She had long had her own suspicions about how much Marie-Antoinette understood, but she suddenly thought of something else.

"Uncle Farley? Who's, um, who's *steering*?"

Uncle Farley smiled. "That, at least, is one question I *can* answer. The house has its own piloting mechanism. Once a course has been plotted, it takes you right there."

Susan studied her uncle closely. He was staring at the floor, a poorly concealed grin curling up one side of her mouth.

Susan put her hands on her hips. "Where did you go?"

With his toe, Uncle Farley traced a curved line in the carpet. The action threw him off balance on the rocking waves, and he had to catch himself on the wall.

"I beg your pardon?"

"You must have gone *somewhere*, or you wouldn't know how the house steers. Or how to program the radio. Or the fact that we wouldn't feel anything when we *sluiced*. Or did you find an *instruction manual* somewhere?"

"Rak," Marie-Antoinette croaked quietly. "Man-u-al."

Uncle Farley's fingers drummed the wall. "When I was a teenager—not much older than you are now—I used to love to go to Renaissance fairs. The jugglers and the bards and the costumes! The richly colored velvets, and the capes, and the hats, and the leggings! They had a real sense of deportment back then, instead of running around in, in *Dockers*."

Susan looked her plump uncle up and down, trying hard not to smirk. "You wore *tights*?"

"Not *tights*, Susan. *Leggings*. Cotton, and not at *all* stretchy."

"You wore tights! And those funny little elf boots! Oh, I'm going to make Mum show me pictures as soon as we get back!"

Uncle Farley frowned. "Well, let's concentrate on getting back and worry about pictures later."

"Never mind that! Where did you go?"

And now a strange smile crept over Uncle Farley's face. A smile of such rapture and wonder that Susan felt as if she were looking inside her uncle's soul.

"I went to see Shakespeare."

Susan clapped a hand over her mouth. Through her fingers she said, "You . . . met . . . *Shakespeare*?"

Uncle Farley shook his head. The faraway look was still on his face, and his voice was equally distant. "Oh, I wanted to, but I thought it would be too risky. What if I spilled the beans about something that happened in the future and he put it in one of his plays? The course of history could literally be changed. Electricity might have been discovered during the reign of James I rather than George III. No, I went to the see *The Tempest.*"

Susan was dumbfounded. "You traveled five hundred years to see . . . a *play*?"

"Not just a play, Susan. *The Tempest*, as Shakespeare wrote it and Shakespeare staged it. In the Globe Theatre, with the smell of urine rising up from the pit, and stale beer, and the audience catcalling the actors." Uncle Farley laughed. "The truth is I didn't understand half of it because of the Elizabethan accent, but it was still magic, I tell you. Just . . . magic."

Susan had a hard time imagining how a play performed without any lights or special effects could be particularly "magical," especially to a man who lived in a house that could sail the Sea of Time. And the smell of urine? Blech! But she could tell from Uncle Farley's face he wasn't faking it. He had witnessed something no one else alive had. And suddenly she wanted that too. Maybe she wouldn't have picked the Greenland Vikings out of all the peoples and places of the past, but still, they were the first Europeans to come to America, and they had almost disappeared from history. It was kind of the opposite of Shakespeare really. Everyone knew about Shakespeare. But hardly anyone knew about the Vikings on Greenland. She would learn things no one else in her time even dreamed of.

As it turned out, she would learn it sooner than she expected.

"Susan?"

The eldest Oakenfeld followed her uncle's pointing finger. There was an odd expression on his face. Nervous yet eager. Awed. Winsome. (*Don't say "winsome,"* Susan heard Charles's teasing voice in her head. *It's affected.* She *did* hope he was okay.)

Uncle Farley nodded at the windows beyond his niece's head.

"Look."

Susan turned. Although she knew where they were going, she was still surprised to see that the ocean had an edge now: even a few hours on the open sea can convince you that land is just a trick of memory. But there it was. A wavy ribbon of brown and green stretched between the steel-gray water and the cold northern sky. The deep green hills reminded Susan of nothing so much as the Island of the Past, but even from a distance she could sense the difference. The density. These weren't hollow vaults housing all manner of creatures. They were dense piles of rock to which a few feet of soil clung desperately, held in by a net of grass that, however green, looked coarser and colder than the grass on the Island of the Past. Even the beaches were rocky and forbidding, and between several hills lay sparkling stripes, water possibly, or maybe ice. The place was eerily treeless as well, and Susan's mind flashed on her tree, her redwood, growing in New York City thanks to global warming. Would this place ever be that warm? She knew global warming was supposed to be a bad thing, but she thought a little sunshine and a nice forest would do wonders for the barren land before her.

Susan turned back to her uncle. She didn't know what to say. There it was: the past.

"Let's go to my study. The spyglass is there. We'll be able to see better."

Susan hurried after her uncle, Marie-Antoinette flapping on her shoulder. Once in the study, the parrot flew to a table, and Uncle Farley handed Susan the spyglass.

She stepped close to a floor-to-ceiling window and brought the telescope to her eye. Immediately a second, lower set of hills appeared. Susan twisted the spyglass, focused, and realized with a start that the hills were actually the turf-covered homes she had seen on the walls of the drawing room. Again she thought of the Island of the Past. Had Pierre Marin been inspired by these buildings? Had he come here? But unlike the hollow hills of the Island of the Past, there weren't windows in these low, long structures. Just the occasional door and even more occasional chimney. A thread of smoke, so thin it seemed as cold as the water in the fjords between the hills. An involuntary shiver ran down Susan's back.

"It doesn't look very . . . inviting," she said. "Does it?"

Uncle Farley's voice was quiet when he spoke, serious.

"Well, the colony was founded by Erik the Red around the turn of the first millennium. Erik was a murderer on the run from the law, and he named the place Greenland because it sounded better than Snow-and-Ice-Covered-Land." Uncle Farley shrugged. "I can't imagine five hundred years in this climate has done anything for his descendants' dispositions. We will want to proceed with, um, *caution*."

Susan was about to ask Uncle Farley what "caution" meant in such a context, when something thin and dark burst through the window, shattering the glass of a single pane. It knocked against a marble bust of Beethoven and clattered to the floor. Only when it was still could Susan and Uncle Farley get a good look at it.

It was a spear.

TWELVE

Wendat

THE MORNING DAWNED EARLIER THAN Charles would have liked, and colder too. Bolts of mist snaked through the glade where he'd made camp, congealing to a general fog over the stream; it was too cloudy to even think about lighting a fire. Charles's nest was snug, though, and only the need to relieve himself drove him out of bed. He had never peed against a tree trunk before, and found it less liberating than chilly. Fortunately, President Wilson remained blissfully snoring on his branch.

Charles was well rested but hungry. Last night's meal had been tasty, but there hadn't been anything left over, and somehow he couldn't face the prospect of fish for breakfast. When the camp was clear, he made another attempt at straightening out his glasses, then shouldered his backpack and roused President Wilson. The parrot immediately stretched his wings and said he would fly up to look for the smoke to make sure they set off in the right direction.

"I climbed a tree and looked myself," Charles said. And then, in a nonchalant tone, he added: "They must've put their fire out too. The smoke's gone."

President Wilson eyed the boy suspiciously. Charles was a nervous child, and for him *not* to be anxious about the disappearance of their smoke beacon suggested he had a trick up his sleeve.

"Yes?" the parrot said in the driest tone he could muster—drollery was really more suited to music rooms and mahogany perches than the great outdoors. "How do you propose we set our course then?"

Beneath his lopsided glasses, Charles's face split into a grin. He had obviously been waiting for just this question. Leading President Wilson to the other side of the filled-in firepit, he showed the bird a large arrow that had been pressed into the soft ground with stones.

"My stars! They've marked their path! How convenient!"

Charles frowned. "*They* didn't mark the path. I did—last night, while you were gathering berries."

President Wilson, who would've *loved* some berries at that particular moment, looked at the arrow. It pointed up the hill in a direction roughly perpendicular to the rising sun—north, the parrot realized. They were heading more or less due north. Now the parrot looked back at his human charge and said,

"You have demonstrated your cleverness and resourcefulness many times in the past twenty-four hours, Charles Oakenfeld. But be careful not to add hubris to your list of attributes." And, without waiting for an invitation—he was too tired and hungry to care about his pride—he flew to the boy's shoulder.

Charles realized he *was* showing off a bit. But he could hardly help it. While President Wilson had done little more than ride on his shoulder, he, Charles Oakenfeld, had started a fire from pieces of wood, caught wild trout, erected his own sleeping quarters, and built the bed he slept on. And now, thanks to his own foresight, he was navigating through unknown wilderness! Why shouldn't he be proud?

As if in answer, the book in his bag tingled against his skin. It felt less like wings than like eyes staring at the back of his head, as if Charles were being watched by unseen forces. Pushed even. Guided along a path he only thought he was choosing himself. But the way Charles figured, even if his newfound resourcefulness had come from Mario's book, the book had chosen *him* to share it with. So that meant there must be something special about him, right? And, swatting some branches out of his way, he strode purposefully forward.

"Be careful, Charles! You almost knocked me off your shoulder!"

Then fly like a bird, Charles thought. But he didn't say it aloud.

Three hours later, Charles's confidence had diminished considerably. The climb had been steadily uphill for one thing, over land that was alternately thickly grown, requiring Charles to beat a path with his stick (after four or five thousand whacks the appeal kind of faded) or else over pebbly slopes that kept slipping out from under his shoes. A half dozen times he tripped, and although he never actually fell or twisted his ankle or anything like that, his shoulder took a beating: each time Charles wobbled, President Wilson dug his claws in for purchase, and the last time he actually drew blood.

"Be careful, Charles! You nearly spilled me!"

"*Me* be careful!? You're the one cutting my shoulder open!"

"Well, if you could walk steadily I wouldn't have to grip so tightly!"

Charles looked at the blood on his fingertips and saw red. "You don't like the way I walk? Fine! Fly!" And, scooping the parrot into his hand, he tossed him into the air.

President Wilson dipped and swirled like a ball of yarn swatted by a kitten, then righted himself and flew to a low-hanging branch.

"When . . . your uncle . . . hears about . . . this!"

Charles scowled back at President Wilson. "You just be

careful I don't open the world's first Kentucky Fried *Parrot* franchise."

As soon as he'd said it, Charles wished he hadn't mentioned food. His stomach was so empty it actually *hurt*. Though he'd kept his eyes peeled for anything edible, he'd seen nothing he was willing to put in his mouth all day. Nor had he come across another stream, and his throat was parched.

The only thing to do was keep walking. Occasionally a flash of red would sweep by as President Wilson flew from branch to branch, but the parrot didn't speak, either because he was too angry or too winded.

And it was hot now. The sun wasn't even directly over-head, but the air felt thick and warm, like the air in a bakery. Except there were no doughnuts or muffins. Or napoleons. Or cookies—no gingersnaps or chocolate chips or peanut butter–rum raisin–pecan sandies. No thick slice of red velvet cake or German chocolate or (Charles's favorite, which he had had for his birthday last year) deliciously sweet-crunchy-chewy-flaky baklava. Charles had carried pieces of it to school for the next week, but now, when he unzipped his backpack and rooted around the bottom seams, he found nothing but unidentifiable brown blobs spotting the bottom of the bag. They could have been faded crumbs of phyllo dough, but more likely they were just lint.

They tasted like lint.

He still had the book. Charles paused, letting his palm rest on the enigmatic empty lines. They were palpably warm to the touch, and their electric pulse seemed to bounce the blood in his veins.

It was only after Charles's fingers had sat on the scored lines for several seconds—or minutes, or hours, he couldn't tell—that he realized the title was gone. *The Lost Cities*. Charles felt around his backpack in case the golden letters had simply fallen off, but found no trace of them. And even as he tried to figure out what that might mean, he realized he was no longer alone. He didn't hear anything—no twig or cleared throat. Maybe that's what tipped him off: the birds had all stopped singing, and in every book Charles had ever read there was only one creature whose presence compelled the creatures of the forest to silence.

Man.

Charles looked up.

He saw only one person at first: a boy really, only a year or two older than he was. The stranger was lean and brown, his upper body bare and his lower half covered in soft-looking buckskin leggings, his feet shod in moccasins. A thin string, also leather, crossed his torso, from which dangled a smooth brown pouch about the size of the boy's head, which was also smooth and brown, having been shaved bare. There was also a knife in the boy's hand. It had only a single slightly crude-looking stone blade on it, but Charles had no doubt it could slice right through his empty stomach.

Charles did his best to smile. "Um . . . hi?"

The expression on the boy's face didn't change. But suddenly there were more of him. At first Charles thought he was seeing double through his lopsided glasses—no, triple—because the two newcomers were dressed identically to the boy. But then he saw they were older, grown men with the same lean, oval faces and large almond-shaped, impassive eyes. In addition to knives and pouches, the two newcomers had bows slung across their backs. A dozen feathered shafts poked from each man's quiver.

One of the older Indians spoke now. He was a young man, probably in his mid-twenties, and his tone was harsh. The boy's eyes dropped and his knife curled backward in his hand, as if it too were ashamed. Though Charles couldn't understand a word of the Indian's speech, he was pretty sure the boy was being chastised—probably for allowing himself to be seen.

Suddenly the twentysomething man broke off. He turned and stepped determinedly toward Charles, his right hand reaching for his sheathed knife. Charles fell back in alarm. But before the man could reach him, his younger companion grabbed the man and began speaking in a rapid, pleading tone. Several times the boy pointed to Charles and then he pointed to his own face, and his index fingers traced curious circles in the air around his eyes. At first Charles thought he was indicating the difference in shape between his eyes and the Indian's—round, rather than oval—but then he realized the boy was pantomiming *glasses*, and suddenly a word he had heard the boy say several times became clear to him.

Lunettes.

Glasses. More specifically, French for "glasses." Unlike Susan, Charles had never studied French, and wasn't sure how he knew the word. Maybe his sister had said it sometime? Or maybe—

Charles suddenly remembered the book in his lap. As nonchalantly as possible, he folded his bag closed, and slowly, one tooth at a time, drew the zipper. Whatever else happened, he knew he couldn't lose Mario's book.

The third man spoke. This man was significantly older than the others—in his fifties or sixties, Charles realized, although the strip of hair running down the center of his head was still inky black. His voice was calm and brief. After he spoke, the twentysomething man barked back at him but the older man didn't respond. His expression was stern but unruffled.

A tense moment passed, and then the twentysomething Indian spat something that sounded a lot like "Pah." Charles got the very distinct impression his life had just been saved.

A short time later, Charles found himself marching rapidly behind the three Indians. His hands had been bound in front of him with a length of leather. Charles had never had his hands tied before, and he found it surprisingly difficult to keep his balance on the uneven terrain. But he was more bothered by the fact that the youngest Indian had confiscated his backpack. The boy had glanced briefly at Mario's book, but had been much more fascinated by the working of the bag's zipper, which he opened and closed a dozen times.

The Indians marched single file, the eldest leading, the gruff young man second, the boy immediately in front of Charles. It was the boy who had tied Charles's hands, pulling the cord from the pouch that hung from his shoulder. The binding was loose but the knot itself was tight, and the pace set by the lead Indian was so fast that Charles had to concentrate to keep from falling, and so couldn't try to untie his hands.

Still, as they marched Charles noticed that the two older Indians were getting further and further away, isolating himself and the boy. From the way the boy frequently glanced in Charles's direction, his expression curious and somehow reassuring, Charles guessed he was holding back on purpose. Finally, when the two older men were a good twenty or thirty feet ahead, the boy allowed Charles to catch up to him. He smiled and touched his fingers to his chest.

"Tankort."

It was a pretty universal gesture, and Charles understood at once.

"Charles O—" He cut himself off. One syllable was probably a lot easier than four.

"Charzo!" the young Indian—Tankort—said brightly. And then he surprised Charles by saying, "*Français?*"

Where was Susan when you needed her? She'd practiced her French all year to impress President Wilson (who could not only speak, but spoke English *and* French). And where *was* President Wilson? Charles stole a quick look around before answering Tankort's question—"Nope"—but failed to see any sign of the parrot.

He turned back to the Indian, who was looking in the trees with a slightly troubled expression. Stupid, thought Charles. He shouldn't have been so obvious. Now he smiled as brightly as he could and said,

"American."

Tankort's brows knit together. "Merkin?"

Charles realized that America probably didn't exist yet. He thought for a minute and then said, "English."

Tankort's confusion melted away—only to be replaced by undeniable disgust. Disgust and fury. The boy looked Charles up and down disdainfully. He thumped his fingers to his chest again. "Tankort," he said forcefully, and then he waved his hand at the two men marching ahead, making a gesture that roped the three together. "Wendat."

Wendat. Charles guessed it was the name of their tribe. He'd never heard the word before, but last winter President Wilson had given a bit of a history lesson during which he mentioned that the Iroquois and Huron confederations had been active in the region south of Drift House. Perhaps the Wendat were a part of one or the other? He figured he had a fifty-fifty shot.

"Iroquois?" he tried, doing his best to make his voice friendly and pleasing.

If it was possible, Tankort's face twisted even further, into a grimace of hatred. He made a hissing noise, quiet but sharp as his knife.

"Iroquois? Wendat *hate* Iroquois." And then, thumping Charles on the chest, he snarled, "Wendat hate *English*." Without another word, he stalked ahead.

The rest of the day was pretty much horrible. Tankort rejoined the two older Wendat, and whenever Charles tripped or stumbled the young Indian would turn and say something harsh and mocking in his own language. When at one point the eldest Wendat seemed to chastise him, Tankort made a long-winded explanation that included the words "Iroquois" and "English" several times. Charles wished he'd paid more attention to President Wilson's lecture, so he'd've known what had happened between the Wendat and the English to cause such hatred. And he wished he knew where President Wilson was now—he'd feel terribly if the last human words Drift House's mascot heard were a crack about a Kentucky Fried Parrot franchise.

At some point during the day (late morning? afternoon? evening? Charles had no idea) a fourth man seemed to materialize out of the trees. Charles looked around the undifferentiated forest, amazed that anyone could find anything here, let alone a single insignificant human. Well, not exactly insignificant: the new Wendat was rather plump, although he marched easily enough. And not single either: he had four dogs under his care. The animals were, to Charles's eyes, nondescript: brown, medium sized, with short hair and thin tails like boxers and long snouts like German shepherds. There was a brief heated conference after the dog keeper joined Charles's group. Tankort and the twentysomething man spoke in angry voices and often pointed at Charles. The dog keeper listened to the conversation silently, attending to his animals and shaking his head slightly when his companions' voices grew particularly loud, as if he preferred the quiet company of his four-legged friends. Finally the older Wendat spoke, and then, when his companions' voices continued to rise, held up his hand to stop the debate.

Somewhat huffily, Tankort and the twentysomething Indian stomped a few feet away. They sat down and pulled strips of dried meat out of their bags, and chewed at them with sullen expressions. The older man and the dog keeper ate as well. The latter brought Charles several pieces of the jerky. He had sweet meaty breath and a furry smell, and he loosened Charles's bindings, making it easier for him to eat. Charles assumed the meat was venison, and although he didn't like the idea of eating Bambi he was way too hungry to care. There were more of the tart berries President Wilson had found yesterday, and a skin of lukewarm water from which Charles drank greedily.

The meal hardly took the edge off Charles's hunger though, and his body felt incredibly tired from the hard march. But as soon as the four Wendat had finished, they hitched the dogs to sledlike contraptions and set off again. The sleds were piled with stacks of what Charles thought at first were pieces of rotting wood, but when he got a whiff of them he realized they were in fact flattened animal pelts—recently removed from their original wearers, judging from the smell.

Something came to him then. Hadn't President Wilson said Pierre Marin learned the secret of time travel from Indians he'd dealt with when he traded fur? Charles wished he could remember—he wished he hadn't chased President Wilson away, so the parrot could answer these questions for him. But when he glanced around the forest he still saw no glimpse of red among the endless waves of green.

Charles had no idea how long they walked—how many miles, how many hours. Many miles. Many, *many* hours. The party stopped twice, both times by streams, where a few more strips of meat were washed down with handfuls of cold water, and then they started up again. The shadows grew shorter as the sun rose, then grew steadily longer as it began to set. The light took on a yellowish cast, then thickened to orange, then gold. It was a rich color, but didn't do much to illuminate the ground below the leaf canopy, and Charles found it harder and harder to see his footing. He tripped several times, and one time actually fell and cried out in fear. The men just stared at him wordlessly while he struggled up and retrieved his glasses, which were so lopsided they didn't want to stay on his nose. Had he really twisted them out of shape just to make a dumb fire? Charles couldn't believe he'd been so dumb. He felt so dumb he couldn't even think of another word for dumb.

He was just about to sit down and refuse to go any further when he noticed a flicker between the shadowy tree trunks up ahead. It was hard to get a clear view because of the underbrush, but Charles thought it was—yes! It was a fire!

One of the dogs let out a yelp and the keeper made a sound like a growl, silencing the animal. Or maybe it was the other way around—maybe the keeper had yelped and the dog had growled. The eagerness of the whole party was palpable. Everyone wanted to get home. Charles wanted to get there too, even if they tied him to a tree. As long as he could sit down they could do anything to him they wanted.

There were shadows in the forest now. Shadows that weren't trees. Moving out to greet the newcomers, then pulsing back in. The fire was big now, a ring of light reaching to encircle the humans in its care. Charles slowed, not sure if fear held him back, or some force from the fire, keeping away everything that wasn't Wendat. Then he felt a hand on his arm—the dog keeper—and he was pulled forward. Suddenly Charles found himself in a small clearing. Dozens of figures emerged from the trees, all of them looking at the newcomers and especially at Charles. Charles could see them pointing at him and drawing circles around their eyes. *Lunettes.* Glasses. Charles thought he heard the word several times, but then he heard another word much more clearly.

"English."

The Wendat formed a wall with their bodies, fencing Charles in. The party he had come with melted into the tribesmen and -women, who pressed in closer, their circle flattening and elongating. Frightened, Charles retreated down the ever-narrower chute formed by their bodies. The Wendat pressed in closer until they formed two rows. Without actually touching Charles, they guided him down the corridor. The sibilant hiss seemed to come not so much from them as from the forest.

"English English English English."

Charles's skin prickled with fear. The word surrounded him, bound him as tightly as the ropes on his wrists. Then he saw that the rows of Wendat ended at a small skin-covered tent. Golden light outlined the doorflap, making it seem like a black shadow, a bottomless chasm.

Charles half expected his bound hands to pass right through the door. But it was solid leather, and he pulled back the flap. He had to bend almost double to enter the tent, but once inside he could stand. He blinked against the light and the smoky air. At first it seemed that the voice came from the smoke itself.

"Sit down, Charles."

The accent was perfect, flat, American English, and Charles recognized it as the voice of people on the Sea of Time. Well, the door had looked like a magical portal. Had he somehow passed onto the sea? He peered into the tent but could see nothing besides the fire.

Charles blinked.

He was seated, but he had no memory of sitting down. His hands were untied and the ground beneath him wasn't ground. It was a carpet of leather, through which Charles could feel round poles. What's more, Charles could swear he was moving.

"Relax, Charles. I know the last few days have been trying, but you are safe now."

Charles squinted. The fire still burned, but it seemed insubstantial. It gave off no heat, and through the pale flames Charles could see the person who was speaking: an old, old man draped in deerhide. A thin band held his colorless hair off a high wide forehead, which was itself somehow colorless, or perhaps it was the color of ancient paper, pale, yet dark at the same time. The old man's eyes were two translucent orbs, and they drank in the fire and reflected back luminescent shadows. Underneath them seven lines had been painted on his wrinkled cheeks, each smaller than the one above it. The lines were simultaneously so faint that Charles wasn't sure they were really there, and blazing with a light that made him squint behind his lopsided glasses.

It was the symbol on Mario's book.

"How do you know my name? And how come you have those lines on your face?"

The man's face and voice seemed too old for expression—intimidation or comfort or anything else. One of his hands came out from beneath the deerskin robe and reached across—through—the fire. Charles expected the man's hand to pass through him in the same way, but a solid, blunt fingernail came to rest on his forehead. It seemed to tingle slightly, like Mario's book, and the flames of the fire licked the thin arm without burning it.

"It is time, Charles."

Charles wasn't sure if the man had said these words out loud or transmitted them to his brain through his finger.

The man nodded, as if he had confirmed something, and then he took his finger away. Somewhat relieved, Charles watched the man's mouth move and heard the words come from his lips. But no matter what their source, he still didn't understand them.

"I have a task for you."

"A task?"

The old man nodded again. The lines on his cheeks blazed and his skin seemed to fade until only the lines remained, as empty as the lines on the cover of the book, yet tauntingly full of unexpressed meaning.

The old man's voice seemed to come from the air itself.

"It is time, Charles. It is time."

THIRTEEN

Osterbygd

GLASS EXPLODED THROUGH TWO MORE windows. One of the spears struck a mullion and wobbled through the air, narrowly missing Susan's face. The other pierced the glass cleanly and whizzed through the room, embedding itself in the spine of a book on the opposite wall. It was a hefty volume, but it couldn't support the weight of the real world for very long, and after a moment, spear and book both fell to the floor.

"We're under attack!" Susan screamed. And then, realizing she'd stated the obvious—well, screamed it really—she yelled, "To the cannons!"

"I think retreat might be a more feasible tack at this point," Uncle Farley said, his voice not quite as calm as his words.

"Let's go up to the poop deck and see what we're dealing with."

Since Susan had no idea how to fire a cannon, she followed her uncle to the stairs that led to the roof of the gallery—what Charles had once called (and what Murray repeated endlessly) the poop deck. She was set to burst through the doors when Uncle Farley's hand fell on her shoulder. He was panting heavily, and instead of speaking placed a finger to his lips. He motioned for the two of them to get down on all fours. Only then did he reach up to open the door, just wide enough for Susan to squeeze through, then somewhat more to accommodate his larger form.

"I won't ask you to wait here," he whispered when they were outside, "since I know you'll just disobey me. But whatever you do, don't go sticking your head through the balusters."

Susan wanted to say she wasn't *that* stupid, but she could tell Uncle Farley was only speaking out of concern. And so she said instead, "Don't say 'balusters.' It's affected."

Uncle Farley opened his mouth to protest, then closed it. He grinned. "Do you think his adventure is as exciting as ours?"

"I hope so. Or we'll *never* hear the end of it." And, nodding toward the balusters—or, in honor of Charles, perhaps we should say, the posts—Susan said, "Ready?"

They slithered to the edge of the deck. In fact, Susan

couldn't have stuck her head through the posts if she'd wanted: they were too thick, and set too closely together, forming an effective shield against things coming from outside the ship. Like spears.

She did, however, push her nose between two posts to see the water below. She wasn't sure what she expected—Vikings, dragon ships, horned helmets—but she was quite surprised by the sight that greeted her eyes: five kayaks floated fifteen or twenty feet out from Drift House, each holding a single man. Ships and sailors were uniformly brown and covered in shiny damp leather, and Susan leaned back to hiss: "Uncle Farley! They're not Vikings! They're Eskimos!"

Uncle Farley smiled wanly. "It's not *quite* the time for a lesson in anthropology, but I believe the people in the kayaks call themselves Qaanaaq."

"Qaanaaq?"

"Accent on the second syllable, Susan. Qaa-NAAQ."

"Um, Uncle Farley? Anthropology? Timing?"

Suddenly a sharp cry pierced the air. A split second later the wood of a post splintered as a spear struck it. Susan could feel the vibration, and as she and Uncle Farley scuttled backward heated words passed back and forth below them. Even as they spoke, Susan felt a bump beneath her breastbone, and exclaimed (a little more loudly than she'd intended),

"The translation charms!" She flinched at the sound of her voice. "The charms," she whispered, pulling hers out.

"Saved by a preteen again," Uncle Farley lamented.

Uncle and niece held the innocuous-looking vials in front of them. Though neither said it aloud, the term "Accursed Returner" rang in both their heads.

"What did Bjarki say?" Susan said, stalling for time. "A dab in each ear?"

Uncle Farley nodded. "And a drop on the tongue." He uncorked his test tube. "Let me go first."

Susan opened hers as well. "We should do this together."

While the Qaanaaq continued to argue, Susan and her uncle moistened their fingertips and brought them to their ears. She shivered as the cold wind blew against her dampened skin, then wet her finger again, stuck out her tongue.

"Hea goeth—" She pulled her tongue back in her mouth. "Here goes nothing."

The drop of water was tasteless, but she still made a little face, as did her uncle. She contemplated the idea of becoming an Accursed Returner, coming unstuck in time, always trying to get back to your place. But before she could plumb the depths of that idea, a voice distracted her.

"We can scale the side and enter the vessel."

"It's not necessary," a second voice said. "Can't you see these strange reflective squares are extremely fragile? We can just break one and enter that way."

Susan found herself filled with elation and fear. "It worked!" she hissed. And then: "They're trying to get inside!"

Uncle Farley looked more bewildered than frightened. "There are swords in the trunk in the library. I suppose we'll have to arm ourselves."

They began to inch toward the door, when a new voice stopped them.

"Stand aside, men of Qaanaaq. I mean you no harm, but this vessel is under my protection."

Uneasy laughter floated up from the ocean's surface.

"Look! We are threatened by a boy!"

"In those clothes! In that boat! Take him, men!"

The Qaanaaq war cries almost drowned out a series of faint *boings*, followed by sharp whizzing sounds and hollow thumps. The war cries turned to angry shouts.

Susan couldn't take the suspense. She crept forward to investigate.

"Susan!"

The eldest Oakenfeld didn't respond to her uncle's frightened hiss, nor to his hand on her ankle. A moment later her nose was between the railings, and a strange gasp escaped her mouth.

As the Qaanaaq's shouts had indicated, a sixth boat had appeared on the scene. It was wide, shallow, and flat bottomed, more raft than boat, and even to Susan's landlubber eyes it seemed unsuited for the rolling ocean waves. But the boat was hardly what had caused her to gasp. It was, rather, the boy standing effortlessly on the rollicking surf. He wore pale linen trousers and a tuniclike shirt, and his feet were wrapped in leather sandals whose laces wound up his ankles. Both his clothes and the rich tan hue of his skin made Susan think he'd just come from someplace sunny and warm—certainly not the forbidding beach that lay a half mile off Drift House's port stern.

Perhaps more to the point, the boy held a bow and arrow, cocked but unreleased. Susan looked left, and saw an amazing sight. Two of the kayaks were half sunk, the arrows poking from their leather hulls a clear explanation of what had happened. While two of the remaining kayakers paddled to their comrades' aid, the fifth warrior faced the boy in the rowboat. His spear was hefted, but he didn't release his weapon.

The eyes of the spearman flickered in the direction of the poop deck. The stone-tipped staff wavered in the air, as if he were unsure whom to target.

The boy in the flat-bottomed boat spoke. "Don't even *think* about it."

"My arm is fast, little man," the Qaanaaq replied. He glanced at Susan and Uncle Farley on the railing. "You risk more than your own life."

"My arrow is faster," the boy said in a level, dangerous voice. "I won't aim for your hull this time."

The stalemate lasted only a moment. The Qaanaaq was neither hero nor fool. He whirled his kayak and retreated. The two kayakers in distress had been pulled from their boats, and they shivered athwart the narrow hulls of their rescuers' kayaks, feet trailing in the water. One of the punctured craft had already sunk out of sight, and with a long bubbling sigh, the second followed it down into the dark and extremely cold-looking ocean. After a long moment, the last warrior struck his paddle in the water, and his kayak twisted and skittered toward shore. Somewhat sluggishly, the other two followed.

Throughout all this Susan squirmed with anticipation. She hardly waited until the kayakers had reached a safe distance to jump up and yell the word she'd been holding back ever since she'd seen the lightly clad boy with the boy and arrow:

"Murray!"

She raced down the stairs.

"Murray! Murray!"

Susan shouted her little brother's name four or fifty more times until she was standing with her arms wrapped around his (surprisingly strong) shoulders, and even then she continued to say his name over and over again.

"Oh, Murray! I can't believe it's you!"

Murray took a step back from his big sister—who wasn't much bigger than he was now—and looked down at his feet.

"Smario now," he said, half under his breath.

Just then Uncle Farley panted up. "I beg your pardon?"

Murray looked up, an expression of undeniable anger on his face. "I said, 'It's Ma-ri-o now.'" Uncle Farley looked somewhat taken aback by his nephew's tone, but before he could say something, Murray's—or Mario's—face brightened, and he turned back to Susan.

"Oh, Susan! It's so good to see you!" He threw his arms around his sister, and Susan felt the wiry, strong muscle beneath the tanned skin.

"It's so good to see you too. You can't imagine what a surprise this is. I've got so many questions for you."

"You'd better save the rest of your questions for the boat. We ain't got much time." He turned to Uncle Farley. "I assume you've provisioned your vessel?" His voice was gruff. Cold really. Cold and rude.

"Er, ah, that is, I'm sure Miss Applethwaite can provide—"

"Don't she always?"

It seemed to Susan—and, apparently, to Uncle Farley—that Mario directed his words at his uncle's stomach, and the older man colored under his skinny, sun-browned nephew's judgmental gaze.

"Well, come on," Mario said. "We can't be gabbing all day. *Time*," he added significantly, "is truly a-wasting."

Susan and Uncle Farley exchanged a look behind Mario's back. Physically, he was undoubtedly an older version of the Murray they knew—Susan put him around ten or eleven, which fit in with the boy Charles had told Susan he'd met last fall. Charles had mentioned the salty accent as well, but he hadn't said anything about this new, aggressive personality.

They followed him to the dumbwaiter, which Murray was

already opening. An enormous wicker basket sat inside on the plush red carpet.

"You just had to make it pretty, didn't ya!" Murray called into the shaft with a chuckle. "If you'd been born three hundred years later you'd've made a regular Martha Stewart, you would have."

Susan smiled, somewhat—well, a lot actually—confused. "Mario," she said. "Your, um, accent?"

"Aye." Mario peeked under the basket's lid. A blue-checked cloth was visible, and a delicious odor of roasted turkey leaked into the dining room. "Life among salts'll do that to you, even those as learned as the Time Pirates." He took a deep breath, then stuck his tongue out, twisted it left, twisted it right, then crossed his eyes. Susan wasn't sure if he was making funny faces to get her to laugh, or if this was some arcane magic rite he'd picked up somewhere. "There," he said when he was finished. " 'Ow, er, how's that?"

"I wasn't criticizing—"

"You wouldn't be Susie Oakenfeld if you wasn't hung up on how people talk. *Weren't* hung up." Mario grinned. "Come on, sis. To the boat. We've got to get ashore."

"Mario," Uncle Farley said as he followed his niece and nephew to the back door, "you seem very . . . directed. Have you got some sort of plan?"

"My plan," Mario said, and his voice seemed particularly bitter, "is for you to row."

A moment later, they were seated in the shallow punt, where Uncle Farley somewhat unsteadily took his place at the oars. He looked at his hands, then gripped the splintery-looking paddles.

"I wish I'd thought to bring gloves."

Mario snorted. He flipped up the picnic basket and folded back the tablecloth. There sat a pair of sturdy-looking leather gloves.

"At least someone thought ahead," he said, tossing the gloves to Uncle Farley. He aimed a bit high, and the gloves smacked Uncle Farley in the face.

Mario's hostility rendered Uncle Farley speechless. He put the gloves on and resumed pulling at the oars.

"Mario," Susan rushed to fill the strained silence. "Who were those people back there?"

"Qaanaaq," Mario said. "They thought you were some of Karl Olafson's men, come back to attack them. During the last Nordseta, he got in a skirmish with some of them and took something that belonged to them, then made off to Leifs-budir."

So many strange names. Susan focused on the last. "Leifsbudir?"

"That's in Newfoundland, isn't it?" Uncle Farley added.

Mario glanced balefully at his uncle. "Geography. *That*'ll come in handy."

"I still don't understand," Susan cut in before her uncle

could protest, "why the Qaanaaq attacked us. I mean, why would they associate us with"—she tried to remember the other name—"Karloff?"

"Karl Olafson." Mario paused significantly, looked from Susan to Uncle Farley and back again. "Well," he said finally, "why do you think *I'm* here?"

Susan was wondering not just *why* Mario was there but who, exactly, Mario was. He seemed very unlike the person she'd've expected her little brother to turn into. "Well, we *were* wondering."

"It was that damn squall," Mario said. "Pardon me, Susie. That *cursed* squall. Like to knock me into the Great Drain it did. It's a good thing I wasn't blown to prehistoric times, or worse. Of course, it wasn't no accident I ended up here. Something pulled me to this time and place, as sure as my name is"—and here he broke off awkwardly—"Mar, er, Mur, er, ah . . ."

"Let's stick with Mario for now."

Ignoring his uncle, Mario leaned forward and grabbed Susan's legs. "Oh, Susan! I thought you were dead!"

Susan jumped back. "You, ah . . . I mean, what? I thought Charles told you—"

"Charles? You mean, Charles isn't . . . ?"

"Isn't what, Mario?" This from Uncle Farley, who stared at the back of his nephew's head, sensing they were close to the source of his strange hostility.

Mario looked wildly from Susan to Uncle Farley. All at once his eyes dropped to the floor of the boat and he fell silent.

"Nothing."

"Mario," Susan said, putting her hand on her brother's knee. "What is it? What's wrong?"

Mario pulled a length of cord tied around his neck from beneath his shirt. His fingers were rubbing it nervously, but when he saw Susan staring at his hands he stopped suddenly. Susan was startled: she had expected to see the familiar golden locket that Murray rubbed so often at home, but it wasn't there. The cord around his neck was empty.

"It's nothing," Mario said again. "Nothing I shouldn't be used to anyway. It's just, well, I thought Charles was dead. But it's pretty obvious from your face he ain't. *Isn't*. I guess I should've known that."

"But, Mario," Susan said, confused, "don't you remember seeing him last fall?"

"I . . . saw . . . Charles?"

Mario looked flabbergasted. Susan had a hard time imagining anyone faking that expression—and besides, she couldn't think of a good reason why Mario would lie about something like this. It led to a disturbing conclusion, however: that this Mario was somehow not the same Mario Charles had met last fall.

"What's this about Mario seeing Charles, Susan?"

Susan looked at her uncle, who was staring at her sternly.

Beyond him were the stony hills of Greenland, and all around was the frigid water of the North Atlantic. She realized the time for secrets had passed.

"It happened last fall. Just off the Island of the Past, when you were, um, incapacitated after the battle with the Time Pirates. Mario showed up. That's where the flying carpet came from."

Uncle Farley grunted against the oars. "I thought Pierre Marin gave the carpet to Charles?"

Susan smiled wanly. "We probably should have told you, but Charles and Murray—that is, our Murray," she said, glancing at Mario, "they thought it best that as few people as possible know about Mario's existence, just in case it might . . . influence something."

"I saw Charles," Mario said again, almost to himself. "I saw—*Murray?*"

Susan nodded. "You did."

Suddenly Mario's face brightened. "You know what this means, don't you?"

Susan looked at Uncle Farley, who shrugged.

"It means I make it back! To you and Charles, and Mum and Dad! All of this endless, endless searching finally pays off, and I get to be Murray again!" His voice dropped to a plaintive whisper, and his fingers clutched the empty cord at his throat. "I finally get to go home."

The look of longing on her brother's face was so overwhelming that Susan felt tears sting her cheeks. She put her hand on her brother's knee.

"You're there right now." She smiled. "You have chicken pox. Mum's probably giving you medicine, and Dad's reading you *The Chronicles of Narnia*."

Mario laughed out loud. "Oh, I probably hate that now. After everything I've seen I could never quite buy into something that simple. Do you . . ." Mario's voice broke off.

"Yes, Mario?" Susan said. "What is it?"

"Do you, well, do you know how long it takes? Till I figure it out?" His hands stroked the empty cord around his throat. "Till I find what I'm looking for?"

Susan could only shake her head. "I'm sorry, Mario. Murray's never really said anything about what he did when he—when he was you. I don't think he remembers."

Mario nodded his head, failing to hide his disappointment. "That makes sense, I guess. I forget so much." Suddenly he turned to face their uncle. "I'm sorry I've been so rude, Uncle Farley. It's just that, well, I thought you were responsible for Charles's, well, you know. Death."

Uncle Farley looked at his nephew silently for a moment. As it happened, he knew a little about how long it would take Mario to find his way back home, having briefly met a ninety-year-old version of him last fall. But he kept this information to himself. Somewhat pantingly, he caught Mario up on the temporal wave and subsequent events that had separated Charles and President Wilson from Drift House. When he'd finished, he paused to catch his breath, then said, "I get the feeling you know a bit about this colony."

"Osterbygd?" Mario said, pronouncing it "Oster-bead." "Yeah, I've been there once or twice."

Uncle Farley smiled. "I think it would be prudent if you told us what you know before we arrive."

They were well over halfway to land, Susan saw. The outlines of the grass-covered houses were more visible now, but other than a few white blobs on the hills that she thought were sheep, she saw nothing living. If it weren't for the smoke coming from the chimneys, she could have believed the colony was abandoned.

Mario nodded. "Right. Apparently, during the last hunt Karl Olafson got in a bit of a skirmish with a Qaanaaq hunting party, which got the worst of it. Many men were killed, their ivory and furs confiscated. But Karl also found . . . something. I've spoken to both Qaanaaq and Vikings to try to get them to be more specific, but people have been reluctant to talk about it."

"How did you get them to talk to you at all?" Susan said. "I mean, you don't exactly pass for a Viking, let alone a Qaanaaq."

Here Mario grinned mischievously. "Oh, I've got a few tricks up my sleeve. A few disguises. Anyway, from what I could pick up, the Qaanaaq somehow came into possession of this object centuries ago, and believe it has magic powers."

"Pardon me for stating the obvious," Uncle Farley put in, "but you sound as though you think this object is important."

Susan noticed that her uncle had to work to get out such a long sentence. But the land was close now. She could hear the lap of cold waves on the shore; once she even thought she smelled woodsmoke on the wind.

When Susan looked back at Mario, he was rubbing the empty length of twine around his neck, a thoughtful expression on his face. When he saw where she was looking, he jerked his hand away.

"There are no coincidences in time travel," he said finally. "Accidents a-plenty, but they always fit into a larger scheme whose pattern is always visible, assuming you look at it from the right perspective. I'm guessing Bjarki Skaldisson sent you here because it was in the eye of the squall, no?" Susan nodded; Mario went on. "I was drawn here as well. There's something big going on in this colony, and when you start hearing about magic objects—"

Just then, there was a scraping sound as the keel of the boat washed onto the pebbly shore.

Uncle Farley dropped the oars with a thud. "Finally!"

The boat wobbled from side to side in the current. Susan felt slightly wobbly too: she was perched on the edge of an island inhabited by people who had vanished from history more than five hundred years ago with a brother who, well, didn't seem a whole lot like her brother. All this talk about a magic object, and the way he'd jerked his hand from his neck when he'd seen her looking: Susan was starting to believe Mario had come to Osterbygd looking for the same thing she and Uncle Farley were, but possibly not for the same purpose.

She looked at Mario now, and he smiled pleadingly, as if he were asking for her faith. And Susan wanted to give it to him, but it was hard, when there were events from his own past that he didn't seem to know about and his fingers were so nervously fiddling with that empty length of twine around his neck.

Uncle Farley sighed in the middle of the boat. "No way to do this without getting wet, I'm afraid." He jumped into the ankle-deep water. A weird expression—half pain, half shock—took over his face. "Now that is—what is the word I'm looking for?—*cold*." A shiver shook his whole body, and then he splashed to the bow and dragged the boat farther up the beach.

Susan took her uncle's hand as she climbed from the boat. Mario spotted an outcropping of rock where they could conceal the craft, and the three of them dragged it across the loose pebbles of the beach to the little cove.

"It feels *remarkably* light with no one in it," Uncle Farley said, grinning sarcastically. "And, since the two of you together weigh about as much as one of my legs, perhaps I should take this as a sign I need to go on a diet."

Mario laughed. "I imagine Miss A. will make that difficult. The very word offends her ears. Speaking of which . . ." Mario lifted the picnic basket from the boat. "I think this will go over *quite* well with people who've been living on seal meat for the past few hundred years." He looked at his uncle and sister with a grin. "Well, what're we waiting for? We've got some Vikings to meet."

FOURTEEN

Time Blinks

CHARLES BLINKED.

He lay under a light deerskin covering in a room filled with murky gray light and the lingering scent of smoke.

When he rubbed his eyes he realized first that his hands were untied and then that his glasses weren't on his nose. He squinted. The room looked to be some sort of tent. A skeleton of long poles held a skin of deerhides. Light seeped in through a small opening near the poles' apex. A word occurred to Charles: "tepee." He thought: I have just spent the night in a tepee.

That part was easy enough. But how had he gotten here?

The smell of something savory distracted him. He sat up.

A brown clay bowl containing some kind of stew sat a few feet away. Beside it were his lopsided glasses, and a couple of chunks that looked like rocks but, after he'd screwed his glasses on as best as possible, focused into lumpy pieces of bread. Cornbread, he discovered when he bit into one, bland, but starchy and filling. As for the stew, it was the best—well, the only—meal he'd had since the trout he'd cooked the day before yesterday. But so small! In a moment the food was gone.

Charles was licking the gritty bowl clean when a flap folded back and a bolt of light flooded the tepee. A snort of laughter followed the light into the tent. Charles tossed the bowl aside and swiped at his chin. His visitor was the twentysomething Wendat from the hunting party. The man pantomimed Charles licking the bowl and laughed again, then quickly, roughly, bound Charles's hands much more tightly than either Tankort or the dog keeper had. Charles tried to remain as passive as possible, but when, without thinking, he reached to nudge his lopsided glasses up his nose, the man smacked Charles's hands down and made a sound that seemed more growl than word. He led Charles out of the tepee and tied him to a tree by his ankle, and then looked him up and down disdainfully. After several of the most excruciatingly awkward seconds of Charles's life, the Wendat jerked his thumb to his chest.

"Handa."

Charles, bewildered, frightened, felt his heart lighten. The man was telling him his name! Perhaps—oh please!—he wanted to be friends.

"Ch-Charles Oakenfeld," he stammered, because even he didn't quite believe it.

Handa shook his head. He thumped Charles on the chest with a strong, blunt finger.

"Handa-vey."

Handa-vey?

A pouch hung on a string over the Wendat's chest. Handa pulled it off and tapped it with the finger that had tapped Charles's chest.

"Handa-vey."

He replaced the pouch and pulled his knife from its sheath. He held it in front of Charles and tapped the blade.

"Handa-vey."

Now Handa tapped the tip of the blade on Charles's heart.

"Handa-vey," the Wendat said one more time. He nodded significantly, then turned on his heel and marched away.

While Handa was, apparently, staking his claim on Charles's blood, the rest of the tribe was busily breaking camp. The tepees came down and were folded inside out, making fan-shaped sleds. The Wendat piled bags and baskets and even a couple of children on these conveyances. A few were hitched to dogs, but most were picked up by two or four people. Charles spotted Tankort taking the pole of one of the four-man teams, but saw no sign of his backpack, either on the young Wendat's shoulders or on his sled.

Charles searched the branches to see if President Wilson had managed to follow them to camp, but saw no sign of the bird. A short time later, Handa came back and replaced Charles's sneakers with a pair of moccasins, and then they set off. The pace was slower than yesterday. Charles's legs were tired after two days' hard marching, and his tightly bound hands made it that much more difficult to keep his balance. The moccasins, though, were quite comfortable. Not exactly as springy as Nike Airs, but much better than Charles would have expected.

The march lasted the entire day. The Wendats' moccasinned feet fell noiselessly on the ground, and the rustle of the sleds was only slightly louder than the rustle of the leaves in the wind. Once, as Charles watched, a young man let go of the sled he'd been pulling with three other men and peeled off from the group, unslinging his bow as he faded into the trees. Charles barely heard the *ping!* of his bowstring, followed a moment later by a short, almost shockingly loud crash. Soon enough the Wendat appeared with a deer draped over his shoulders, and a small, proud smile on his face. The deer was loaded onto a sled and the young man resumed his place with his companions.

Charles noticed something else on the young man—a welted, star-shaped scar beneath his right shoulder. Charles was pretty sure this was the scar left behind by a bullet wound, and now he noticed that many of the tribe bore such scars. Charles couldn't imagine what it felt like to be shot, let alone to have a bullet extracted from deep within muscle and bone without anesthesia. He remembered what Tankort had said yesterday: Wendat *hate* English. If the English had done this, Charles could see why the tribe disliked them so much.

As he peered around for a sign of Tankort, he caught a glimpse of a sled that was different from the others. It wasn't a sled, for one thing: it was being carried by men at both the front and back ends by a pair of long poles. In the center of the poles sat a square deerhide cube. The leather sides were laced tightly over their wooden frame, and Charles thought there were symbols painted on the sides. Yellow squares, it looked like, inside of which had been painted . . . lines! Horizontal lines, each smaller than the one above it!

Suddenly he remembered the old man from last night, and the lines painted on his face—the same seven lines etched into the cover of Mario's book! Then he remembered the feeling of poles beneath him, the sensation of moving. Although it made no sense, Charles knew the poles he'd felt were the very poles holding up the deerhide cube. He knew the old man he'd seen was inside that cube, and that he'd been inside it too. But how? When?

Charles looked at the men carrying the poles. Their burden seemed almost weightless. Indeed, when one man let go of his pole to scratch his nose, the other three didn't even notice. Yet Charles was sure there was someone inside the cube. He'd seen movies in which rich people and other august personages were carried in chairs like this. What else could—

Charles blinked. Blue sky glittered through the branches and leaves. Then a Wendat face appeared in his line of vision, a woman, joined a moment later by Handa, panting slightly, as if he'd run up. Although he knew no one spoke English, Charles still couldn't help from saying, "What—what happened?"

"Charzo fall."

Charles looked over. Tankort was there. The hatred was gone, replaced by derision.

"Charzo hit head. Charzo sleep."

Charles's head felt perfectly fine. Confused, but fine. "I did not hit my head. And I didn't fall. I—" But Charles had no idea what had happened. One moment he had been peering at the mysterious deerhide cube, and the next he was on his back, looking up at the sky. He sat up and looked for the cube now, but there was no sign of it.

"English walk like baby." Tankort did an imitation of a toddler's waddle, falling with a loud, theatrical crash to the ground.

The sound snapped the adults out of their inaction. Handa hauled Charles roughly to his feet. A moment later they were marching.

"I did *not* fall," Charles hissed to Tankort. "And I do not walk *like a baby*." But Tankort only rolled his eyes and toddled away.

They marched on. Twice more Charles found himself on the ground. The first time took him by surprise, but the second time he felt it coming. His vision grew blurry, like it does when you allow your eyes to relax so much they become unfocused. Shapes melted, multiplied. Charles took off his glasses and tried to straighten them, but when he put them on nothing had changed. Every Wendat and sled and tree had grown a twin. It seemed at first that Charles was seeing double, but that wasn't quite it. The twins walked or slid or swayed a foot ahead of their original. With a start, Charles realized he wasn't seeing two *things* at the same time—he was seeing two *times* at the same time. Then he blinked and found himself on the ground yet again.

The Wendat stopped long enough to feed Charles, apparently assuming the pale-skinned, delicate boy was not used to such hard marching. Charles munched his dried venison thankfully, but, hungry as he was, he was even more concerned about the fact that he seemed to be coming unstuck in time. Could it be that the stream he'd walked up had only a temporary effect? Maybe he'd end up back in his era? Having never traveled through time before, Charles had no idea what to think, and he was pondering various scenarios when Tankort approached, accompanied by an older Wendat. The man's cheeks bore fresh traces of red and yellow paint, and when he got close enough

Charles could see that the familiar seven lines had been scored on each of his cheeks in bright red dye. Around each of the symbols had been drawn a yellow square, just like those on the deer-hide cube. The squares enclosed the lines, containing them.

Charles lifted his bound hands and pointed. "What do those mean?"

The old Wendat smacked Charles's hands away. He dipped a hand in a pouch and hurled a pinch of yellow powder in Charles's face, causing him to sneeze and sputter for several seconds. The powder fogged Charles's glasses and got in his eyes, but he was too scared to wipe it away, and he blinked uncontrollably.

The old Indian barked something at Tankort, who turned to Charles.

"Votav says if you speak he will cut out your tongue to keep you from casting spells."

"But I didn't—"

A shower of powder cut him off. When Charles could see again, he saw a long stone knife in Votav's hands. The old man's eyes were cold above the yellow and red symbols on his cheeks. He spoke quietly, looking directly at Charles.

"Hold still, Charzo," Tankort translated, "and you may yet speak your children's names."

Charles had never really thought about his tongue before, but it suddenly seemed like a *terribly* important part of him. As he watched, Votav produced a pair of small wooden bowls. He poured a few drops of water from a leather sack into each of them, then tipped some yellow powder into one, red powder into the other. He mixed the contents of each bowl with either end of a smooth white bone. Charles hoped it had come from a deer or a bear or something, and not a person. When Votav had two smooth pastes, he dipped his bone into the yellow dye. He brought it to Charles's face and traced a square on each cheek just beneath the rims of his lopsided glasses. The wet paste felt funny on Charles's skin, and he had to fight the urge to wrinkle his nose, or scratch.

Votav dipped his bone in the red paste. Charles counted the lines as they were etched on each of his cheeks. One, two, three, four, five, six, seven, the last so short it was practically a dot. The seven lines on the cover of Mario's book were now on his cheeks, just as they were on Votav's, and on the man from last night, and on the cube that contained him.

Suddenly a memory floated up from the depths of his brain. When he was four years old, he had gotten his first pair of glasses. His father had taken him to an optician, who had produced Charles's lenses with a flourish. He slipped them onto Charles's nose, and it was only after Charles had blinked and focused and looked around at the new, crisp edges of things that he realized the world as he had known it had been blurry. He'd never realized it because he hadn't had anything to compare it to.

Charles looked around at the gathered Wendat. They were

somehow sharper than they'd been, the ground beneath him was firmer, the smells of soil and pollen and his own sweat more distinct. No, it wasn't the other things that were sharper. *He* was sharper. Somehow, the symbols on his cheeks had brought him into focus. Charles wondered if the symbols possessed this power themselves, or the dye from which they'd been made, or Votav.

The old Wendat was wrapping his tools in a roll of deerhide. He said something to Tankort and walked away.

Tankort looked at Charles. The derision was still in his eyes, but there was curiosity too, as if he was realizing Charles was more than what he'd thought he was.

"Votav say you not fall," Tankort said finally. "Unless you *are* baby."

They marched the rest of the day. There were, indeed, no more falls, or blinks, as Charles thought of them, and no more rests either. If anything, the Wendat quickened their pace to make up for lost time. Charles tried to figure out what was happening—what the connection was between Mario's book and the painted deerhide cube and the Wendat tribe and Drift House and the wave that had crashed off the Sea of Time, but he was so tired he couldn't quite pin it all down. A dozen stars were winking above the leaves when the party finally stopped. Fires were lit; the deer that had been killed earlier was skinned and gutted and carved into steaks that were soon sizzling over the flames. Charles, again tied to a tree by his ankle, was given another bowl of the stew he'd had for breakfast, as well as another lump of cornbread.

When he'd finished eating, Handa untied Charles and led him to a small circle of men gathered around a fire. In the first tier of the circle sat Tankort and the dog keeper, and Votav, draped in an impressive deerhide cloak trimmed with shells and feathers. The older man who had been in the party that picked Charles up was also there, and two other men Charles had not met before. Along with Votav, about half the men had the squared lines painted on their cheeks. The fresh paint glistened in the firelight.

After he'd seated Charles, Handa went away again, returning with eight skewers of freshly cooked deer meat. These he handed around the fire one at a time, to Votav first, and then to the older man who had been in the party that picked Charles up, and then to one of the new men, and so on down the line. Tankort was the last Wendat to receive a skewer, and the final one was handed to Charles, which gave him a pretty good idea of his status in the group.

For a long time, the contented sound of chewing was the only noise in the forest, and the occasional sizzle as someone warmed their meat in the fire. Charles nibbled at his. It was delicious, but he was too nervous to concentrate on it. Shadows moved in the trees as more and more Wendat came to sit around the fire.

At length one of the Wendat took his half-eaten skewer and

stuck the meatless end into the ground. His cheeks were un-painted, his lips moist and shiny with meat juice.

"Handa has claimed your life," this man said in thickly ac-cented but perfectly clear English, "because he was the leader of the party that brought you among us. If you perpetuate any mischief against the Wendat, he will be held responsible, and he will also have the responsibility of determining your pun-ishment. You will remain Handa-vey, Handa's blood, until you have shown yourself trustworthy."

Charles was conscious of dozens of pairs of eyes on him. Speaking as respectfully as he could, he said, "You speak En-glish. How?"

"My own story is one that would break your heart," the English-speaking Wendat said after a long pause, "as would that of any of the individual men and women who make up the remnants of my nation. Once I had a wife and children, but now I have only myself. All of the people around you have lost wives or husbands, children, parents, their home. Tonight I speak to you on behalf of all of them, to tell you our story, and to find out if you are enemy or friend."

Charles took a moment to process this information, then said in the politest voice he could muster, "Can I at least know your name?"

"I am called Grabant. Only recently have I taken on the role of speaker for the Wendat, since my predecessor was killed in the wars between the English and French."

Charles saw heads nod and shake around the dimly lit circle as the names "English" and "French" were spoken, and he said, "Were you . . . I mean, are you Huron?"

Heads shook at this word too, sharply, negatively, but only Grabant spoke.

"We are Huron in the same way that you are Handa-vey: because someone more powerful chose to call us by a name of their choosing. Huron is a French word, not ours. We are Wendat."

Charles nodded. "I know about this war. You fought with the French, against the British and the Iroquois."

When Grabant answered, his voice was quiet and serious and edged by some sharp emotion that could have been anger or pain. "At first we fought because we were foolish enough to believe the French would help us if we helped them. But then we just fought for our lives. In the end we realized that all you can do in war is try to survive."

Charles felt chastised by the Wendat's words. "My friend told me all the Hur—all your people were killed."

"That is very nearly true. Once the Wendat were the most numerous people to live on the northern shores of the great waters that divide us from the Iroquois. Our villages were clean and well tended, with great longhouses in which we ate and slept without fear, working our gardens and turning to the forest for meat. This tiny number that you see today is all that remains."

"How many—"

"One hundred seventy-two. Once we were numberless, but now we number one hundred seventy-two."

Charles was silent for a long time. He wasn't sure what to say, so he touched a finger to his cheek. The dried paint on his cheeks felt like paper.

"Is this to protect me? Or protect you?"

The Wendat glanced at Votav, who continued to stare impassively into the flames.

"It is a precaution," Grabant said. "Time flickers around you strangely, and these symbols will keep you—and us—in one place."

Charles glanced around the circle. "Not everyone has the symbols. You don't."

"Not everyone believes time is as easy to shape as Votav does. We have heard the stories for generations, but none of us has ever slipped ourselves, let alone journeyed through the fog."

"The fog? Where are you going anyway?"

Grabant's eyes narrowed, almost as if he'd been expecting this question. "We are being led far away. To a place no English- or Frenchman will ever come to. As the deer must stay with deer and the wolf must stay with wolves, so our people and your people must remain forever separate."

At these words, Charles's mind flashed to visions of what he knew lay in the future: Europeans spreading unchecked west, south, north across the continent, with the native populations confined to reservations encompassing a fraction of the land they'd once lived on. In a way, Grabant's desires would come true, Charles thought. But probably not in the manner he or his people were hoping.

"Your presence is troubling to us, Handa-vey," Grabant continued. "Our people have already wandered far from the places we knew. These lands are colder than the ones we left. But neither French nor English have ever been seen in these parts, and we had hoped to stop soon. There is still time to plant squash and beans and corn for the fall harvest. Time to build warm shelters for the winter so we won't have to huddle in tents to keep from freezing. But if your presence is a sign that others like you are not far behind, we shall have to keep going. And, perhaps, we shall have to leave a warning behind."

Charles gulped. "Warning?"

Grabant paused, contemplated his words. "The Wendat are not a warlike people. We have always lived in peace with our neighbors until the French came, and the British, and the Iroquois. But we will fight if we have to, to protect ourselves. Our ancestors say, if you have to go to war, do not leave your spear at home, or your bow, your hatchet, your knife, or your wits. Do you understand?"

"I'm not sure."

With a flick of his finger, Grabant made the piece of skewered meat in front of him wobble like a metronome. "There are some among us who want to mount your head on a stake as a warning to any who come after you. The Wendat are not yet helpless, Handa-vey. If you think otherwise, you are much mistaken."

Although he was only ten years old, Charles had had his life threatened before, by the mermaid Queen Octavia. But the mermaid had been careless—at any rate overconfident—and, as well, Charles had had his uncle to help him, and Susan and Murray, not to mention Pierre Marin and the Time Pirates. But Grabant had spoken in a calm, matter-of-fact voice about beheading Charles, who was suddenly, acutely conscious of the circles of hostile eyes ringing him, and the empty forest beyond them.

"I, um, that is, well—"

Suddenly a voice rang out of the dark trees.

"Stay where you are!"

Instantly, knives appeared in the hands of every Wendat seated around the fire.

"Drop your weapons!" another voice cried out. "Back away from the boy!" There was a pause—during which, Charles noted dismally, no one did any backing away—and then a third voice called out, "We have you surrounded!"

On the other side of the fire, Grabant made subtle movements with the fingers of his right hand. Although Charles didn't actually see anyone move, he had a sense of fewer shadows around the fire.

"Do not delay!" a fourth voice cried. "Step away from the boy or my men—RAK!"

Charles, who had been as mystified by the voices as the Wendat, suddenly understood. A moment later, a young man appeared carrying President Wilson. He held the parrot upside down by the legs, like a chicken. As always when he was stressed, President Wilson resorted to a stream of abuse.

"Unhand me, you foul miscreant, or I will flay the flesh from your bones with my talons!"

It was pretty obvious that President Wilson was in no position to do anything of the sort, but given the fact that his captor probably spoke no English, it was a particularly hollow threat.

At the sight of the bird, another murmur went through the circle. Charles thought it was directed at President Wilson's strange appearance—he was sure the Wendat had never seen a parrot before, let alone a bird that could talk. But the situation turned out to be somewhat different. Grabant leaned over and spoke to the man next to him. As he talked, he made the circles around his eyes that Charles had seen so many times in the past few days, and Charles thought he detected a distinct expression of relief on his face. The second Wendat nodded, glancing at Charles with what seemed to the boy a look of newfound respect, then slipped off into the darkness.

Grabant turned back to Charles. His expression had changed yet again: there was a cautious smile on his face.

"It would seem Tankort was right about you after all."

The last time Charles had spoken to Tankort, the young

Wendat had voiced his hatred of Charles, then made off with his backpack. Charles wasn't sure he wanted Tankort to be "right" about him.

"Are you deaf, imbecile!" President Wilson was still screaming. "You continue to hold me at peril to your own life!"

Grabant nodded to himself. "He insisted you were of the trader's kind. That is why Handa let you live in the first place."

Charles felt he almost understood what the Wendat meant, but not quite. Too much had happened too quickly—he couldn't add it all up. President Wilson's screaming in his ear didn't help matters any.

"Curse you, cretin! Release me or they'll need to use dental records to identify your body!"

"The trader?"

Grabant's brow furrowed in confusion. "Perhaps you did not realize our name?"

Now Charles really was confused.

"Your name is . . . Wendat. Isn't it?"

Grabant nodded. "Yes. Wendat. It is an old, old word in our language. It means 'People of the Floating Island.'"

People of the Floating Island? Did he mean the Island of the Past? And the trader? Pierre Marin had been a fur trader, before he discovered the secrets of time travel. President Wilson said Pierre Marin had learned to navigate time from the Huron. Could it be . . . ?

Just then the Wendat who had left the circle reappeared

carrying a long pole. One end was sharpened into a stake, and Charles, who remembered Grabant's threat to mount his head on a pike, felt a shiver travel down his back. But the man only stabbed the sharpened end of the stake into the forest floor, allowing Charles to see a horizontal bar mounted at its top. The bar was about a foot long, and scored with familiar-looking scratches.

"Is that a—" Charles was too overwhelmed by the odd turn of events to finish his question.

"Come, Xerxes," Grabant said now. "I apologize for the undignified way we have brought you among us. But it has been so long since we have played host to you or anyone else from the Sea of Time that we have started to disbelieve our own memories. This man did not know who you were." And, gently taking President Wilson from the boy who held him, he set him on the well-used perch.

President Wilson glared balefully at the circle of Wendat. His plumage, Charles saw, was ragged and ruffled, making him look simultaneously bigger and smaller than the parrot Charles was used to seeing.

"Xerxes?" he said finally, in a mightily aggrieved voice. "I'll *show* you Xerxes."

FIFTEEN

The Amulet of Babel

AFTER ALL THE PREPARATION OF getting to Osterbygd, meeting the actual Vikings took less time than Susan would've imagined. They'd barely left the punt behind the rocks when a woman came around the side of one of the hill-like houses carrying a small bundle of sticks. They seemed to see each other at the same time: the woman's bundle clattered to the stony soil, and she lifted her skirts and ran screaming for the nearest door. Her cries carried clearly over the flat land.

"Pirates! Pirates!"

"Well, I guess we know these are still working," Uncle Farley laughed, touching his vial beneath his jacket.

"Nothing to do but keep walking," Mario said. "Running'll just confirm her fears."

"Good point," Uncle Farley agreed. And, shifting Miss Applethwaite's heavy picnic basket from his left to his right hand, he continued trudging over the pebbles.

A moment later five men burst from the house, carrying between them an ax, a bow, and three spears. Well, no, Susan realized, the spears were actually shovels, or maybe hoes. And the bow was just a curved piece of wood. Even the ax head looked small and kind of dull. The woman followed them out, but remained crouching in the safety of the low doorway.

The men were short—the largest was only an inch or two taller than Susan—but they were broadly built, and their heads and faces were covered with hair that ranged from pale yellow to reddish to dark brown. All of them had on leather trousers and ragged, coarsely woven woolen shirts. Most were barefoot, though one wore a pair of fur-lined boots. The boots were unlaced and the wearer had trouble keeping them on as he walked, suggesting he'd run out in a hurry. This was the man carrying the curved stick of wood.

The men surrounded the newcomers and brandished their weapons. Several made threatening noises as you would to a wild animal. The man in the boots even smashed his stick on the ground. Unfortunately it broke in two, but he recovered quickly, picking up the second half and brandishing the two short, splintered stubs.

"Yar!" he said.

Susan wasn't sure if she should be worried or start laughing. The men's thick beards made it hard to read their facial expressions, but Susan thought one man, a middle-aged individual with glittering, sober blue eyes, was trying not to smirk. He was the man with the dull-looking ax, and after a moment he let his weapon drop to his side.

"Perhaps you should try speaking to them," the blue-eyed man said dryly, "instead of just saying 'yar.' "

Susan bit back a giggle. There was a bluntness to the man's speech. She couldn't tell if it was his natural manner or the literalness of the translating charm, but in either case, he did good deadpan.

At the sound of her stifled snort, another man peered at her with slitted eyes, as if he was trying to figure out if the strangers could understand Norse. He had big holes in his trousers, through which Susan could see a pair of knees black with dirt. The man brandished his hoe at her, and Susan noted that, like the ax, the hoe's blade was worn down to a rusty stub. Nevertheless it was dirty and jagged, and she took a step backward.

The man with the blue eyes put a hand on the hoe's gnarled shaft, staying his companion.

"Who are you, and how have you come to Osterbygd?"

"Please," Uncle Farley said, setting the picnic basket down and opening his empty palms before them, "we come in peace."

"He speaks Norse!" the man with the boots exclaimed.

The man with the holes in his knees said, "And his hands! They are as soft as a woman's!"

"Their clothing is a bit delicate as well, if it comes to that," said the man with the blue eyes.

Susan glanced at her uncle and brother. Mario was still wearing the linen trousers and tunic (she marveled that he wasn't freezing, but he seemed perfectly content), while she and Uncle Farley both wore jeans and polar fleece jackets—hers was dark purple, Uncle Farley's bright red.

Now a man with a beard as red as Uncle Farley's jacket spoke.

"Do not think we are fooled by empty declarations of peace. If you have come to raid us you will find Osterbygd more than a match for such a paltry crew, no matter what weapons you conceal in that carrying case of yours."

"Gunnar," the man with the blue eyes said in an impatient tone. "A boy, a girl, and a man with soft hands. Clearly piracy is not this group's objective."

"Aye, Iussi," the man called Gunnar said. "It is their very lack of weapons and warriors that has me worried. Who but magicians would send children and porters among strangers? How do we know these aren't devils Karl Olafson conjured with that charm he stole from the Qaanaaq?"

"Now see here," Uncle Farley cut in. "I am not a *porter*, nor do I have womanly hands."

"I'll say he doesn't," the woman in the doorway threw out now. She emerged from her cubbyhole and thrust a pair of calloused, dirty hands in front of her. "A little girl's hands, maybe, not a hardworking woman's. Speaking of which—" She plucked the pair of broken sticks from the booted man, then turned to retrieve the rest of her fallen faggot. "I'll be having those, Hejnryk Jenison. A woman's got work to do while menfolk gossip the day away."

"I'll have you know I just rowed all the way from—" Uncle Farley turned and pointed at Drift House floating on the open waves. "From there. Look, I've even got a blister."

While Uncle Farley tried to get everyone to notice the little welt on his pinkie, Susan, along with the rest of the party on the beach, turned and looked at the distant ship. How stately Drift House looked as it bobbed on the water! The cannons gleamed on the upper deck and the glass of the solarium was like a beacon reflecting the brilliant cold light of the northern sky. To her it was a comforting sight, but to the Vikings the effect was somewhat different.

"Saints preserve us!" said the man with holes in his knees. "I think you are right, Gunnar. I have never seen such a craft as that. They must have strong magic indeed to make so fine a vessel."

Even the woman seemed to be cowed by the sight of the ship, and, giving the newcomers a wide berth, she scooted into the house with her firewood.

"Is that pointed part . . . glass?" Hejnryk, the man in the boots, said now.

"It's the solarium." Susan nodded. "It's fantastic. It's almost as big as your whole house, and it has the most amazing banyan tree you've ever seen, and orchids and vines and—"

"Susan," Uncle Farley cut her off in a low voice. "I don't think now is the time."

With a sinking feeling, Susan realized Uncle Farley was right. The men seemed impressed by what she had described, but not in the good way. Rather, they seemed intimidated, and as such, frightened and mistrustful.

For the first time, Mario spoke. "We are neither magicians nor pirates. Nor are we allies of Karl Olafson. In fact, we've come to help you against him."

"Karl Olafson is gone," said Iussi, the man with the blue eyes and the ax (which, Susan noted, he no longer held loosely, but in front of his chest).

"Karl Olafson has gone to Leifsbudir," Mario said. "But he's taken your fishing boats, hasn't he? He can come back and raid you anytime, but you are trapped here."

The Greenlander peered at Mario. Through the healthy coating of grime on his hands, Susan could see his knuckles whitening as he tightened his grip on his weapon. "How do you know so much about us?"

Yes, Susan wondered. How *did* he know so much? But it wasn't Mario who answered her question.

"I told him," a new voice said.

Susan and everyone else whipped their heads around. A boy about her age had emerged from the shadow of something she'd taken for a small hillock with concave sides but now realized was a collapsed building, so densely covered in grass that it looked like part of the landscape.

"Traitor!" Hejnryk spat at the boy. Shorn of his splintered sticks, he waved his empty fists.

"Hejnryk," Iussi said, "there's no need to announce our business to strangers—though they do seem to know quite a bit about us already. Certainly much more than we know about them."

"You can't keep secrets from them," said the boy Hejnryk had labeled a traitor. "These people are from the future. I told you they would come."

"You said your father would open a hole in the sky too," Iussi said, "but I do not see that."

"It's true," Mario said.

"Er, Mario," Uncle Farley said. "Ixnay on the ime-tay avel-tray. I don't think it's wise for us to be putting such ideas into the heads of fifteenth-century ikings-Vay."

Gunnar snorted. "Vikings?"

With a start, Susan realized the translation charm had worked on Uncle Farley's Pig Latin exactly as it had on his English. Fortunately, Gunnar seemed much more interested in Uncle Farley's comment about Vikings than about time travel.

"*Vikings?*" he said again. "Don't taunt me, stranger, lest I strike your ample body with my hoe and use it to fertilize my fields. Our ancestors were Vikings, roaming the world, conquering villages, taking what they wanted and striking fear in the hearts of men. We are Greenlanders—farmers and fishermen, and prisoners of a barren land."

"You are prisoners of your own ideas," said the boy. "This land is harsh, yes, but hardly barren. Your imagination is far less fertile than the hills behind us and the sea before us."

"I can sow you next to the fat one, boy," Gunnar snarled. "We will see how fertile *you* are."

With a snort, Iussi lowered his ax. "This has turned into an argument among children. You, sir"—he nodded at Uncle Farley—"perhaps while these *boys* are squabbling, will accompany me inside. There are nets to mend, and while we knot you can tell me how you came to be in our remote part of the world. Are there any *men* who wish to join us?" Iussi looked sternly around the group.

With varying degrees of head-hanging and grumbling, the men turned and headed inside. Susan made as if to follow, but Iussi held up a hand.

"While I sense you are not like our females"—he glanced at Susan's pants—"still, this is a conversation for men. Unless you wish to help Eirika with the meal, I suggest you let Iacob divert you while we talk."

Susan opened her mouth to protest, but felt a hand on her arm. It was Mario's.

"Not *now*," he said, giving "now" the broadest possible meaning. "And besides, two groups can gain twice as much information as one." And he nodded at Iacob.

"I thought you already talked to him."

Mario grinned. "I haven't got your charm, Susie, let alone your cross-examination skills."

"Mario," Susan said, fighting hard to keep a grin off her face. "Stop calling me *Susie*. And don't think I'm happy about this," she added, loud enough for Iussi, Gunnar, Uncle Farley, and the other men to hear.

"Girls never are," Gunnar said, clapping a hand on Uncle Farley's back. "Gunnar Thorvaldsson," he said in a fraternal tone of voice.

"Farley Richardson."

"Well met, son of Richard."

"Her mother is my older sister," Susan heard Uncle Farley say as he lifted Miss Applethwaite's picnic basket and walked toward the entrance of the grass-covered building. "Believe you me, I know where Susan's independence comes from."

Gunnar laughed aloud. "The women of your country strike me as exceptional in many ways. Your wife must be a truly gifted weaver," he said, reaching up and squeezing Uncle Farley's fleece-covered shoulder. "And I cannot imagine what your mother fed you, to produce such a giant of a son."

"Just wait'll I open this basket. Have you ever had a turkey sandwich?"

"Turkey!" Gunnar exclaimed. " 'Tis the food of legend!" And, smacking his hands, he and the other men vanished inside.

Susan turned to face Iacob. The boy looked at her with eyes that, like the ocean, were gray and deep—cold, yes, but also warm. Alive, in a way that none of the other men's eyes were. It suddenly occurred to her to wonder why *he* hadn't been invited inside either. What was this traitor business, or the stuff about his father opening a hole in the sky?

With a start, Susan realized the boy was staring at her as intently as she was examining him. His expression was neither curious nor defiant. Merely . . . appraising. Behind him stood a dozen or so buildings in various stages of disrepair, and beyond them were the fjords and the hills, the streams, the rocks, the sheep, the swiftly moving clouds; behind them the ocean swooshed and a stiff breeze clattered grains of sand across the beach. Iacob stood in the midst of all this, and yet he seemed distinct from it as well, an immigrant only partially suited to this environment. This image jogged some memory in Susan's brain. And then it came to her: her tree. The redwood in Manhattan. Capable of living on the East Coast only because of a mistake in climate, yet adding beauty and grace to the land from which it grew. The motionless boy struck Susan as not quite of his world, but something she couldn't imagine anywhere else either.

Standing up straight, Susan did her best to return the boy's appraisal, taking him in from his blackened bare feet up to his shock of dirty brown hair, which stuck out from his face in a thousand different directions. Just give it five hundred years, she thought, and that hairstyle will finally be in style.

Susan laughed at her private joke. Iacob raised his eyebrows but didn't say anything. She took a step toward him and stuck out her hand.

"I'm Susan Oakenfeld."

Iacob looked at her hand, and then he looked back at her face.

"He is my father."

After a long moment, Susan realized the boy wasn't going to shake her hand. Maybe he wasn't being unfriendly, she thought hopefully. Maybe they just don't do that yet. She shoved her hand in her pocket.

"Who is? Iussi? Gunnar?" Somehow she knew neither of these was the man Iacob was referring to.

"Karl Olafson," Iacob said, his voice level and deep. Deep as his gray eyes. "Karl Olafson," Iacob Karlson repeated in a voice as deep as the cold, cold ocean. "The man you have come here to kill."

Susan opened her mouth. Closed it. Opened it again. Closed it one more time. She shook her head in confusion.

"We wouldn't . . . I mean, I could never . . . I mean, kill someone? We just wouldn't *do* that."

"People will do anything," Iacob said. "Under the right conditions, for the right reasons. Even kill."

"No," Susan protested, but her voice was weak. Bjarki had said that as long as the temporal squall raged they would be unable to return home, and it was starting to look more and more likely that the charm Karl Olafson had stolen from the Qaanaaq was at the center of it. But was it worth taking someone's life to get it back?

While she was pondering this, Iacob whirled on his heel and started walking away from her. He walked slowly though, not as if he was leaving, but as if he wanted her to follow. Just as she caught him up, he said,

"You and your companions speak my language better than anyone I have ever heard."

Used to being the one who asked the questions, Susan felt distinctly off balance. Now, stalling, all she could come up with was, "We do?"

"You do."

Gravel gritted beneath Susan's shoes and, less loudly, beneath Iacob's bare feet. They reached the corner of the long house, and Iacob paused. He looked at the sea for a moment, then turned and started toward the hills. As she set off after him, Susan suddenly realized he was taking her on a tour of his home. He was showing her where he lived.

She looked at what he was offering her. The ground between the houses and the fields was covered in patches of grass and pebbles, and a thin stream snaked its way out of a cleft between two hills. Three more houses curved off to the left. Stingy threads of smoke came out of the chimneys of the first two; the third looked as though it had collapsed at one end. There was something that looked like a stone-walled corral beyond the last house, and then there was a fourth building, not as long as the houses, but taller, with two small windows on the side, their tiny panes filled with some opaque material. Its stone walls cut a sharp outline against the empty sky, but it wasn't until she discerned the cross shape worked with white stones into the brown that she realized the tiny building was a church. A pair of sheep grazed in a fenced churchyard strewn with tiny piles of rocks—no, not piles of rocks, but tombstones. Many more tombstones than the number of living people Susan had seen.

It was suddenly impressed upon her that she was looking at something no one else from her time had seen: a thousand-year-old Norse settlement, the first-ever European town in the New World. The buildings were small, but the fact of their existence seemed disproportionately large. This was history, and she was seeing it. She was a part of it.

Susan realized Iacob was staring at her, waiting for an explanation of how she'd come to speak his language so well.

"Well, Uncle Farley's research has taken him to all sorts of places—"

"He has never been *here*," Iacob cut her off. And then, leaning close to her in a gesture that could have been threatening or simply conspiratorial, he hissed, "I think you are assisted in your smooth speech by the same magic that has claimed my father. What I want to know is, do you work this magic, or does it work you?"

Susan tore her eyes from the graveyard. "Wh-what makes you ask that?"

"Because after my father found what he found, he was suddenly able to understand the speech of the Qaanaaq, and not just the words we had picked up from trading with them. One time I even heard him speak to a Qaanaaq he had captured, and though it seemed to me he spoke *our* language, the prisoner seemed to understand him equally well, and was even in the act of answering him when my father slit his throat."

Susan gulped. The ruse was up. "We believe your father has stumbled across something that is beyond his power to control. But we, that is my uncle Farley and my brother Mario, have studied these things, and we can help."

"The boy is your brother?"

Susan didn't give herself time to consider the question. "Yes," she said firmly.

"There is something different about him."

"Well, he's my half brother."

"Not that kind of different. Not"—and here Iacob reached out a hand and touched Susan's short dark hair—"not a difference in hair color."

The edge of Iacob's hand brushed against her cheek when he touched her hair, and Susan felt a blush heat up her skin. She could feel her heart beating in her chest and she wasn't sure why. To her surprise, Iacob blushed too, and he pulled his hand away and turned back the way they had come. With a start, Susan realized the tour was already over. In a hundred paces, they had seen everything.

"Um, yes," Susan said, "there is something different about my brother. I would explain it to you, but I'm afraid I don't really understand it myself."

Iacob nodded. "It changes you."

"It?"

Iacob waved a hand. "The magic. My father was always a hard man, but he worked for the good of our community. For as long as I have been alive he has led the Nordseta, risking his life to bring back enough food to see us through the winter, as well as such rarities as people from the Old World might desire, should they ever come here again. But now he has put all our lives in jeopardy. He has taken our boats, he has made the Qaanaaq our enemy. He is a murderer."

"Maybe the magic doesn't affect everyone the same way," Susan said desperately. She didn't want to believe her own brother could become as corrupted as the man Iacob was describing to her. Could slit someone's throat.

Iacob squinted at her. "I think you know no more about the amulet than I do."

Susan tried to keep her voice neutral. "Amulet?"

A look of confusion crossed Iacob's face, and Susan, fingering the translation vial beneath her jacket, found herself wondering what word he'd really spoken, and what word he'd heard from her mouth. But all he did was make a circle of the thumb and forefinger of his right hand and bring it to his throat, as if indicating a charm hanging from his neck.

"You understand?"

"Yes." Susan's nod felt jerky to her. "What, um, what'd it look like?"

"You don't know?"

Susan had anticipated this question. "I just want to find out if it's the object we're looking for," she countered smoothly.

Iacob peered at her. The trace of another grin curled his lips, but Susan couldn't tell if he was on to her. "My father showed it to no one, not even me. But I caught a glimpse of it once." He paused, as if debating whether or not to describe it, then nodded. "It was golden. Shaped like an arrowhead, and marked across with lines."

Susan had a flash. They had come back to the front of the houses, and she looked around for a stick but didn't see one, so she dropped to her knees and used her finger to draw in the stony soil. She drew the seven lines that had been impressed into the cover of the book Mario had given her and Charles.

"Did it look like this?"

Iacob's eyes went wide. "So it *is* yours!" For the first time, Susan heard a trace of childlike eagerness in his sober adult voice. Eagerness, but also suspicion: this amulet had turned his father evil, after all.

"Actually," Susan admitted, "I don't know who it belongs to. Mario might, but I think even he knows only part of the truth. But we, that is, my other brother, Charles, and I, we received something that was marked with the same insignia. And we think it's somehow causing problems in our—" Susan was going to say "time," but changed her mind. "In our world."

Before Iacob could respond to this, a loud voice split the air.

"Heathen!"

Susan whirled around. A wild-haired figure was striding rapidly toward them from the direction of the church. Tattered robes flapped from his body, and something glittered in his outstretched right hand. Susan thought it was a short sword at first, then realized it was a cross.

"Devils! Demons! Away with you!"

"Father Poulsen," Iacob whispered to her. "He carries his cross with him at all times, because he is convinced Gunnar would melt it into a rake if he ever set it down."

"Step away from the witch-girl, Iacob Karlson!" Father Poulsen said now, waving his cross as if he were swatting at flies. Susan could see that the priest's vestments had once been richly embroidered but were now tattered and held together with bits of twine and leather patches. Beneath the dirty hem, his feet were as bare and black as Iacob's. But something that looked like a ruby glittered on the bar of the thick silver cross, and it was almost as big as her fist.

"She is no witch, Father. Just a traveler from Ropia."

It took Susan a moment to realize this last word meant "Europe." Of course, Iacob would think that anyone who possessed the material goods she and Uncle Farley did must come from the Old World. She wondered why the translation charm hadn't fixed it, though. Maybe it was attempting to render his lack of knowledge? Or maybe it was wearing off? It would be awkward to have to reapply it in front of Iacob, let alone the raving newcomer.

"Bah!" the priest cried now. "Black magic swirls about her, from the tips of her shorn raven tresses to her shadowed ankles, which are as delicate as a reindeer's."

Everyone looked down at Susan's ankles, including Susan. She was wearing black socks, which she guessed was what the priest meant by "shadowed."

"Is it magic you see about her?" Iacob said in an amused tone of voice. "Or merely a temptation to renounce your vows?"

For the second time in their brief acquaintance, Susan felt

her skin grow hot. The priest, however, was not amused, and he stuck his ruby-fronted cross right in Iacob's face.

"Watch your tongue, child. Between the sins of your father and your affection for the Qaanaaq, you are but a half step from damnation yourself."

At the mention of his father, Iacob's face went cold and his hands balled into fists. Susan was afraid he was going to strike the priest, but fortunately another voice broke the standoff.

"Here now," came Iussi's levelheaded call. "What's the commotion?"

Susan turned and saw Uncle Farley and Iussi and Gunnar walking up from the house they'd gone into a half hour ago. The picnic basket, apparently empty, swung lightly from Uncle Farley's hand, and Iussi had both hands on his stomach and was rubbing contentedly.

She jumped when she felt a thump on her shoulder: Father Poulsen had "tapped" her with his cross, which was every bit as heavy as it looked.

"This witch-girl is casting spells!"

A frown crossed Iussi's lips, still greasy with what appeared to be turkey gravy. "Spells?"

"Look!"

Susan gasped. The priest was pointing at the ground where she had just drawn the symbol that had been on the cover of Mario's book. But then she gasped again, because the symbol was gone, smeared out by several long foot-wide swathes.

The priest whirled on Iacob. "Don't think you can hide the evidence of her sorcery, boy. I saw her scratch her satanic design into our soil. This land is cursed now. Cursed!"

Iacob turned and looked at the sheep on the distant hillside. A thin, innocent whistle passed his lips.

"This land has long since been cursed," Gunnar said, although his voice was not particularly concerned. His lips glistened with the last traces of Miss Applethwaite's meal, and his beard was full of breadcrumbs. "Neither God nor devil has much use for it as far as I can see." He stifled a burp. Well, actually he didn't stifle it. He just burped.

"Silence your blasphemy," the priest declared, waving his cross wildly, "lest I accuse you of being in collusion with the devils as well!"

"Er, Father Poulsen," Iussi said. "We *are* in, um, collusion with them." His voice was fat and lazy, and he licked his fingers with visible relish.

The priest took a giant step backward, holding his cross in front of his chest.

"Not you, Iussi!"

Iussi nodded, switching from the fingers of his right hand to his left. "They have come to help us against Karl Olafson."

"The only help against Karl Olafson can come from God. If these strangers claim power to rival his, its source can only be in Satan."

"Then Satan has a good cook," Gunnar said. "I have never

tasted ambrosia or manna, but if this is the food they serve in hell, get me a shovel."

The priest recoiled in horror. Yet at the same time he licked his lips, as if the thought of good food were enough to tempt even him. Susan wondered how long it had been since these people had had a meal they genuinely enjoyed. Something besides—ugh!—seal.

Uncle Farley took advantage of the priest's confusion to say to Susan, "The combination of Miss Applethwaite's picnic basket and your brother's negotiation skills proved very persuasive. Apparently this Karl Olafson has gone to Leifsbudir," Uncle Farley continued, "on Vinland. What we know as Newfoundland."

"Aye, Vinland," Iussi said again, a slightly confused expression on his face. "Leif Erikson landed there four and a half centuries ago, and it has been almost that long since any of our kind visited it."

The priest shook his fist. "Iussi Karlgren! At the price of your almighty soul, I demand that you cease your interactions with these agents of the devil!"

Iussi looked at the priest benignly. "Forgive me, Father, but it is a risk I have to take. We have agreed to journey with this off-lander to Leifsbudir and recover the artifact that Karl Olafson stole from the Qaanaaq."

"Journey? How?"

Before anyone could answer, the priest strode a few feet

toward the sea and shielded his eyes with his cross. "By the saints! You cannot think such a vessel is any but the devil's barge!" He whirled around. "Iussi, Gunnar. You are men of sense. Their food must have bewitched you! I beg you. Tell me that you will abandon this accursed plan."

Iussi turned from the priest. He stared out at Drift House for a long time without speaking. Finally, he looked back to the assembled group.

"I admit that I cannot fathom how people who can build such a vessel could want anything that such as we possess. Even your clothing surpasses my understanding," he said, running an admiring hand over Uncle Farley's jacket. "Soft as a hog's intestine, and yet it doesn't putrefy!" He looked back at Susan and the others. "And yet there is a compelling honesty to the way you speak, and you offer us much as well, and not just in the way of victuals. I cannot vouch for the other men, but Gunnar and Ulvaes and Hejnryk and I will accompany you. Father Poulsen," he added, "I entrust the safety of Osterbygd to you in our absence."

"It is the Lord who shall protect Osterbygd, and the Lord who shall forsake you, when you leave the shelter of sanctified land." The priest dropped to his knees. Susan thought he was going to pray, but instead he used the silver cross in his hands to draw its twin in the sand, where formerly Susan had drawn the insignia that had been on Mario's book. When he finished he pointed his spiritual pencil at her.

"We will see if your magic can prevail against the power of the Lord." And, rising, he stalked back to his church.

Susan waited until the priest was gone, then turned to Mario.

"I believe it when Uncle Farley says you negotiated the deal. You could always convince Mum that buying your favorite flavor of ice cream was in *her* best interest."

"Frozen sugar milk?" Iussi murmured.

Gunnar's tongue danced over his lips. "Sugar?"

Susan ignored them. Mario's face had gone ashen at the mention of their mother. All the self-possession that made him seem more like the grownups than like Susan and Iacob vanished, and he stood there, a ten- or eleven-year-old boy who terribly missed his mum.

"How is she?" he said. "And Dad? Oh, Susan, you don't know how much I've missed them!"

"They—they're well," Susan said, taken aback. Mario's loneliness was so desperate it hurt even to witness it. She took a deep breath, then decided to give voice to her earlier suspicion. "Mario," she said carefully, "do you think Karl Olafson's amulet is the one you were wearing—"

"Susan!"

Uncle Farley's voice was unexpectedly short, but Susan didn't take her eyes from Mario, who refused to meet her gaze.

"Mario," Susan pressed on, "can we both use it? Or do we— do you have to choose? Between us getting back, or you?"

"Susan, please," Uncle Farley insisted. "You know we can't discuss these things. It might influence the future."

Suddenly Mario whirled on his uncle. "None of you understands what I've been through! How many times I've opened my eyes and looked to see if Charles was awake, only to realize I was alone. How many times I've looked in the mirror hoping to see me—five-year-old *me*—but instead I see *this* person." Mario pinched and pulled his skin as though it were a costume he wished he could rip off. "The Amulet of Babel is the only way for me to go home."

"Amulet of Babel?" Uncle Farley's brows lowered.

"Bjarki told us to look out for something from Babel!" Susan said to her uncle, then turned back to Mario. Conscious of the Greenlanders' stares, she lowered her voice. "I'm right, aren't I? Only one of us can use it to go back to our time?"

Mario looked at his sister pleadingly. "You've got to understand, Susan. It's *the only way* I can get home."

As the full weight of the truth sank in, Susan felt . . . awful. Just awful. "But don't you see, Mario? If you take it and go home, *we* won't be there."

Mario looked back and forth between his uncle and sister, his eyes wet with barely contained tears. "It's not fair. It's just not fair."

Susan reached for her brother's hand. "You *do* get back, Mario. Somehow. Eventually. You *come* home."

Mario's hand hung in Susan's for the longest time, limp, defeated. "But I want to go home *now*. I'm so . . . alone."

His head swayed back and forth for a moment. Then, suddenly, he pulled his hand from Susan's and stood up straight. The mask of confidence and control was back on his face, although his eyes were still wet. He turned to Iussi.

"You have enough boats to get your men to our vessel?"

Iussi hesitated. The last few minutes had clearly shaken his faith in the strangers. Finally he nodded. "One boat, yes. And the raft. It will take a few trips, but we can manage it."

"Good," Mario said. "I will see you on board." And, without looking at Susan, he trotted off toward the punt.

Susan started to follow him, but her uncle caught her arm.

"Let him go, Susan. He has a hard decision to make. We can't make it for him."

Susan stared after her brother's retreating form, but it was Iacob who spoke next.

"The magic is stronger than him."

All eyes turned to look at the Greenland boy, who, like Mario, had been made an orphan by time's magic.

"It will take him, just as it took my father."

"Iacob," Susan said, "do you think Mario will betray us?"

Iacob shook his head. "Not Mario. The amulet. The Amulet of Babel. It will betray us all."

SIXTEEN

The Wanderer of Days

CHARLES BLINKED.

He sat in front of the old man he'd seen his first night with the Wendat. His cheeks itched terribly, and he scratched at them with his fingernails.

The old man was staring at Charles. "It's happened again, hasn't it?"

Charles sat cross-legged in a dimly lit cube about four feet on a side. It wasn't until he felt the logs beneath him that he realized he was in the deerhide box he'd seen—earlier today? yesterday? He had no idea, just as he had no idea how he'd gotten inside it. He looked around for an opening, but saw none.

The deerhide seemed to be lashed tightly—permanently—to its frame.

The poles vibrated beneath him, and Charles realized they were moving. He looked at the old man, but before he could say anything the man smiled patiently and said,

"It's called a litter."

Charles rubbed at his painted cheeks some more, peering at the markings on the old man's face. "Can you read my mind?"

"I cannot read your mind, either with or without the symbol Votav painted on your cheeks. But you have asked me this question before, with exactly the same expression on your face." The old man smiled. "It is unusual for the blinks to be this pronounced."

"Blinks? That's the word *I* used."

"No doubt you remembered me saying it." In response to Charles's befuddled expression, the old man continued: "Think, Charles. We had our first encounter last night, when you arrived in the Wendat camp. You blinked forward to this very moment, then back again. Your memory retained a shadow of what you experienced here. As I said, it is unusual for the blinks to be so pronounced, but the object you are carrying emits a very powerful energy. As do I, for that matter. I'm afraid you have been—how do the people of your time put it?— caught in the crossfire."

Charles suddenly realized he was wearing his backpack. He pulled it off and felt the hard outline of Mario's book.

Mario.

Charles looked again at the old man's face. At the wrinkled skin and pale hair and thin lips and especially at the eyes. Could it be?

The old man's smile grew wider, yet no less wistful. "You asked me that too. And you looked relieved when I told you the answer was no. I am not—and never was—your brother."

Charles did feel relief. That would've been too, well, weird. Beyond weird. Freaky. Super-freaky.

"Look, um, sir, mister, whoever you are. Who, well, who *are* you?"

The old man sighed breathlessly—as in, no air seemed to leave his body. "I have been known by different names in different places and times," he said with an air of someone who has said the same words too many times to count. "In this life, to these people, I am known as the Wanderer of Days."

"You're not Wendat?"

"Not exactly."

Charles wasn't sure how one could "not exactly" be Wendat, but all he said was, "Are you—what Murray is? An Accursed Returner?"

" 'Accursed' was a word added by the mermaid queen Octavia, who found the idea of limitless lives horrifying, and wanted only one existence, unchanging and eternal. But yes, I am a Returner. Like Murray."

For some reason, Charles didn't like the way the Wanderer

said "like Murray." He wanted him to say "like your brother."
It was hard to think that someone who was "like" this man
could be related to Charles—to anyone human. This man
wasn't "like" anyone Charles had ever met.

"Why do I keep blinking? It has something to do with
Mario's book?"

"Something to do with the book you carry, yes." The Wanderer nodded. "But also something to do with me." The
Wanderer paused, considered. "Every living being is made
up of a tiny piece of time and a tiny piece of space, con-
joined: that is all life is. Some people use the words 'soul'
and 'body,' but regardless of what you call it, I am not so
much body anymore. As such, my presence upsets the regular flow of time. If you think of time as water, as the Sea of
Time encourages us to do, then I am solid water. Ice. And
when you brush up against me, there is a ripple."

"A ripple."

"You have been jumping forward in time, a few seconds, a
day. Sometimes two times have been laid over each other simultaneously, as on the night you arrived."

Something flashed in Charles's mind. "But I thought—I
mean, Pierre Marin said you can only go backward in time. You
can never go beyond the present."

"That is what distinguishes the Returners from everything
else in the universe. We can. And we can take others with us."

Charles, thinking of Murray again, didn't like the way the

Wanderer referred to Returners as things rather than people. For a long time there were just the sounds of forward motion— the slight creak of the tightly laced deerhide, the panting of the men carrying them—and then it dawned on Charles: they weren't just moving, they were going somewhere.

"Where are you taking me?" he asked the Wanderer, trying to keep the panic out of his voice.

"To meet your brother and sister, of course. And your uncle."

"Murray's with Susan?"

"I believe the one with her calls himself Mario. You met one of them, didn't you?"

"'One of them'? What does that mean? What does being a Returner really do to you?"

"A soothsayer might tell you that Murray is fulfilling his destiny or some such, but that smacks of superstition. Murray is simply living his life as it was always going to be lived. It just so happens that it is a very different life from the one you and your sister lead. Very different lives."

"What do you mean, 'lives'?"

The Wanderer smiled patiently, almost fatherly. "You understand the basic principle of Returning?"

"You . . . die." Charles had a hard time saying the word, since it applied to his brother and to the man sitting across from him, neither of whom seemed dead. The Wanderer didn't seem quite alive either, but that was another story. "You die," Charles repeated, "and then you're born again?"

"Not quite. Rebirth implies reincarnation, or magical trans-formation. Phoenixes are reborn, and Hindus, and in a certain way, Christians. Returners simply . . . return."

"Return to what?" Charles said.

"To the moment at which the Returning aspect of their na-ture was revealed. For your brother, that was the day he hid in the dumbwaiter inside Drift House—what your uncle refers to as Miss Applethwaite. She showed Murray who he was, and so it is to her that he always returns."

"She . . . Miss Applethwaite is real? A real person?"

"She was. And in her own time she still is. Her story is a complex one, however, and not something we can go into here. I need to finish telling you about Mario, and then I need to tell you about the time jetty, and the mirror book, and the Amulet of Babel."

Time jetty. Mirror book. Amulet of Babel. When Charles had gotten separated from Drift House, he had thought he was setting out on an adventure like the one Susan got when the mermaids took her to the bottom of the Great Drain. But it was starting to look less like an adventure and more like a vo-cabulary test. But the Wanderer was still speaking.

"Murray, as I've told you, will live many lives. Each life will remove a trace of his material essence, but it will take many thousands of Returnings before enough of his body and mind have been stripped away to allow him unimpeded access to the temporal aspect of his being."

Charles blinked. Not in the temporal sense. He just opened and closed his eyes rapidly.

"You mean . . . you mean he'll forget what happened? It was like that last time. With the mermaids. Murray thought Susan would do a favor for the mermaids that would get her killed, but it was actually the mermaids who wanted to kill her."

"Exactly," the Wanderer said, "but that is just the tip of the iceberg. As a Returner, Murray is still very new, and as such he is liable to be confused, impetuous, and often angry. He is still bound to his material psyche, you see, and this may lead him astray."

Charles thought about this.

"You mean," he said finally, "you mean, he's still human?"

At this word, some emotion flickered over the Wanderer's face. Something almost wistful.

"Yes, that is the very word, Charles. Human." But he didn't make it sound like a good thing.

"You mean, we shouldn't always trust him?"

The Wanderer smiled—grimly, but also, Charles thought, a little proudly. "Above all, the one called Mario is driven by the urge to be the five-year-old he was before his true nature was revealed—to be Murray again, so that he can live with his mother and father and sister and brother. These feelings will cloud his judgment."

"But Mario—Murray does get home again. He's there now. With chicken pox."

The Wanderer nodded. "You know this. And unfortunately so does Mario. And he is impatient. You must see to it that his desire to get home does not interfere with his other tasks."

The litter jolted then, slightly, and the shells on the Wanderer's cloak rattled. He stared at the deerhide walls as if he could see through them, then turned back to Charles.

"Our meeting draws to a close. Listen to me carefully, Charles. The object in your possession is called a mirror book. You have noticed that it is missing the seal on its cover. I myself removed that seal thousands of years ago, to mute the book's power. But in a very short while the seal and the book will be reunited, and when that happens the resulting shockwave will open something called a time jetty. The jetty is like the opposite of the Great Drain. If the drain is a whirlpool, the jetty is a waterspout—a concentrated burst of time that destroys anything it passes through."

Something clicked in Charles's brain. "The lost cities! They were all destroyed by the jetty!"

The Wanderer nodded.

"But that's all in the past," Charles said. "My past. What can I do about it?"

"Indeed you can do nothing about the past," the Wanderer said, as if the destruction of Troy and Pompeii and all those other fabled places was of no consequence. "But," he continued, "if you act wisely, and in time, you can still save your own city."

"My own—New York?" It says something about Charles that he didn't panic when the Wanderer spoke of the destruction of his home. He knew the old man wouldn't be telling him this unless there was some way to prevent such a catastrophe. And so he said, "What do I have to do?"

"I am going to help you obtain a second mirror book. You must take the two books to the end of the jetty, and open them in each other's presence. Only one mirror book can undo what another has wrought."

Before Charles could ask another question, the Wanderer opened the deerhide draped over his shoulders. Charles gasped. For the Wanderer's chest wasn't there. Or, rather, it was there, but it was translucent, like the fire Charles had seen his first night. And through the old man's see-through ribs Charles could discern—

"Murray!"

His little brother was curled up in a tiny chamber about the size of the one Charles sat in. He seemed to be asleep. Or . . .

"Is he . . . ?"

"The book, Charles. The book!"

Charles squinted. And then he saw it: Murray's head rested on a large book. The chamber he was in was dark, but it seemed as if the book were a bright red.

"There is no more time for doubts and disbelief, Charles. *Reach in and take it.*"

The words rang in Charles's ears. This man wanted him to

reach into his chest and pull a book from beneath his brother's head. Gulping, he stuck out his hand, but the Wanderer said, "Wait!"

A light suddenly appeared, and in the light Charles could see Uncle Farley peering in at Murray. And all of a sudden he realized:

"He's in the dumbwaiter! Murray's in the dumbwaiter!"

It was true: Charles was looking at the day last fall when Uncle Farley had found Murray sleeping in the dumbwaiter after the children's momentous game of hide-and-go-seek. Now his uncle reached in to grab his nephew. As his broad back bent over, Charles could see his own face looking on, and Susan's, and through the dining room windows behind them he could see the wide open sky of the Sea of Time. Uncle Farley lifted Murray out of the dumbwaiter, and as he stood up the doors fell closed behind him, leaving only the red book lying on the plush base of the dumbwaiter.

"Now, Charles, now!"

Charles reached without thinking. He felt a strange coldness as his hand passed through what should have been the Wanderer's ribs. His hand seemed to reach and reach, stretching out like the arm of Mr. Fantastic or the Elastic Man, forever and ever, and then, almost as if he were reaching into a grab bag, Charles felt his fingers close over the edge of the book. He grabbed it firmly and snatched his arm back just as the dumbwaiter's doors opened again. Uncle Farley peered into the empty chamber. It seemed to Charles that Uncle Farley looked him right in the eye, and then the Wanderer drew the deerhide closed around his hollow chest.

And Charles had the mirror book in his lap. There was the seal missing from his own book: a golden blob, slightly heart shaped, into which those seven lines had been scored. Other than that, it didn't seem at all like the book Mario had given him. It was brown, for one thing, and smaller too—less like a pizza box and more like a volume of an encyclopedia. It didn't tingle either. In fact, it seemed pretty much like a normal book, and idly, Charles reached to open the cover.

A very solid hand stretched out from the deerskin cloak and pressed on the cover of the book. When Charles looked into the Wanderer's face, it seemed to him that the man was concentrating to keep his hand solid. Charles took his hand off the cover, and the Wanderer's arm vanished beneath his cloak, but not before it . . . faded slightly and became slightly transparent.

"It will tempt you that way. When you don't even realize it."

Charles was about to say something when he suddenly noticed that the slight rocking had stopped. The litter was no longer moving.

"Put the book in your bag, Charles. Do not let anyone see it or take it from you."

A glimmer of light appeared in one corner of the litter. Charles realized that the Wendat were unlacing the straps that held the deerhide closed.

"But what do I do with it?" Charles asked, stowing the book in his bag next to Mario's.

"Murray will know what to do with it."

"Murray? Mario?"

"*Murray*, Charles. You need to be able to tell the difference."

The flap opened wider. As light poured into the chamber, the Wanderer of Days seemed to fade in the glow.

"But where? When?"

"When it is time, Charles."

The flap folded open. A pair of spears were thrust in, separating Charles from the Wanderer, penning him in. Charles stared up at the old man's face imploringly, but the Wanderer only repeated himself.

"It is time, Charles."

In the bright shaft of daylight Charles could see that the boxed lines had been painted across the spears' stone blades. And now a face appeared in the open side of the litter, just as Uncle Farley's had appeared in the side of the dumbwaiter.

"Charzo?" Tankort said. The anger had left his face, and he stared into the litter's shadowy interior with a mixture of fear and awe. "I take you to your family now."

SEVENTEEN

The Parrot Speaks

KARL OLAFSON HAD MADE OFF with Osterbygd's three largest ships, leaving the colony only a rickety boat that was basically a long canoe, and a second craft that looked as though it had been cobbled together from pieces of driftwood. Susan opted for the canoe (it had sides for one thing, and the waves had grown choppy as the day progressed) but she regretted her choice once she climbed aboard and her tennis shoes splashed in two inches of icy water. The wood was crumbly and smelled like gym socks, the bung corked with a fistful of grass. The craft survived the journey, however, and once in Drift House she, Mario, and Uncle Farley met with Iussi, Gunnar, and Iacob for a brief conference in the music room.

Iussi stood in the middle of the room and stared at the rug and the chandelier and everything in between. He wandered to a table and picked up a glass paperweight.

"Amazing! Your land must be fantastically wealthy."

"Um, yes," Uncle Farley said. "I suppose it is. And my own family is blessed with a certain amount of luxury. But perhaps we should discuss the, ah—"

"The Amulet of Babel," Susan put in, impatient to learn more.

Iussi nodded. He set the paperweight down. "There is little to tell. Karl Olafson came back with it from the last Nordseta. He had taken it from the little people—"

"The Qaanaaq," Iacob cut in here. He was standing in a corner, and Susan had almost forgotten he was in the room.

Iussi glanced at him uneasily. "Yes," he said, "the Qaanaaq. I myself did not see it. Karl Olafson guarded it jealously. He wore it beneath his shirt, on a length of seal intestine."

Gross, Susan thought. Just—*gross.*

"Karl was a different man after he came back," Iussi continued. "Swaggering and starting fights with anyone who crossed his path. Then stories began to come from Karl's house. They said he had stopped sleeping. That he stopped eating as well, and spoke languages no one could understand."

At this, a look went around the room, from Susan to Mario to Uncle Farley, but none of them said anything. Iussi's eyes followed the silent exchange, at the end of which he smiled slightly and nodded.

"I see these stories are significant to you. Very well then, I will not ask you to tell me about things of which you are loath to speak. If someone will show me where the firepit is, my men and I will begin to prepare a bit of sustenance for our journey. We have dried fish. If you have water, we can reconstitute it."

Uncle Farley made a bit of a face. "Actually, you can hold on to your, ah, dried fish." He put his hand around Iussi and steered him toward the door. "I have a rather remarkable woman in my employ who can whip up the most *amazing* dishes from seemingly nothing."

"If they are like the 'pick nick' you served us earlier," Gunnar said, smacking his hands together, "we shall be most grateful indeed."

"Oh, that? That was just a snack." And, beginning to describe some of Miss Applethwaite's specialties to the two Greenlanders' jaw-dropping amazement, Uncle Farley led them from the room.

Susan hoped that Mario might speak more openly now that the adults were gone—if not about the amulet, then about his life as an Accursed Returner—but all he said was, "I'd better set up camp too. We're going to need all our energy in the morning."

"Are you going to sleep in the room you shared with Charles?" Susan smiled weakly. "Or are you big enough for your own room?"

"Nah. I'll get a sheet from Applethwaite and set up in the solarium. Ever slept in a hammock, Susan? The sea'll rock you to sleep every night."

And then it was just Susan and Iacob. They looked at each other helplessly. What strange positions they were both in! He was helping her in an expedition that might very well end in his father's death. And she was fighting with her brother for an object that could get only one of them back to their own time (although *how* that worked was still a mystery). When you tried to sort out the rights and wrongs and the emotional allegiances, it all ended up a muddle. Lacking any clear plan, Susan fell back on good manners.

"C'mon. I'll show you around."

They wandered from room to room. To Susan, everything in Drift House was old and quaint, and yet to Iacob the objects and artifacts were still far in the future. He was fascinated by the wonders possessed by the "Ropians," but almost every time he asked Susan what this object was, or who was that figure in a painting, she didn't know. It was as if they were not only from different worlds, but there was a whole world between theirs, one that was lost to Susan as much as it was off-limits to Iacob. Reencountering the broken Pompeian cast in the drawing room, she felt how truly large the past was: how much it had given the people of her time, and how much of it had disappeared, never to be recovered—not even to the owners of Drift House.

Eventually they ended up on the poop deck. The cold southern coast of Greenland lay before them—along with a dozen Qaanaaq. They sat in a long umiak that looked to have been carved from the trunk of a single tree. Since there were no trees on Greenland, Susan assumed it must have come from the mainland, which raised a question that had been bothering her ever since she'd first heard of the colony. Pointing to the Qaanaaq vessel, she asked Iacob,

"How come you never moved to the mainland? I would think there's much more of what you need to live there."

Iacob stared at the long, narrow vessel floating on the water. "The Qaanaaq go back and forth between our island and the big land to the west," he said finally. "They say it is very different from where we live. The water bathes only one edge of it, and it stretches west and south farther than a man can walk or row in his lifetime. There are great forests there, and grains, and other food-bearing plants they have tried to describe to me, but who can understand a food he hasn't tasted? And there are other people there, other tribes, many of which far outnumber the Qaanaaq, as the Qaanaaq far outnumber us."

Susan knew that if she wanted to she could go downstairs to Drift House's library and find out the tribes' names—not just their names, but where they came from, and what became of them in the centuries after this one. But she stayed where she was, feeling that Iacob's perspective, though so much more limited than her own, still offered her something she would never discover through an encyclopedia.

"They say that Leif Erikson, the son of our founder and the man after whom Leifsbudir is named, visited the big land and saw this richness for himself. It was Leif's idea that we move from the island Erik the Red had brought us to and instead make our home in this other place, which he too considered more suited to our way of life. The Ropian way of life. But Leif rashly attacked the people who lived on the big land, and was lucky to escape alive. We have not returned since."

"So he trapped you," Susan said, waving a hand at Greenland's rocky, treeless coast.

"Trapped?" Iacob laughed slightly. "I suppose we are trapped, but not by Leif Erikson. Centuries have passed since that first encounter. Wrongs can be righted, sins forgiven, or forgotten. The only thing that traps us now is our unwillingness to change."

"What do you mean?"

Iacob laughed again, a bitter laugh that seemed old beyond his years.

"The last boat from Norway came years ago, when my father was a boy. It was the first vessel from the Old World that had been seen in nearly half a century. And do you know what my father and his generation did? They bought linen. Cloth. Because cloth was one of the things that separated us from the Qaanaaq. Made us think we were better than them. They bought metal too—blades for knives and hoes, and one plow that Iussi thinks is the only thing that stands between us and oblivion. Decades of ivory and white fur and feathers traded for a few trinkets of dubious value, a few yards of cloth that offer almost no protection against the cold. But the most expensive thing they bought?"

He paused, obviously waiting for Susan to guess. But Susan had no idea, and she just shook her head.

"A Bible."

"A Bible?" she repeated, not sure why he'd said the word with such vehemence. Father Poulsen flashed in her mind. Perhaps it was the priest he disliked.

"The men traded nothing less than a live polar bear cub for it," Iacob sneered. "For that price, they could have bought a dozen swords. But they traded it all for a book."

"Well, it is a religious book—"

"It could have been a book of spells for all the difference it made. No one in Osterbygd can read!"

"You can't *read*?"

Susan didn't mean for her question to come out, well, snotty. Iacob's face turned a bright shade of red, but he recovered his composure quickly.

"For the same things, the Qaanaaq would have given us parkas and kayaks, which we could have studied and learned to make ourselves. But no, we must catch our fish in our own rickety boats, in woven clothes that absorb the moisture rather than repel it, and sit shivering in our church staring at a book whose pages are enjoyed only by termites. The way I see it," he went on, "there is always 'some place better.' Some place where the air is warmer, the sea full of more fish. But the Qaanaaq have taught me that people must learn to make their homes where they are, to measure happiness not by the things your world brings to you, but by the things *you* bring to your world."

Susan slept fitfully that night (although "night" was a relative term, since it never actually got dark that far north in early June). The North Atlantic swells heaved the house about. Every time she dozed off she woke up immediately with the sense that she was falling out of bed. Uncle Farley had given her a chamberpot "just in case," but fortunately it never got that bad.

At one point she opened her eyes and saw that the light had changed from the yellowish haze of night to the icy gray of morning. Beneath the comforter her body felt warm, but the tip of her nose registered the chilliness of the air. Last fall, Mr. Zenubian would have had a fire going before she woke up. Her robe would have been hanging on its peg near the firescreen, toasty warm and awaiting her. As she stared at her breath fogging the air, she almost would have welcomed his sour odor, if he'd been there to build a blaze for her.

From somewhere she remembered how Charles had christened her Captain Susan, and she called on that strong, independent girl to take charge now, get up, get dressed, get her ship ready for the extra crew members who were sleeping on the next floor. She dashed out of bed, ran to the dresser and pulled on pants and a long-sleeved T-shirt, and her fleece, which was the best she could do in the way of warm clothing (it was summer vacation, after all, and she hadn't thought she'd need to bring her winter coat and, like, mittens). She put on socks and shoes, then headed downstairs.

She walked down the hall quietly, staring at the glass cases that lined the hall. The objects in them were a little jumbled, but nothing had fallen to the floor, and it occurred to her that that was why everything was behind glass—to keep it in place while sailing. And even as she thought that, she realized that the house's wild motion had ceased considerably.

"We've stopped!" she said out loud, then immediately clapped a hand over her mouth. No sense waking everyone before they were ready. Uncle Farley had been up late, after all, preparing beds for nearly a dozen men, so she should let him get his sleep. She would wake him after she'd done a little reconnoitering.

Moving as quickly and quietly as she could, she skipped to the window at the end of the hall. Thick bolts of gauzy fog lay over the water, but through it she could see a dark green strip of coast stretching as far as the eye could see in either direction. The coast seemed to be covered by a dense coniferous forest, with only a thin strip of rocky beach separating the trees from the ocean.

"Why, we're here!" she said out loud again, and then she laughed at herself and whispered, "Stop talking to yourself, Susan."

Downstairs she went to the dining room first, for breakfast. She was a little surprised when Miss Applethwaite offered her only a big cup of steaming hot chocolate. A little disappointed too: she'd thought she wanted a nice buttery crumpet or two. But in fact she was too jumpy to sit down to eat. The chocolate was thick and filling and warm and, most important, she could carry it from room to room.

She went to the drawing room next, but its walls still seemed to be broken. That is, the swirling darkness had lost its swirliness, and was now merely dark. As she stood sipping her chocolate and staring into the blackness, Susan remembered her previous voyage in Drift House, when the drawing room's walls had also gone dark. The family had thought the walls were broken then as well, but Susan later realized the darkness actually depicted the lightless bottom of the Sea of Time, where the mermaids had taken her. Was that the case here, she wondered. Was she destined to end up in another black place?

She set her cup down and went to a window again. The fog was already thinning, and Susan could make out more of the landmass in front of her. The island—presumably Vinland— or Newfoundland as it was known in her time—was densely empty, crowded with rocks and trees. Nothing suggested human habitation. although the mist did make it hard to see very far inland.

As she stepped back from the window she noticed Marie-Antoinette on her perch. It seemed to Susan that the parrot's eye flickered slightly, as if she were shutting it just as Susan turned. Susan walked over to the elegant, dainty bird.

"Good morning, Marie-Antoinette," she said—but quietly, in case the parrot really was asleep.

Marie-Antoinette shook herself. A yellow eye opened, took in Susan and the gray light in the room, then closed again.

"I don't understand why you persist in this charade," Susan continued. "Don't you ever want to talk to someone?"

A long breathy sigh escaped the parrot's nasal slits, but other than that she didn't stir.

"I mean, I'm sure it's fun to torment President Wilson and all that. It's always fun to tease boys. But it's just us girls right now. Come on, you can confide in me. I promise to keep your secrets."

Throughout Susan's speech, Marie-Antoinette's fluffed plumage had gradually settled back into place. The parrot's head and tail drooped, and her breathing settled into an even rhythm. Susan wondered if the bird had actually gone back to sleep.

"Oh, come on, Marie-Antoinette. There are a dozen Greenland soldiers sleeping upstairs, and Uncle Farley, and Mario, and Iacob." Susan wasn't sure why she separated the boy out from his fellow Greenlanders, but she heard the stammer in her voice and felt her cheeks grow hot. "I get so tired of being the only girl aboard. Can't we have a little female solidarity? Can't—"

Susan broke off. A dark shadow had floated across the window behind the porch. Since the morning had grown perceptibly brighter, the shadow was distinctly noticeable—and ominous.

One of Marie-Antoinette's eyes flickered open again, but Susan didn't care now. She stepped back to the window and pressed her eye to the slit between curtain and wall and peered out. What she saw sent a chill down her spine.

A long Viking ship lay ten feet off Drift House's starboard side. It was so close Susan could see the barnacles stubbling the boat's hull, not to mention the bearded faces of the sailors on deck, all of whom brandished clubs and spears, and stared at Drift House with malevolent expressions.

When Susan stepped back from the window, she started a second time. Marie-Antoinette was facing her, and the look in her eye was anything but ignorant.

"We must hide, Susan. Now."

Susan didn't remark on Marie-Antoinette's decision to speak finally. "We have to warn Uncle Farley and the others!"

There was a soft thump as something, the prow of the alien ship or perhaps a towline, struck the side of Drift House right by the front door.

"There's no time, Susan," Marie-Antoinette hissed. "They're here!"

"Marie-Antoinette!" Susan hissed back. "Our crew could be slaughtered in their sleep!"

Marie-Antoinette slitted her eyes in frustration. "Humans! So much trouble! All right then, stand back!"

"What—"

But Marie-Antoinette had already stood up tall on her perch. Flapping her wings like a rooster bringing in the morning, she opened her beak and a piercing wail erupted from her tiny body. Susan had to cover her ears to shield them from the noise (which sounded, she couldn't help but notice admiringly, *exactly* like a New York City police siren).

"Now," Marie-Antoinette whispered while hopping deftly from her perch to Susan's shoulder. *"Hide."*

"Where—"

Marie-Antoinette pointed with her wing. "The radio."

As Susan ran across the room for the shelter of the large tombstone radio, she heard commotion all through the house. Footsteps thumped above her, the stairs creaked with heavy treads.

Closer to her, and more frightening, was the loud smash of something against the front door, followed by the tinkle of falling glass. There was a second smash, and Susan heard the door slam against the other side of the drawing room wall. She practically dove behind the radio as a *THUD—THUD—THUD* announced the arrival of three Viking soldiers jumping into the hall.

Susan squeezed herself into the tiny space between the side of the radio and the corner of the room. A shout rang out from what sounded like the stairs; there were answering shouts from the doorway. With a start, Susan realized she couldn't understand what was being said.

"Marie-Antoinette! I forgot my translation charm!"

"What, and you think *I* can translate for you?" Marie-Antoinette made a thin sound like a snort. "Keep it down, Susan. You don't exactly need to *talk* to them."

Susan couldn't believe she'd forgotten something as important as her translation charm. How careless of her! Her Captain Susan days were long past.

Footsteps ran down the hallway. Thuds and smashes and more thuds, all punctuated by unintelligible shouting. Viking—Greenlandish? Norwegian?—was certainly a fearsome-sounding language. It had sounded perfectly civilized when she'd understood it.

Now there was another shout. Though she couldn't see anything, the voice was so loud Susan knew it was coming from right in front of the door. And, though she couldn't understand what was being said, Susan could tell from the tone that it wasn't particularly nice.

"Susan, look!" A red wing reached into her peripheral vision. "This panel seems loose."

"Really, Marie-Antoinette," Susan hissed. "Let's leave the radio repair to Uncle Farley and Charles—"

A loud crash cut her off, followed by a terrible scream—not of anger or fear, but pain. Before the sound had run its course, it changed to a strangled gurgle.

Susan tried to speak again, couldn't. She looked down at Marie-Antoinette helplessly.

"I think we can get inside, Susan," the parrot said in a calm, matronly tone of voice. "It might be our only chance to get out of this with both wings intact."

The gurgle gave way to a keen moaning, over which the shouts and smashes still sounded.

"Wh-what?" Susan said.

Marie-Antoinette slipped a few feathers in the narrow seam between the side and back panels of the radio. "I can't do it myself, Susan," she said, her voice still calm, although a thin edge of panic was audible. "We need fingers. Now get yourself together or I'll bite your ear off."

Susan nodded, tried to tune out the moans of the man on the other side of the radio. Dazedly, she prized her fingers into the crack and pulled. The wood stuck a moment, and then slid open about six inches. Susan could see a dark empty chamber within.

Suddenly there was a different shout in the hall outside.

"Get off my ship, you ruffians."

"Uncle Farley!" Susan said, in close to a normal voice.

"Sshh!" Marie-Antoinette hissed. "You can't help him. Get inside *now*."

"I warn you," Uncle Farley went on in a forceful voice, "I was an alternate on the Sorbonne fencing squad! I know how to use this!"

"But, but—"

"Susan"—Marie-Antoinette snapped her beak threateningly—"now!"

Susan gave the panel one more pull. It opened wide enough for her to squeeze inside. She hesitated, then felt the sharp edge of Marie-Antoinette's claws on her rump, and wormed her way through the opening. Turning around, she saw Marie-Antoinette slip through after her, then reached and pulled the panel closed. It snapped back into place so quickly she had to jerk her fingers out of the way to avoid getting them pinched.

Suddenly everything was different.

"Bjorn!" a thick deep voice cried. "Take Henni back to the ship and see to his wound. Bow-legs, search the lower chambers for the talking box. The rest of you, help me take the stairs. We shall throw these weaklings from the deck of their lumbering vessel and set it alight on the water like a funerary barge!"

Susan realized the radio was somehow acting as a translation charm, allowing her to understand what the renegade Greenlanders were saying. Of all their words, the two that stuck in her mind for some reason were "talking box."

"MARIE-ANTOINETTE! KARL OLAFSON'S MEN ARE LOOKING FOR THIS RADIO!"

"SQUAWK! SQUAWK! SQUAWK! SQUAWK! SQUAWK!"

Susan had thought she was hissing her words, but her voice exploded out of the radio, followed by Marie-Antoinette's even louder shrieks, amplified as if through a loudspeaker. Well, not so much a loudspeaker as the sound system for a rock concert. When her voice faded, she could hear the pictures still rattling on the wall, followed by a crash as something fell to the floor. Everything else had gone silent.

"Men," said a slightly startled, slightly amused voice. "I believe it's in here."

Suddenly there was a crash. A smash. The bash of one club against another, and then:

"Lecki! Onno! Hold off the giant! He has the strength of one and a half men!"

Uncle Farley! Susan thought. But she was too preoccupied to fret about this, because she heard footsteps run directly toward her, followed by a loud thumping as someone knocked on the side of the radio.

"We have it, Myrki!"

"To the ship with it! We will hold off the giant's crew while you move it out!"

Later Susan realized she should have braced herself. But at the time all she could think was that the men were stealing the radio—with her inside it. She was paralyzed. Paralyzed, but not, unfortunately, rooted in one spot, and when the radio suddenly tilted backward so did she. The last thing she heard before she hit her head was an impossibly loud

"SQUAAAAWK!"

And then: blackness.

Just as the drawing room walls had predicted.

EIGHTEEN

Return to Drift House (Redux)

"I *AM* SORRY, PRESIDENT WILSON."

Silence came from the front of the slim canoe, where President Wilson stood like a masthead, shrouded by fog and darkness.

"I didn't know how to get a message to you. And I didn't want to give away your existence, or else you might have been captured too."

"Steady, Charzo," Tankort said from his position in the rear of the canoe.

Charles made firmer strokes with his paddle. The fog was so thick he couldn't see the water it stirred, though he could hear its faint plash—and feel it too, on his feet, in the damp bottom of the canoe. Charles had decided that the bottom of the canoe was damp before he got into it, because he didn't want to think about the possibility that the thin shell of bark separating him from this vast body of water had a slow leak in it.

"And I *certainly* didn't mean to exclude you from my conference with the Wanderer of Days. I'm *sure* you could have been of use there. You'd've thought to ask him far more pertinent questions than I did."

Charles thought he heard the parrot "hmph."

"To tell you the truth, President Wilson, I'm not sure how I ended up in the litter in the first place. The Wanderer said the book Mario gave me has a funny reaction when it's around him. It causes a little, um, ripple I think he called it, in the temporal flow. So I was kind of blinking ahead every once in a while, sometimes a few seconds, sometimes a few hours."

Charles couldn't be sure, but it seemed that the parrot's shadow thickened slightly. The bird must have fluffed his feathers against the coolness of the foggy air.

There was the sound of a throat clearing behind him.

"This is why you fell, isn't it?" Tankort said in a hushed voice. Charles wondered if it was him the Wendat didn't want to disturb, or the sea—or whatever might be living in it. "When I made fun of you for being clumsy?"

In his relief, Charles hardly noticed that Tankort's English seemed much improved. "Exactly!" he said.

"I am sorry for teasing you."

Charles was impressed. He and Susan so rarely apologized to each other for much bigger offenses. "Thank you," he said now, turning slightly. "I appreciate it."

"Steady, Charzo," Tankort said as the boat wobbled. "Or we'll end up in the wrong place."

Something in Tankort's voice made Charles think that the place he referred to was more than just geographical. Turning his head as gently as he could—the canoe was so slight that even the tiniest movements affected its course—Charles peered into the fog. But the swirls of mist gave back nothing. Within a few feet all was blackness, and now Charles found himself wondering if he and Tankort were not paddling on the edge of the Atlantic Ocean as he'd assumed when they set out, but had in fact navigated onto the Sea of Time. That would certainly explain the Wendat's expanded vocabulary.

When he'd emerged from the litter, he'd seen that the tribe had marched to an immense body of gray water Charles assumed had to be the Atlantic. As soon as he got out, a pair of men immediately sewed the litter shut again. From the outside, Charles could see that the deerhide was laced tight as a drum to a frame of sturdy beams—though in truth the leathern square seemed less like a drum than a cage. The outside of the litter was painted with the boxed Amulet of Babel over and over, as well as several other strange symbols in ochre and indigo. Charles wondered if the symbols actually gave the Wendat some sort of power over the man inside, or if perhaps they were there to protect them.

It was Handa who led Charles and Tankort to the canoe, where President Wilson was already installed, along with a pair of paddles. The paddles worried Charles: he had used the rowing machines in the gym in the basement of his building, and never managed to go for more than ten or fifteen minutes without getting tired (not to mention bored).

Handa said something that Tankort translated.

"Handa says, since you are leaving the tribe, you are no longer Handa-*vey*. He says the two of you are free of any obligation to each other."

Charles nodded at this. "Please tell him I say thank you."

Handa took the sheath that held his knife and held it out to Charles. He spoke again; Tankort translated.

"Handa offers you his weapon of his own free will. Not as *vey*, blood obligation, but man to man. He says for you to use it in safety and necessity."

Charles took the knife solemnly. It was very light, but weighed heavily on his mind. "But what will he use?"

Tankort didn't quite manage to suppress a laugh. "He has five more just like this one, and after another winter of quiet nights around the fire he will have another five."

Charles nodded. The sheath had a long thin length of braided cord attached to it, and he slipped it over his shoulder diagonally, like a military sash.

"Tell him I would give him something as well, if I had anything to give."

Tankort gave Charles a funny look. "I am not sure he would take anything that comes from your world, Charzo. Somehow gifts from the English never seem to be free."

The two boys climbed in the canoe then, and Handa ran them out into the water. Tankort took the stern to steer, occasionally correcting Charles's form. Paddling a real boat was nothing like the machine in the gym. For one thing, each boy only got one oar, which was short and made of wood. Years of use had worn a depression in the shaft, and Charles's left hand fit naturally into this groove; his right rode the flat end of the shaft, pushing down to complement the pull of his left hand, and with slow, even strokes, the boys propelled the craft into the open water. The sky was banded in shades of blue and orange and black that merged imperceptibly with the dark water at the horizon. Charles stared out at the open water for a long time, conscious that his arms—his and Tankort's—were piloting them into that endless expanse.

Certainly a part of him was afraid. The canoe was so tiny and frail, the ocean huge and inexorable. In some ways it seemed much bigger than the Sea of Time. It was certainly more present in the tiny boat, as opposed to Drift House's carpeted and wallpapered rooms. The swells were more pronounced, the occasional drops of water splashing into the canoe on Charles's skin were much colder, and the smell of salt was everywhere.

But Charles had learned to acknowledge his fear, rather than repress it and let it get the better of him. The swells were bigger, but they also had a regularity to them, and if you paddled across them they didn't rock the canoe too alarmingly. And, too, Charles had faith in Wendat technology. It was strange for a boy used to airplanes and subways and computers to think of canoes and paddles and moccasins as technology, but they were, in fact, intelligent human adaptations to the environment, and they worked perfectly. Charles's feet stayed warm and dry despite the dampness in the bottom of the canoe, and the boat cut evenly through the water, not just propelling the two boys away from the shore, but propelling them toward Drift House, toward Uncle Farley and Susan and the comforts of home. That was enough to keep Charles from feeling truly afraid, and as he stared at President Wilson's back he imagined that he was looking at Drift House's coat of arms, and let that be his guide.

He hardly noticed as the color of the sky darkened, thickened really, as though night were being stirred into it like soup, the stars glowing like phosphorescent bits of pasta. By then, too, Charles was tired. Tankort had kept the pace slow, and periodically had the boys switch which side of the boat they paddled on, so no part of Charles actually hurt, but all of him was a little achy and fatigued. Though Charles hadn't asked to take a break, Tankort had at one point volunteered that it was unsafe for them to stop rowing, because without any forward motion the boat could run afoul of the swells, and so Charles rowed with the knowledge that rest wasn't possible until they reached their destination. When the fog started rolling in, he watched it impassively, noting only in the farthest depths of his mind that the mist was warmer than he would have suspected, and that the water beneath the boat seemed to have calmed somewhat.

"Tankort," he said, "are we on the Sea of Time?"

"Steady now, Charzo. Even strokes."

Charles moved the paddle from his right side to his left. "Are you piloting us through time?" he tried again. The silence went on for so long that he thought Tankort wasn't going to answer him. But then:

"Do you not know? The thing you carry—it sets the course. You have only to listen to it." He paused a moment, as if listening. "It is not very far now."

Charles listened, but didn't hear anything. The bag was on the floor of the canoe behind him, and he could see it in his mind's eye, see through it to the pair of mirror books it contained. The whole one he had taken from within the Wanderer's chest, and the second one with the missing lines scored deep into the front cover, each of the seven grooves as dry as an empty riverbed waiting eagerly for the next rain to fill it. It seemed to Charles that a wind blew the cover of his book open, riffled the pages till they showed the Tower of Babel, pyramiding into a swirling purple sky one enormous step at a time . . .

Charles suddenly realized you didn't always listen with your ears.

"Wow," he said.

"It is missing part of itself," Tankort said. "It wants to join again. It has wanted to do this for a long time. The two parts call to each other."

Charles thought of the vibrations he had felt from Mario's book when he'd first held it. These vibrations hadn't been in the one given him by the Wanderer. Yes, it was just the first book that was calling out. The first book that had desire.

"And you can hear it too?" he said to Tankort, remembering how he'd justified hiding the book from Susan by telling himself that it spoke only to him.

"I do not think 'hear' is the right word, exactly. But I cannot think of a better one." Suddenly the quiet sound of Tankort's paddle stopped. "Look, Charzo."

"At what?" Charles also pulled his paddle from the water. "Where?"

Tankort didn't answer, and Charles peered into the mist. It seemed thinner. No—lighter. With a steady pace, a glow spread over the hidden ocean, and beneath it the mist seemed to dissolve. In what seemed like no time at all—though it didn't happen particularly quickly—the air was clear and Charles and Tankort and President Wilson sat in their canoe off the coast of a dark green island. And there, some distance beyond the port bow, rocked the familiar galleon shape of—

"Drift House!"

With a great flap and flutter of wings, President Wilson stirred himself in the front of the bow, and now Charles had the real explanation for the parrot's silence: he had been asleep.

"Why-who-what? Where is the enemy? I shall slice him stem—"

The parrot broke off when he was drowned out by Charles and Tankort's laughter. He began combing his feathers nonchalantly, then suddenly broke off.

"I shall fly ahead and alert Farley and Susan to our arrival. Perhaps Applethwaite will prepare something more substantial than dried meat and berries," he added, looking at Tankort. And, flapping his wings, he lumbered into the air and wheeled in the direction of Drift House.

It took almost another hour for the canoe to reach the house. The swells had increased again, and the current pushed toward the shore. The boys had to row against it, and it was obvious from the sound of Tankort's labored breathing that he was as tired as Charles was. For the first time since they'd set out, Charles's shoulders began to hurt. And his upper arms. And his forearms. And his hands, and his fingers too. But Charles didn't care. The solarium glowed in the morning light like a warm fire, calling him home.

But when, finally, he reached the house, only a grim-faced Uncle Farley reached a hand to help him from the canoe.

"Where's Susan?" Charles said immediately.

"Come inside," Uncle Farley said nervously. "I'm sure Miss Applethwaite can whip you up—"

"WHERE—IS—SUSAN?!"

Uncle Farley cringed at the volume of Charles's voice, even as his nephew pushed into the house. Charles had, without realizing it, unslung his backpack, and now, despite the preciousness of its cargo, and the lengths he had gone to in order to get it, he dropped the bag to the floor.

For the elegant entrance hall of his uncle's home had been destroyed. Not a single table remained in one piece, their splintery remains stacked under the staircase in a forlorn pile of jagged sticks of wood from which poked a brass handle or a bit of gilt. The white marble bust (Charles had learned it was Herodotus, although he'd been too shy to ask who "Herodotus" was) had been overturned and lost its nose and one ear, and the giant portrait of Pierre Marin had been slashed twice, once through the treasure chest and again through the chest of his purple velvet frock coat. The scarred canvas had wrinkled, causing the body of Drift House's founder to wilt as though with age, and the eyes that had once seemed to follow everyone who walked through his hallway now stared in slightly different directions.

But most disconcerting of all was the blood.

It had splashed and splattered more or less everywhere. The walls were misted reddish brown, and one of the rugs had a dark stain on it the size of a bath mat. There was a big hand-print on the doorframe to the drawing room, and the broken lattice of the door was covered with dark smears, as though a careless painter had failed to wipe the excess liquid from his brush.

"Uncle Farley!"

"No, no, Charles," Uncle Farley said immediately. He pulled Charles to him and ran his hand soothingly through the boy's mop of hair. "It's okay, Charles. She's okay. She's just, um, been kidnapped."

Charles pushed back. "Just! Been! Kidnapped!" He shook his head incredulously. "We've got to do something!"

Uncle Farley smiled softly at the creature before him, half little boy, half wild beast. "Yes, yes, we're making a plan. But, ah, your friend? In the boat? I think he wants to speak to you."

"Tankort!" Charles had forgotten all about him in the confusion. He ran back to the doorway.

The young Wendat had pushed the canoe back a little ways from Drift House—just far enough to prevent anyone in the house from boarding it.

"Tankort," Charles said in a quieter voice. "You're not leaving?"

"Yes, Charzo." Tankort shrugged, as if he would say more if he could, but off the Sea of Time his English had become limited again.

"But . . . but . . ." Charles didn't really know what his "but" was. He just knew he didn't want Tankort to leave. "I wanted you to meet my sister."

Tankort looked in the direction of land, then turned back to Charles. "You find her."

"But how?" Charles said, knowing his question was pointless.

Tankort only nodded again. "You find her," he repeated. With deft movements of his paddle, Tankort began rowing the canoe backward.

Charles realized the Wendat would not be stopped from going. And so, standing up straighter, he said, "I'm sorry we got off on the wrong foot. I would have liked to get to know you better. I think we could have been friends."

Tankort shrugged, and Charles wasn't sure if he'd understood. "Friends," he echoed, then smiled. "Yes. Friends."

The canoe glided away from Drift House.

"Thank you," Charles called across the widening body of dark water between them, "for bringing me back to my family."

The gap between house and canoe had grown quite large by then. Charles could hardly see Tankort's face, but he continued to stare at the canoe. The Wendat's last words were oddly articulate, as if the canoe were in the real world and on the Sea of Time simultaneously.

"Thank you for showing me that not all English are the same." Tankort's voice floated to Charles, and then the canoe sank into a hollow between two waves and disappeared. After a moment, Charles realized it was gone. He stared at the empty sea for one more moment, then headed inside to find out what had happened to Susan, and how they were going to rescue her. He retrieved his backpack from the top step and walked through the door, only to stop short when the first person he saw was—

"Mur—Mario?"

"Got it in one," Mario said with a grin. "One and a half. Nice war paint," he added. "And I love what you've done with your glasses."

Rubbing at his cheeks, Charles rushed forward to embrace his brother, but Mario stepped rapidly backward in the wrecked hall, almost as if Charles had pushed him. He held up his hands.

"The, um, things in your backpack."

"The mirror books?"

"Can't get too close to 'em. They're a bit like Kryptonite to me."

"But . . . but didn't you give us one?"

Mario took a long time before answering. "If I did, it wasn't a whole one. You resourceful guy, you."

Charles wasn't entirely sure what this meant, but he couldn't quite hold back a smile. "It's been a pretty eventful few days."

Throughout this exchange Uncle Farley had stood silently

in the shattered, blood-spattered doorway of the drawing room, giving the brothers their moment. But now he cleared his throat.

"Mirror book? Is that the thing you so jealously guarded right before we were separated?"

Charles turned to his uncle, nodding sheepishly. "I'm sorry I ran off."

"I shall have to ground you for the rest of the summer," Uncle Farley said, but he had a grin on his face as he said it. "An explanation will suffice."

"They're, I don't know, magic or something. Apparently they can do all *sorts* of things, but we need them to close the temporal jetty."

"Jetty?" Uncle Farley said. "Is this related to the squall?"

"Squall?" Charles said. "The Wanderer didn't mention a squall. He only told me about—"

"Who is this Wanderer? The boy in the canoe?"

"No. That was Tankort. He's a Wendat—a Huron. Like the lake. But their real name is Wendat."

"And this Wanderer is one of them?"

"Not exactly," Mario said now. "He's more like..." He shrugged beneath the gaze of his brother and uncle. "Well, their god. But a god they don't particularly trust. He knows more about time than, well, anyone. He's been pretty much every place a human being can get to, and a few they weren't supposed to. He has a long, um, *association* with the Wendat"—Mario flashed a knowing look at Charles—"that ended late in the seventeenth century, shortly after Pierre Marin encountered them. I guess Charles has been there too, now."

The sound of footsteps on the stairs disturbed them. A moment later a small blond-haired man appeared at the upper landing and barked something in a language Charles didn't understand. Uncle Farley answered the man in English, telling him that he would be right up. Glancing briefly at Charles, the man ran back upstairs.

"Charles, I have to attend to the wounded. Mario, perhaps you could get Charles something to eat, and fill him in."

As Uncle Farley ran up the stairs, Mario turned to his big brother—who was about an inch shorter than he was.

"Charles, could you? I mean, your bag?"

"Oh, right." Charles stashed his bag on the bottom shelf of a dresser in the music room while Mario went to get him something from Miss Applethwaite. The tray from the dumbwaiter bore a large soup tureen and a covered pie plate, but Charles's nose immediately told him what was in the two dishes.

"Consommé and apple pie!"

"Our first meal here."

Charles sipped the first delectable bite of broth. "That seems like a long time ago."

"And it's only five hundred years in the future!" Mario said. "Give or take a decade."

The two brothers looked at each other for a moment and then simultaneously burst out laughing.

"Oh, Charles, I've missed you and Susan so much. Even more than Mum and Dad, I hate to say. But you seem different. Older. Tougher."

Charles blushed, and took a few quick bites of soup to cover it. He continued to eat while Mario told him about the squall and everything that had happened on Greenland, finishing up with his and Uncle Farley's conjecture that Susan and Marie-Antoinette must have hidden in the radio when Karl Olafson's men came aboard, and so were carried off when the raiders stole Drift House's last remaining transtemporal navigating device. Charles was well into his apple pie by then, but he stopped chewing long enough to say, "Wait a minute! If Mr. Zenubian has the little radio, and Karl Olafson has the big one, does that mean Drift House is—*stuck* here?"

Mario nodded. "We've got to get one of them back somehow. Since Mr. Zenubian is presumably still in the twenty-first century, and Karl Olafson is only on that island, he's obviously our best bet."

Charles gulped down the last of his pie. "So what are we waiting for? Let's go!"

Mario grinned at his older brother's enthusiasm. "Karl Olafson's men outnumber us two to one, and they have the advantage of a fortified position. With Drift House essentially engineless, we can only bring men to shore three at a time in my punt."

"Which is very dangerous," Charles said, immediately understanding. "Karl Olafson can just pick us off as we come. So if we can't attack him outright, we need to try"—a twinkle glittered behind Charles's bent glasses—"subterfuge."

Mario's eyes widened in surprise. "Charles Oakenfeld! When did you become such a strategist?"

Charles blushed a little. "After I saw the Trojan Horse on the Island of the Past, I went home and read the *Iliad* and the *Odyssey*."

"Homer! I love Homer!"

Charles paused. His little brother had said he loved Homer in the way you say you love an uncle you don't get to see often enough, rather than a writer who had lived almost three millennia ago.

"Yes, so, I read Homer. And, um, we need some kind of plan like that—something sneaky. Something they won't expect, or know how to deal with."

Just then a loud crash came from above them, followed by protracted yelling. A moment later, Uncle Farley's voice echoed down the stairs.

"Charles! We need you up here!"

Charles and Mario followed the sound of yelling to the third floor. A throng of strange and slightly smelly men made it hard for Charles to see the floor in their midst, but then he realized the yelling man was not, in fact, on the floor. He was on the ceiling.

He was, more accurately, pinned to the ceiling by the flying carpet, which he must have stepped on and activated by accident. His lumpy form could be seen writhing through the thick cloth of the carpet, which the tiny strangers were unable to reach and pull back.

"Coming through, coming through." Uncle Farley's voice cut in now. He appeared in the hallway with a stepladder. "Make way, please." As he set the ladder up, Uncle Farley said to Charles, "You do know how to work this, yes?"

Charles nodded. He climbed to the top rung of the ladder, standing on the step labeled NOT A STEP, and tapped the underside of the moon on the carpet lightly. The carpet descended slowly, and the trapped Greenlander rolled immediately to one side and fell to the floor, knocking over three of his companions like bowling pins.

Uncle Farley turned to Charles. "Perhaps we should put this out of the way to avoid another mishap."

"My room?" Charles said hopefully. A plan was hatching in Charles's head, and he snuck a glance at Mario, who nodded in understanding.

Uncle Farley saw the look that passed between the Oakenfeld boys and shook his head.

"I think perhaps Susan's room is best. We don't want any more *mishaps*."

They rolled the carpet up and carried it downstairs. Charles was surprised to see his sister's bed unmade, her dresser drawers hanging open and clothes strewn about. He kicked a pair of jeans to one side with his moccasinned foot before unrolling the carpet.

"Uncle Farley!" Mario exclaimed. "Susan left her translation charm." He was pointing to a small vial on a string on her bedside table.

"Is that how you can understand the Vikings?" Charles said.

"They prefer to be called Greenlanders," Uncle Farley answered, "but yes." He pulled his own vial from his shirt and told Charles how it worked. "I suppose you should wear it now."

Charles slipped the cord over his head, unstopped the vial, and tentatively touched his finger to the liquid inside.

"It's okay, Charles, it's quite safe. I've done it several times now."

Charles nodded and touched his finger to his ears first, then his tongue. The clear spot of damp had no taste, and he felt no different. As they exited Susan's room Uncle Farley stopped and pulled a roll of keys from his pocket. He locked Susan's door, securing the carpet from "any more accidents," and he looked significantly at Charles and Mario.

Charles was disappointed—he'd thought the carpet was the perfect thing for a nighttime rescue operation. But when he glanced at Mario, his brother surprised him by winking conspiratorially. He held back a step behind Uncle Farley, and whispered, "Don't worry about that. I've learned a thing or two about picking locks in my time."

Charles wanted to pull his little brother aside to ask him if he had a plan, but they were interrupted by shouts yet again— this time from below. Immediately, Charles knew the potion was working, for he heard an unfamiliar voice shout:

"Traitor!"

Charles and Mario and Uncle Farley ran for the stairs. Charles could feel a draft as he descended, and as soon as they rounded the bottom of the stairs, he saw why: the back door stood wide open, and a single red-haired Greenlander was standing in it.

"Stop, traitor! You won't get away!"

Charles pressed into the doorway, where he saw a small flat-bottomed boat being rowed by a boy about Susan's age. The boy wore an expression of grim determination beneath dark, unkempt hair, and he didn't respond to the calls from Drift House until Uncle Farley called,

"Iacob, please! We won't hurt you or your father. Just come back."

The boy in the boat stopped rowing and looked at the crowd gathered in the doorway.

"I am sorry, Mr. Farley. But only I can get through my father's defenses. Only I can stop him."

"Stop him?" Uncle Farley said. "But how?"

But Charles understood. He ran to the music room where he'd stashed his bag.

It was gone.

"Nooooooo!"

As he ran out of the room he ran smack into Mario.

"He's got the mirror books!"

Charles hadn't really thought about how Mario would react when he said this, but in his wildest dreams he never would have guessed what his little brother said next.

"Maybe it's better this way."

Charles stared at his little brother, dumbfounded. It was only when Mario pulled on a string that was tied around his neck that he understood.

"The Amulet of Babel. It—it's your locket, isn't it? It's what you need to get back to our time? To be five years old again."

In answer, Mario only shrugged. He had started to rub the empty cord around his neck.

Charles grabbed his brother's hands. "We can still get it back! We can take the carpet and—"

Mario shrugged again. "Perhaps we can get it back. Perhaps we can stop Karl Olafson from opening the jetty. But don't you see? You can use the amulet to end the temporal squall, which will allow Drift House to get back to the twenty-first century, or I can use it to become a little boy again, which will allow me to finally go home. But we can't do both."

Charles wanted to protest, but the look on Mario's face told him it was pointless. Mario squeezed his big brother's hands now and said, "We'll go tonight. When everyone's sleeping. It'll be fun," he said. But there was no fun in his voice.

At the door, a group of Greenlanders were apparently trying to lasso the fleeing boy—to no avail, judging from their groans and curses. Uncle Farley stepped away from them now and approached Charles and Mario. He looked back and forth between their serious faces.

"I hope you two aren't planning any shenanigans. It's bad enough that Susan's in trouble. I don't need you two in danger as well."

Charles looked at his brother, who met his eyes with a happy-sad expression that was old beyond his years. Charles couldn't believe that it had to be this way—that the amulet could only save Mario, or save Drift House and its occupants. It seemed like a cosmic prank.

As if reading his mind, Mario half grinned, then shrugged it away. Turning to their uncle with a bright, false smile on his face, he said, "Of *course* not, Uncle Farley. We wouldn't *dream* of such a thing."

NINETEEN

Karl Olafson

SUSAN LAY IN THE DARK for a long time with her eyes closed, because she didn't realize she was awake. The world was nothing but sounds: the strange chant of men-at-arms, the creak of their paddles as they turned in the oarlocks, the obsequious voices of servants (as well as the occasional roar of a displeased ruler). And then, strangest of all, Iacob's voice.

"Father."

She opened her eyes. For a moment she forgot she was in the radio, so she couldn't understand why the light was so dim.

"So. You have come at last."

If Iacob answered his father, Susan didn't hear, because when she sat up she heard an ominously loud rumbling. She froze.

"The wooden box makes strange noises," Karl Olafson said after a moment. Susan heard a tinge of fear in his voice, and was relieved. Hopefully he wouldn't go prying off one of the side panels anytime soon.

"The people from the water have trapped dangerous spirits inside," Iacob answered his father. "The spirits are eager to get out and wreak their revenge on the first people they see."

Bluster added itself to the fear in Karl Olafson's voice.

"Let us hope they don't get out then. You are closer to the box than I." There was a pause, and then Karl Olafson said, "I sense that you have brought me something, my son."

What was this? Susan sat up as quietly as she could, feeling a twinge at the back of her head. I must've been knocked out, she thought. Cool. She blushed hotly in the shadow of the radio. "Cool" was never a word she would have said out loud.

A sliver of light came through one side of the radio. Susan figured it was the tuning band between the two dials. The band was plastic, and transparent. She'd never noticed before, probably because the inside of the box was dark. But now she found that if she rested on her hands and knees she could put her eyes up to the slot and see out perfectly.

As she leaned toward the band, she heard a clacking noise and felt something soft and small scramble out of her way. Marie-Antoinette! Susan reached a hand through the dark to try to touch the bird reassuringly; a determined peck drove her hand away. Susan almost chuckled. Captivity certainly hadn't cowed Drift House's disgruntled second bird.

She leaned all the way into the slot now, and found herself looking at a shadowy space lit only by a pair of flickering torches and one large bonfire. It was a cave, Susan realized, narrow, but stretching back farther than she could see. The walls appeared to be wet-looking black earth, with creepy roots sticking out like something from a horror movie. The floor was earthen too, though here and there wide flat boulders poked from it, and these had been turned into stone tables covered with animal hides and wooden tools and clay jugs and things. Sitting on one of the smaller stones sat a thick hairy-faced man draped in something Susan assumed was a polar bear skin, although it was so dingy with dirt and smears of grease that it was less white than dark, dark gray. Standing before this man, with his back to her, was a thin boy she assumed was Iacob. At any rate he was barefoot in leather breeches, as she remembered him, but there was an eerily familiar shape hanging off his shoulders: Charles's backpack.

"CHARLES!"

Susan's voice boomed out into the empty space. She smacked her hand over her mouth, and even that tiny sound was amplified into a thunderclap.

Iacob whirled around, the backpack half falling from his shoulders and tangling in his arms. It was funny to think of someone who didn't know how to wear a backpack—but Susan was much more concerned with how Iacob had come to possess it in the first place. It seemed unlikely that Charles would have given it to him. Had Iacob taken it for some reason? And most important, how had Charles managed to join them in the fifteenth century?

Meanwhile, Karl Olafson was looking at his son with a skeptical expression. "Spirits? It sounds more like a child to me. And a girl at that. Guards!"

"Father, no!" Iacob whirled back to Karl Olafson. "It is not, uh, safe."

Karl Olafson ignored his son. He spoke to someone Susan couldn't see. "Pry open the side of that box. I think we have a spy in our midst."

"Father, please! If the magic gets out—"

The radio jerked to one side, and Susan fell against a wall. Fortunately she didn't hit her head this time, but her hand came down hard on a squirming, feathery bundle.

"SQUAWK!"

Marie-Antoinette's annoyed cry reverberated like a gunshot, and the box went still. Susan couldn't see anything, but she could imagine Karl Olafson's men jumping away from the strange sound.

"Sire! The box! It's haunted!"

"Sire?" Susan thought she detected a note of sarcasm in Iacob's voice. "Have you crowned yourself, Father?"

"Nonsense!" Karl Olafson said. It was unclear to whom he

spoke. "It is no more magical than a flute or a lyre. It makes noise because someone is playing it. In this instance, the person playing it is inside the box."

There was a moment of silence. Then:

"Sire? What is a flute?"

"Or a lyre?"

"Yes, Father," Iacob said. "What are these . . . musical instruments? And how have you heard of them?"

"Don't be coy, my son. The amulet is mine, and shall be yours upon my death—if you have indeed returned to be my heir. Do you have the book?"

There was a brief pause, and then Iacob said, "I think you know the answer to that question already, Father."

As quietly as she could, Susan inched back to the tuner slot. Dimly, she could make out Marie-Antoinette motioning with her wing for Susan to remain still, but Susan had to see what was going on. Iacob was more or less in the same place, the backpack in his hands now, but Karl Olafson was standing. The polar bear robe had fallen off his left shoulder, exposing a kind of woven leather tunic that was a bit like armor, and the military aspect was enhanced by a large dagger that hung from a sheath draped across his chest. Father and son stared at each other with looks of determination on their faces.

"They call me king," Karl Olafson said in a level, slightly menacing tone of voice, "and they will call you prince, and one day king, as well—if you demonstrate your fealty."

"Fealty?" Iacob's mouth had trouble with the word. "Flutes and lyres and . . . fealty? You know much more than you did the last time I saw you."

Karl Olafson put his hand to his chest and stroked something. Susan thought it was the cord holding up his dagger, but then she realized it was something beneath the tunic. The two halves of a string hanging from his neck disappeared beneath the leather. With a thrill of both horror and excitement, Susan realized it must be the Amulet of Babel!

"I know more than you can imagine, my son."

Iacob brought the backpack closer to his chest. "Like the contents of a closed sack?"

"Like the future, my son! I can show it to you as well. All you have to do is give me what's in that bag."

Susan could see that Iacob's hands were white knuckled from clutching Charles's backpack so tightly, but his voice was firm and—mostly—level. He nodded now, in Susan's direction. She caught her breath lest he expose her, and a sound like a snapped bowstring reverberated through the cave.

"The box," Iacob said. "It controls the strangers' ship."

"It does more than that, my son."

"I do not care about those other things, Father. Without it, the strangers are trapped."

A smirk, barely visible through the thick beard, twisted the side of Karl Olafson's mouth.

"Without it, we are also trapped, my son."

Iacob opened his mouth, then closed it. He shook his head. "I do not understand, Father. You have Osterbygd's boats and most of its weapons as well. And you have the amulet. How are you trapped?"

"You know what I mean, Iacob. Our people have been having this discussion for generations. Greenland is vast, but there is still nothing there. No place to go, nowhere to live. It is a prison, and it is time we broke free."

"Free? To what, Father? Where? Iceland? Norway?"

"There is no place on earth fit to deny us, and with the help of that box"—Karl Olafson pointed, and Susan involuntarily flinched—"we will soon be able to go wherever and whenever we choose."

Whenever? Did Karl Olafson know about the radio's temporal powers? But how?

Iacob apparently had the same question.

"When-ever?" he said, awkwardly repeating the word.

"Yes, my son. *When*ever." Suddenly Karl Olafson reached a hand to his throat and pulled on a string that hung there. Susan almost expected a fanfare after all this time, but the gold pendant slipped into view without a sound. She was surprised— she thought it would be tiny, like the one Murray wore around his neck, but it was almost as big as a tea saucer, and thick too. Maybe it's not what Mur—what Mario needs after all, she thought. Maybe we'll be able to get home and he'll be able to be a five-year-old again, and we won't have to choose. Her brother's lonely pleas to go home came back to her, and she prayed she was right.

Karl Olafson's voice broke into her thoughts. "The amulet has given me terrific visions, my son! It has shown me how to open a hole into the future! A hole we can step through as though it were a doorway, and through which we can bring back the most remarkable objects! Firearms that can propel bullets through the air a thousand times faster than a spear or an arrow, airships capable of carrying hundreds of warriors at heights and speeds no bird could ever reach, and computers that can outthink a thousand men. And so much more, from medicines to weapons to power sources. With them we can dominate the whole of the new world! Not just the islands of Greenland and Vinland, but the vastness of the two continents that lie to the west of them!"

Although the translation ability of objects associated with the Sea of Time was generally unnoticeable, there were times when it produced odd effects. Susan understood everything Karl Olafson had just said (and was terrified by it as well), but Iacob, who shared a language with his father, only stared at him in incomprehension—but his terror was just as palpable as Susan's.

"You speak of madness, Father!"

"How can you accuse me of madness, when you have just journeyed five hundred miles over the open water in a manor house with no visible means of propulsion? You know I speak the truth."

"It is not the truth of your words that frightens me, Father. It is your intention. You wish to upset the natural order."

"Iacob." Karl Olafson shook his head in a disappointed manner. "My son. The world is full of things we Greenlanders are too ignorant to understand. But that doesn't mean they don't exist, or can't be claimed by someone strong enough to grab them. I tell you we *can* go to the future, and we can bring back weapons that will allow us to conquer the whole of this world, compared to which Greenland is as a postage stamp on a letter."

Again, Karl Olafson's words, so clear to Susan, left his son confused. "Post-age stamp? Letter?"

Karl Olafson brought the pendant to his lips and kissed it. "The words, Iacob! The words I have heard and the things I have seen thanks to the Amulet of Babel! My head is full to bursting with all of it!"

"I think it *has* burst, Father. I thought you were open to reason, but that pendant has taken you past human negotiation."

"Enough! I grow tired of your insolence and disloyalty. Give me the book, so that I can rejoin the amulet to its berth and open the temporal jetty." And Karl Olafson took one hand from the necklace and placed it on the hilt of his knife.

"Neither your words nor your weapons will get this book from me, Father. Not until you return the box to the strangers' ship."

"You are brave, my son, but foolish. Do not think the bond of blood will keep me from spilling yours."

Karl Olafson took a step toward Iacob, who jumped back and grabbed one of the torches so quickly it was obvious he had planned his move. Way to go! Susan thought, but she was still terrified for him. Karl Olafson had his knife, after all, and there were the two guards she couldn't see, presumably armed as well. She was desperate to help in some way, but trapped in the radio all she could do was cross the fingers of both hands for luck.

But Iacob didn't waver. "Stay back, Father, or I'll destroy it, and all your plans with it."

Karl Olafson paused. Then, smiling grimly, he pulled his knife from its sheath almost casually. "It is not necessary for you to die, my son. Give me the bag, and everything will be forgiven."

Like all the Greenlanders' tools, Karl Olafson's knife was worn and small, more hilt than blade. But what was left was sharp and wickedly curved, like the claw of a lion, and looked more than long enough to slit the throat of a thirteen-year-old boy.

Iacob took another step backward and pressed himself against the wall of the cave. "I *will* do it, Father!"

Do it, Susan thought. Just do it!

Karl Olafson continued to advance on his son. He held the knife in front of him, as if showing a toy to a child.

"Look, my son, at what we have been reduced to. These little slivers of steel, when there are mountains of iron—and silver and gold and precious jewels—awaiting us. Would you deny your fellow countrymen the chance to live in comfort? With food to fill their bellies and medicine to heal their illnesses, and light, so they do not have to skulk in murky caves like the men of a thousand years ago? Do you really find our poverty so ennobling?"

"You use the word 'comfort,' Father, but what you mean is 'conquest.' You speak of food and medicine for our people, but it seems to me we can have none of these things for ourselves unless we take them from someone else. Light, Father?" Iacob waved his torch, causing it to sputter and smoke. "You don't want light. You want fire, to burn away everything you see!"

Karl Olafson snorted derisively. "This sounds like the nonsense you have learned from talking to the Qaanaaq."

"The Qaanaaq say that our kind are like termites in a house. We eat and eat and eat until everything is rotted away and the structure collapses on our heads."

Karl Olafson leveled the knife at his son. "I will give you one last chance, my son. The bag, or your blood."

Iacob hesitated for so long that Susan thought he might actually surrender. He stared at the blade in his father's hand as if hypnotized. But then, finally, he blinked, and looked in his father's eyes. "I am sorry. You leave me no choice." And quickly, before Karl Olafson could stop him, he brought torch and bag together.

The flammable nylon caught fire immediately, burning with a noxious orange flame. The sight was so captivating that it took several moments for Susan to realize that Karl Olafson had made no move to stop his son. Instead, he sheathed his knife, and his smile grew wider as he stared at the growing flames.

Iacob's eyes flickered between his father and the burning bag in his hand. His face was filled with confusion as he waited for an attack that didn't come. When the bag grew too hot to hold, he dropped it to the floor, where it burned smokily. The smoke wafted across the floor in dense spirals, and when it drifted through the radio's grille Susan had to bite her hand to keep from coughing. Marie-Antoinette, however, had no hand to bite, and her thin parrot cough blared out of the radio like a burst of gunfire. Susan heard the unseen men on either side of the radio moan in fear at the strange sound.

If Karl Olafson heard, however, he gave no sign. He stood looking at his son with an expression of eerie patience. It seemed that once he'd freed the amulet from his shirt he couldn't stop touching it, and both hands stroked it constantly, the way a young child will stroke the head of a sleeping kitten over and over again. Susan found herself wondering what would happen when the amulet woke up.

Occasionally his eyes flickered to the burning bag, but he

made no move to put it out. Soon enough Susan saw why: Charles's backpack burned away, leaving the book Mario had given them uncovered—and unscathed. And then, squinting, Susan saw that there wasn't one but two books. Something about this sent a thrill of fear up and down her spine, and she heard her sigh amplified into the room like the wail of an approaching tornado.

Karl Olafson seemed to see the second book at the same time Susan did. He looked up at his son with an openmouthed expression, of wonder and triumph, and also, Susan thought, of madness.

"Oh, my wayward son. You have brought your father so much more than you realize. Guards, seize him!"

The two men seemed only too eager to get away from the moaning, shrieking box. They ran across the room and one of them grabbed the torch from Iacob's hand and the other seized the boy by both arms and held him fast. Iacob, who seemed to have run out of ideas, didn't struggle, but only stared at the unburned books on the ground.

"What have I done?" he said. It seemed to Susan that his eyes glanced in her direction. "I'm sorry. I have played right into his hands."

Karl Olafson knelt before the smoldering books, but the flame was still too hot for him to touch them. "Talking to the 'spirits' inside the box, my son?" His laugh was short and rude.

"You said the amulet allowed you to see things that had not

yet come to pass. I see now it is true: you knew the fire wouldn't harm your precious book."

Karl Olafson could hardly look away from the burning books. Again and again his hand danced toward them, only to retreat to the amulet when the flames licked at his fingers.

"Yes, my son. I knew you would bring it to me, and I knew you would fail in your attempt to destroy it."

"And yet you seemed surprised by something. Could it be the fact that there were two books in the sack?"

Karl Olafson failed to hide his consternation. He took a hand off the pendant long enough to wave his son's words away.

"It is nothing. The amulet only shows me those things that are important."

"Is that true, Father? Or could it be that the amulet only shows you what it needs to get you to do its bidding? You think you are using the amulet, Father. But what if it is using you?"

Karl Olafson looked nervously at the two books. His hands held the amulet so tightly that Susan could see the cord biting into the skin of his neck. He made a visible effort to steel himself. "You will not frighten me out of opening the jetty, Iacob."

"Do you even know what the jetty is, Father? You speak of traveling to other lands, other times even, but how—"

"Enough!" Karl Olafson shrieked. It was obvious that Iacob's questions had frightened him. "The Amulet of Babel has guided me perfectly to this point. It will not fail me now.

You," he added, pointing to the guards, "gag him if he attempts to speak again."

Karl Olafson unsheathed his knife and Susan stifled a gasp. But he only used it to flick away the last burning threads of Charles's backpack. As he reached toward the pair of books, Susan looked all around the room for something—anything—to stop him. But there were only the two guards and Iacob, who was struggling so hard it took both of them to hold him. Desperate, Susan used the only resource available to her: her voice.

"KARL OLAFSON!"

Susan had shouted. The radio turned this shout into a sonic boom. A tankard of ale on one of the flat-topped boulders clattered to the ground and the smoke coils were pushed against the far wall like cats shying from a barking dog. But Karl Olafson only started slightly, then sheathed his knife and reached toward the pair of smoking books.

"DO NOT ATTEMPT TO RELEASE THE MAGIC, KARL OLAFSON, LEST YOU UNLEASH MY WRATH!"

Susan shouted with all the force of her lungs, but Karl Olafson's face was so transfixed she couldn't tell if he'd even heard her. His eyes glistened as his right hand stretched out slowly but eagerly, even as his left hand stroked the amulet at his throat. A look of ecstasy passed over his face as his index finger stroked the seven grooved lines on the cover while the thumb of his left hand stroked the matching lines on the amulet. His eyes closed, his lips moved as if he were praying. If he *was* praying, Susan didn't want his prayer to come true.

Suddenly the radio began to rattle like a boiling pot. Susan had to splay her hands and feet to stay upright. Outside the radio, the pulsations seemed to be even stronger. It was hard to tell if they actually knocked over Iacob and his guards, or if they were simply cowering in fear, but at any rate the two men and the boy were on their knees. The men covered their faces, but Iacob's eyes were fastened on his father. The energy seemed to swirl all around Karl Olafson, rippling his hair and waving the polar bear skin that cloaked his shoulders. But he kept his finger on the smoldering mirror book and continued to move his lips soundlessly.

"Father, no!" Iacob screamed.

"NO!" Susan screamed with him.

The metal tankard clanked as it bounced across the floor. The torches flickered wildly. Their smoke seemed to be coiling away from the wall now, circling Karl Olafson. Susan had never felt more afraid in her life, and Marie-Antoinette had taken to her wings within the narrow confines of the radio and was flapping and screeching crazily.

"NO! NO!" bird and girl screamed together.

"No!" Iacob screamed at his father.

And then their voices were echoed by an answering shout: "No!"

And again:

"NO!"

Susan's heart raced. She would know those voices any-where! But were they in time? Were they saved?

Pressing her eyes to the slot to see as much of the cave as she could, she yelled, "CHARLES? MARIO?"

She couldn't see her brothers, but Karl Olafson could, for he'd suddenly snatched the two smoking books and held them in his arms. He was staring right at her—no, not at her. Past her.

Susan beat at the sides of the radio. "CHARLES! MARIO!" she screamed. "YOU HAVE TO STOP HIM!"

A blurry form four or five feet in the air shot into view. At first Susan thought her brothers had somehow been catapulted into the room, but then she realized they were on Charles's fly-ing carpet, which swooped straight for Karl Olafson. For his chest, where the two mirror books hovered a mere inch or two away from the Amulet of Babel hanging from his throat. Sud-denly Susan remembered Karl Olafson's words about rejoining the amulet to its berth, and she realized it mustn't come into contact with Mario's book.

"NO!" she screamed, so loudly that the rock table split in two.

Or perhaps something else split the table, for even as Susan screamed, the carpet crashed into Karl Olafson's chest, forcing book and amulet together. There was a blinding flash of light, and something that felt like solid noise pulsed through the room.

THROOM!

Even when she could focus again, Susan could only catch glimpses of what was happening in the cave. The carpet fluttering like a piece of silk in a hurricane. Karl Olafson falling backward and losing hold of one of the books. His smirk of triumph shining like a beacon—then transforming into a snarl of pain and fear.

For the room was . . . was melting. Collapsing, crumbling, swirling, fading. Disappearing in a gale that splintered rock itself.

Yet not even that was as scary as what was happening to Karl Olafson.

It seemed as though someone had turned on a light inside his body. At first it just came out the holes—ears, mouth, nostrils—but then his eyes seemed to burn away, and then his skin seemed to turn black even as white lines began to show up, bright glowing tiger stripes that showed even through his shirt. Karl Olafson's mouth was open wide but the only thing that came out was a beam of light that seemed to shine through the fading walls of the cave. And he was fading too, or being consumed by the light that shone out from inside his body.

And then, quite suddenly, he was . . . gone.

Susan blinked. But she didn't have time to wonder what had happened to Karl Olafson, because her eyes caught sight of Charles, who was hanging on to the carpet with one hand even as his other clasped something close to his chest. Mario's book! But where was Mario? And Iacob? Susan couldn't see her youngest brother anywhere, but she spotted the Greenland boy. He seemed to be wading against a tide as his hand reached out toward something—the second book!—that hung in the air, its pages flapping wildly like a bird's wings. But before his fingers could close around it one of the guards grabbed his ankle and tripped him. And then Mario appeared as if from nowhere. He launched himself at the guard and knocked him off Iacob. Susan could hear his voice above the growing din in the room.

"Get the book and get on the carpet!"

Even as he spoke, the second guard ran to the aid of the first. He grabbed Mario and tried to pull him off his friend, but Mario refused to let go.

Iacob looked between Mario and the book. He seemed about to go to Mario's aid when Mario managed to look up at him.

"Go! Or all will be lost!"

There was something so commanding in his voice that Iacob didn't hesitate. He leapt for the book and caught it, then seemed to roll through the air and catch the edge of the carpet. Charles was there, and hauled him aboard. As soon as he was on the carpet, he turned for Mario, but he was already far away and still grappling with the two guards. And now Susan saw something glint in the hand of one of them. A knife!

The cave was gone now. In its place was just a vortex. The carpet with Charles and Iacob on it spun at one side while Mario wrestled with the guards at the other.

Something flashed. The guard with the knife had raised his hand in the air.

"MARIO, LOOK OUT!" Susan screamed.

Mario looked up from the two men who held him, directly at Susan. Despite the roaring in the cave, she heard his voice clearly.

"You were right, Susan. I'll find another way home."

The blade flashed down, disappearing into Mario's chest.

Susan screamed again, even as a second and more blinding flash of light seemed to travel up and down the jetty. It was as though a new star were being born. The explosion spun the box wildly, Susan fell away from the slit, Marie-Antoinette squawked, Susan hit her head again. For the second time that day everything went black. But this time Susan, who had just witnessed the death of one of her brothers, welcomed the darkness, and wished it would never end.

PART THREE

In and Out of Time

TWENTY

Babel

THE FIRE IN THE PIT turned into yellow ribbons.

The walls and floor of the cave turned into sand, and then into water, and then into wind. The wind swirled all around Charles like a tornado, but what Charles thought about was the Great Drain, emptying the Sea of Time into the next world—the world from which nothing returned. But unlike a tornado, or the Great Drain for that matter, the swirled blur that had been Karl Olafson's cave made no sound at all.

And Karl Olafson.

Karl Olafson made no sound either.

Nor did he move, after the carpet had knocked the book in his arms against the pendant hanging from his neck.

The Amulet of Babel.

Charles had seen what was going to happen even before Susan shouted from the radio. He stomped his feet on both sets of arrows to stop the carpet, but it was too late: the carpet slammed directly into Karl Olafson, and crushed mirror book and pendant together, reuniting them after more than two thousand years apart.

Then, motionless, soundless, Karl Olafson still somehow . . . changed. He began to glow. And, though he didn't move, something told Charles that the glowing wasn't painless. It was like a fire had been lit deep in Karl Olafson's belly and was burning its way out of him. As he watched, the man that had been Karl Olafson flaked away like an incinerated stick, leaving behind only a formless light that swirled into the whirling nothing that had been the real world.

Only a few things held on to their shape: Charles, for one thing, and Iacob. And the two mirror books, and Drift House's radio, out of which came unintelligibly loud shrieks and squawks.

And Mario. Mario stayed real, along with the two guards, and the knife in one of the guard's hands.

Suddenly Iacob flashed close to Charles. Acting on instinct, Charles grabbed Iacob's hand and hauled him onto the carpet, and so he was spared the sight of the knife plunging into Mario's chest. All he saw was the flash of light that illuminated Iacob's face so brightly that Charles thought the Greenland youth was going the same way as his father. But then the light faded and Iacob was still there, staring over his shoulder with an expression of dumbfounded horror. Charles turned, and saw only the two guards—the two guards and the knife and a rapidly dissipating glow he knew had been his brother until a moment ago. Then the light was gone, and the two guards spun away, flung to the outer edges of the vortex, their mouths open in soundless cries of fear.

The jetty was expanding now, in diameter, in length, in speed. The bottom spiraled down into an inky blackness while the top opened up into electric white. Already the guards had disappeared, but the radio was more or less directly across the void from the carpet. Charles looked at the wooden box that contained his sister, then turned to Iacob, fixing the traitor with a stern eye.

"Hold on."

"To what?"

Charles didn't answer. At that particular moment he didn't really care if Iacob fell off the carpet or not, since by his reckoning it was Iacob's theft of the mirror books that had created this situation. He slammed the right arrow and the star at the same time. The arrows turned the carpet sharply, the star boosted its speed. The rug shot over the center of the spiral toward the radio; Iacob tumbled backward but managed to stay on the carpet.

Before they'd gone even a few feet, however, something

went wrong. The carpet began spinning wildly. It was an odd sensation, because there was no centrifugal force accompanying it: neither Charles nor Iacob were thrown toward the edge of the carpet as they should have been. The carpet began to sink rapidly. Again, there was no sensation. Charles didn't feel it in his stomach as he did when he fell backward on the school trampoline—but he did have a sinking feeling in his heart as he and Iacob fell down and down and down the huge whirling spiral, while the radio, with Susan inside it, shot up and up and up into the celestial emptiness.

Still, Charles managed to keep his head. The carpet was spinning clockwise, so he pressed hard on the left arrows. Slowly the revolutions decreased, and when they'd stopped spinning Charles pressed the forward arrows and inched them toward the wall of the vortex. Once in the outer channel, the carpet seemed to sink into a groove, spinning in a spiral that was so slow and wide you had to look at the far-flung walls of the vortex itself to realize you were moving in a circle.

"Charles?"

Charles looked at the boy at the other end of the carpet. He tried to think of something to say but nothing came.

"I'm sorry, Charles."

The boy held the mirror book he'd taken from his father. The cover was turned out, and Charles could see the golden seal, a blobby triangle with seven scored lines on it, floating amidst the deep red leather of the cover. Charles assumed that was the book the Wanderer had directed him to take from under Murray's head, until he looked down at the book in his hands and saw that it too was red, and titleless, its cover marked only by the seven-lined seal. The two books were indistinguishable now.

"I thought if I gave my father the books," Iacob continued, "he would return the box that controls your ship, and of course Susan as well."

Charles stared at the mirror book a moment longer. He'd been to bookstores a million times, had seen multiple copies of the same book. But these volumes were identical—were, indeed, mirrors of each other.

"Some plan," Charles said, finally tearing his eyes away from the amulet on Iacob's book. "We lost Susan *and* the radio, and Karl Olafson got to open the time jetty. Everything worked out *perfect*."

"It would appear that my father also lost something, Charles. His life."

Charles fell silent, chagrined. Then: "I've never seen anyone turn into light before."

Iacob managed a small, mirthless laugh. "It is not so common on Greenland either."

"Is that what happened to Mar—to my brother?"

Iacob paused a moment, then nodded.

"Maybe they didn't die," Charles said quickly. "Maybe they were just . . . transformed."

Iacob shrugged. "Maybe your brother was. I don't think your brother is made from quite the same stuff as you or me, or my father."

"That's probably true," Charles admitted. "Well, um, I'm sorry too. About your father. You tried your best, I guess."

Charles looked into the whirling vortex now. It seemed to have thinned, and through it he could see a galaxy of stars— above and below and all around the carpet. Measured against their limitless expanse, the spiral, which had seemed so large a moment ago, now seemed like a fishing line dropped into the ocean.

Iacob cleared his throat. "Should we look in the books?"

"No!" Charles said quickly. Then, more calmly: "I think opening them would be dangerous."

"Why? What do they do? What are they for?" Iacob dropped his eyes. "I have to tell you that I . . . I don't read. No one on Greenland can read anymore. Not even Father Poulsen, the priest."

Charles smiled. "It's not the words. I don't even know if there *are* words in them. One of them used to have pictures, but might have changed now that the amulet is on it. Anyway, the Wanderer said we should only open them at the end of the jetty."

Iacob peered down into the seemingly infinite spiral. "So there *will* be an end?"

Charles shrugged. "I hope so."

Iacob stood up and walked gingerly across the carpet, as if the view might be different from the other side.

"Careful," Charles said, when Iacob's foot landed an inch or two from a symbol of some four-legged animal, possibly a dog or a wolf. Charles had no idea what pressing it would do.

"Thank you, Charles. But I do not think I will fall off."

Charles laughed. "No, I didn't mean that. I don't want you to step on one of the controls."

"Controls?" Iacob looked down at his feet in confusion. Charles looked at Iacob's feet too: boy, were they *dirty*.

He pointed at the thin-stemmed tree woven down the center of the carpet. "See all these symbols at the ends of the branches? They control the way the carpet flies. The arrows turn it left and right, the sun makes it go up, the moon makes it go down."

"Ah," Iacob said. He seemed to comprehend the design woven into the carpet's fabric for the first time, the leaves at the branches' ends with the symbols embedded in each one. "And this?" He pointed his blackened toe at the symbol below the wolf/dog. It looked a bit like an Easter egg.

"Careful!" Charles said again. "I dunno what all of them do. It could transport us inside a volcano or something."

"A mountain of fire?" Iacob said, and Charles realized that must be how the translation charm had rendered "volcano" in Iacob's language. "There are strange things in your world."

"There are volcanoes in your world too. You just never saw one."

"I don't mean mountains of fire. I mean carpets that fly, and that can harm you if you use them incorrectly. Do all the amazing things in your world come with so many hidden dangers?"

Charles was about to say "Of course not," then suddenly heard his mother and father's voices in his head, warning him from touching the stove while it was hot, shelving certain medicines in high cabinets, installing filter programs on his Internet connection to keep him off certain websites—and of course sending him to live with Uncle Farley last September.

"I, um, I guess that's what happens when you invent complicated things. You have to be careful. I mean, cars—"

A skeptical frown creased Iacob's face. "Speeding four-wheeled carts with no visible means of propulsion?"

Charles returned Iacob's frown. The translation charm was one of those things that worked perfectly and invisibly—except when it didn't, in which case it didn't really work at all.

"Okay, um, ships. Ships help you travel great distances. But sometimes they sink and people drown. It's just a risk that comes with them. Anything can have negative as well as positive effects. I mean, even food. If you eat too much you get fat."

"No one I know has 'eaten too much,'" Iacob said in a slightly mocking tone, "for many hundreds of years." Iacob paused, then went on thoughtfully. "When the ship from Norway came during my father's youth, people marveled at its size

and speed and strength. There was much talk about the supe-
riority of Ropian life over our own, and over the Qaanaaq. But
the sailors took all our stored furs and ivory and gave us only a
Bible and a few iron tools in exchange, and that winter three
people froze to death just walking to church, because there
was not enough fur to make winter garments for them. But
when spring came we were able to dig their graves just fine,
with the shiny new shovel."

Charles didn't understand the point of Iacob's story, and he
said so. Iacob carefully stepped around the symbols on the rug
and came to sit beside Charles.

"The sailors from Ropia told us that their vessel was nothing compared with the ships being built by other countries. I
think the people they singled out were the Spanitch? They
spoke of marvels created in Italia and Francia—churches bigger than our village, and small sticks that eject a lump of iron so
quickly it can pierce a man's heart. I think even you would be
amazed by such marvels. But it seemed to me that these mira-
cles did not work for their inventors as much as their inventors
worked for them. In the same way years of my village's stored
furs were traded for a few measly tools that gave them food but
not warmth, these people had to roam the world in search of
treasures they could take back to Ropia to trade for different
kinds of treasures. All in all, it did not seem to me that they
lived a life any better than the Qaanaaq. Only a life with more
things in it, and more dangers, and more work."

Before Charles could come up with a response, Iacob exclaimed, "Charles—look!"

Charles peered in the direction of Iacob's downward-pointing finger.

"Is that a . . . a building?" The Greenland boy's voice was filled with awe.

Maybe it was the funny angle, but Charles didn't recognize it at first. They were above it, after all, and all the pictures Charles had seen naturally showed it from the ground, even the ones in the mirror book. But finally he realized what the enormous edifice below them was.

"It—it's the Tower of Babel!"

The sentence was both the most plain and the most strange thing Charles had ever heard himself say. The Tower of Babel! The most famous building in history—in religion, even. And it was there, before his eyes!

The most famous building in the world. But not, apparently, to Iacob.

"I don't understand. You know this building? Are we in your time?"

"N-no," Charles said, daunted at the very thought. "It's, like, *way* before that. It was built in biblical times."

"Then are *we* in the Bible?"

For an illiterate kid, Iacob could sure ask tough questions. Charles, who had not been raised religiously, found that even thinking about Iacob's idea made him nervous.

The two boys stared at the building for a long time. From this angle, you could see the terraces at the top of each level, as well as the wide flat top and the small temple erected there. An incredibly steep staircase ran up one side. There were more steps than Charles could count, but then a number flashed in his mind: 999.

He glanced at the book in his hand. He knew it had put the number in his head. But then his eyes were caught by the lines on the amulet. Seven of them. He looked back to the building and counted the terraces, and wasn't surprised when the number was also seven. He realized that the rune was the tower, only turned upside down.

Charles looked up at Iacob. "The Tower of Babel was built by people who wanted to reach heaven."

Iacob stared down at the awe-inspiring building, which seemed more like a shape that had been carved out of a mountain than a structure erected on a flat plain. Even though they were above it, the tower still seemed taller than one could imagine. Living in New York City, Charles knew he'd seen much taller buildings, but this structure had a massive base as well. At the bottom, it appeared to be even wider than it was high. And, as well, there was nothing around to diminish the perspective. All the other buildings were just one or two stories tall, barely visible in the shadow of the enormous ziggurat.

Charles blinked. He suddenly realized he was looking at a city of the ancient world. The Tower of Babel. So this must be . . . Babel, right? Babylon? The sight made Charles so nervous that he resorted to an old habit: he pushed his glasses up his nose. But when he did so he felt the bent nosepiece for the first time in a couple of days. He took them off and cleaned them, remembering his ingenuity in building the fire in the forest. He knew he was going to need that ingenuity now, and a little bit of luck too, and maybe some magical assistance. He, Charles Oakenfeld, was looking at the fabled city of Babylon.

Suddenly Charles remembered the vision of the tower the mirror book had shown on that far-off day in the tree above Drift House, and he understood what was going on. He wasn't just looking at the tower. He was going to go inside it. He was going to go *under* it, and close the jetty.

"Charles?" Iacob said in a quiet voice, as if afraid to interrupt his thoughts. "We're about to land."

It was true. After an eternity that had lasted only a few minutes (or a year, or more accurately, two thousand), the time jetty appeared to fade away into nothingness just above the uppermost level of the tower. As the carpet spiraled gently out of the jetty, Charles tapped on both sets of arrows at the same time, bringing them to a stop a few feet above the terra-cotta tiles that lined the floor of the terrace. Half-built walls made of large, squat, somewhat crumbly looking bricks rose up on all four sides, shielding them from the view of anyone who might be looking up—assuming they could even see that high.

"They are making it still higher?" Iacob said. "I wonder, when will it be tall enough?"

"According to the Bible," Charles said, "the tower was never finished. The Babylonians kept building it higher and higher, until finally God destroyed it."

"We'd better hurry then."

It took Charles a moment to realize Iacob was joking, and when he did he laughed—nervously, but he laughed. What else was there to do?

Now, tentatively, the two boys stepped off the carpet, as if their feet might go right through the floor. But the tiles were firm and smooth beneath the moccasins the Wendat had given Charles, and he padded across them to one of the half-built walls. The crumbly bricks were basically large rectangles of dried mud, and a good-sized stack of broken ones suggested they weren't the most durable things in the world. It was hard to imagine that such an enormous structure was basically just dirt, cut out of the ground and stacked up on top of itself.

Charles climbed atop the unfinished wall. The city below was small and dark. In the distance, he could see lights twinkling on a low wall that seemed to ring the city. No lights twinkled from windows though. Only the occasional flicker here or there defined a public space, or perhaps a person carrying a torch or lantern. Did they have lanterns this long ago? Charles didn't think so, but the lights were too faint and far away for him to see.

When Charles turned back to Iacob, he saw that the Greenland boy hadn't moved from the center of the terrace. There was a small, frightened look on his face.

"We do not belong here," he said in an awed voice. "It is not right."

Something about Iacob's words made Charles look at the mirror books, which were still on the carpet. A thin, golden light glowed from the amulets on their covers. The light was simultaneously ominous and reassuring, though Charles couldn't have said why it produced either sensation.

He turned back to Iacob. "We might not belong here," he said, "but I don't think we ended up here by accident either."

Iacob turned, looked at the glowing mirror books for a long moment, then turned back and pointed across the terrace to Charles's left. Four stone pillars stood there, supporting a flat, thatched roof. Beneath this shelter a square hole had been cut into the floor, and Charles could just glimpse the top of a staircase descending into darkness.

Pitch darkness.

"You said we had to open the books at the end of the temporal jetty." Iacob pointed at the opening. "Is that the end?"

Charles knew that the answer to Iacob's question was yes, and he knew that Iacob knew it too. You didn't have to open the mirror books, didn't even have to hold them in your hands, to feel what they wanted now. Their desire for the dark hole was as palpable as smoke. And so, shrugging silently, he crossed the terrace and climbed back on the carpet, and after a moment Iacob joined him. The two boys placed the mirror books at the front of the carpet, standing them up like headlights so that the pair of glowing amulets could illuminate their path. When Charles touched his book, he felt a new sensation. It was more than the little tingling charge he'd felt when he'd first handled the mirror book. It seemed to be *in* him, as if the mirror book's hunger were being reproduced in his own body. He felt its yearning for a dark place far below the tower—dark not simply because it was buried under hundreds of thousands of thick mud bricks, but because it was . . . dark. Cold. Inhuman.

Charles glanced up at Iacob. It was clear the Greenland boy was feeling the same sorts of things from his book. Iacob looked up at the faint, tattered spiral of the jetty above them. When he looked back at Charles, his eyes were filled with grim determination, and Charles knew he was thinking of his father, and how opening the jetty had killed him.

"We will close it, yes?"

Charles nodded. "That's what we're here for."

"Then what are we waiting for?" And, crossing his arms, Iacob sat down on the carpet and stared fixedly ahead.

Charles studied Iacob's profile. His mouth was set in a frown of grim determination, and Charles was glad the Greenland boy was working with him, not against him—he looked capable of anything.

Charles turned forward now. The two thin beams of light shot out from the mirror books at the front of the carpet, and now Charles thought they looked less like headlights than like a pair of tow ropes, as if the books were pulling the carpet to its destination.

Charles tapped the star. Slowly, silently, the two boys eased into the darkness.

TWENTY-ONE

Food for Thought

Susan.

The word came from everywhere and nowhere. Through her ears, but through her mouth too, and her nostrils, and her eyelids. Through her skin. The experience was so disorienting that she didn't even think to ask herself how skin could hear.

"Susan, wake up."

Susan emerged from . . . sleep. It wasn't quite the right word, but her head ached too much for her to think of a better one. She opened her eyes. A beak as big as the entrance to a cave opened and closed. Words came from the beak.

"Are you awake?"

Susan blinked. Now a bird's head came into focus. It was

the size of a bowling ball—red like a stoplight, red like a ripe apple—and it filled up the entirety of her vision. She blinked again. Slower this time, letting her eyes stay closed for a long time. When she opened them again the bird's head had shrunk until it was smaller than her fist, the beak as tiny as an uncooked pasta shell.

"M-Marie-Antoinette?"

Now Marie-Antoinette blinked and fluffed herself slightly.

"Thank goodness. I didn't know if you'd be able to wake up once we left the temporal universe."

Susan used the fingers of her right hand to check for the fingers of her left. She found her feet then, her limbs, her stomach, finally pressing—tenderly, tenderly—on the sore place at the back of her head. This last, more than anything else, brought her fully back to herself, and she took stock of her surroundings. She was in a clean, bare, wooden room about ten feet wide and fifteen feet long, whose high ceiling stretched to a cathedral point at least thirty or forty feet overhead. A large window stretched the length of one of the long walls, but it had been covered with some kind of delicate lattice and filtered the clean white light to a soft dun. The shape of this room was familiar, as though it were a church she'd been in before, but she couldn't quite place it. She turned back to the parrot.

"Are we on the Sea of Time?"

"Over it, actually."

"Over it?" Susan suddenly noticed the room was shaking ever so slightly. Bouncing really, like a boat on the water—or an airplane in the sky. She eased herself to her feet and walked to the window. There was no glass, she saw, just the lattice, and she hooked her fingers through the diamond-shaped openings and peered out.

What she saw took her breath away: an enormous icy blue vortex, as big around as . . . as . . . Susan couldn't even begin to say how big around it was, and Susan had been in the Great Drain of the Sea of Time. She could see that the vortex was spinning ferociously, and yet she and Marie-Antoinette seemed to ride it in their floating room as smoothly as the aforementioned boat or airplane.

"Are we, I mean, in the—"

Marie-Antoinette shook her head. "The drain? No. I am not sure what this is, but it is not the Great Drain."

Susan nodded and turned from the lattice, rubbing more liberally at the sore spot on the back of her head. (Well, spots, really, since there were two distinct bumps. Knocked out twice in one day, she told herself. Way to go!) She looked down at the parrot.

"What happened to the radio?"

Marie-Antoinette did one of those uncanny things Susan had occasionally seen on the parrots of Drift House: she appeared to smile.

"Susan," she said in a light tone. "We're *in* the radio."

Susan gasped. She realized immediately that this was true. The room's shape was exactly that of the tombstone radio. "But . . . it's *grown*."

"Correction. It is growing."

And Susan realized this was true too: the room did seem palpably larger than it had when she'd first opened her eyes.

"I don't suppose you have any idea how this happened?"

"None at all," the parrot said. "I'm afraid chronology doesn't hold that much interest for me."

"I think you mean temperology."

The parrot shrugged. "Temperology, chronology. It's all Greek to me."

Susan frowned. Since there didn't seem to be anything else to do, and since Marie-Antoinette was finally feeling talkative, she figured it was time to get her story. "So how did you end up with the Time Pirates anyway?"

The parrot stared up at her with a cocked head. "Can't you guess?"

Susan could only return the bird's stare in confusion, and then all at once understanding filled her slightly sore cranium. "Are you? I mean, were you destined for the Island of the Past?"

"*Ara tricolor*," Marie-Antoinette said in a flat voice. "The Cuban macaw. The last of my kind disappeared just as President Wilson"—Marie-Antoinette snickered a little, but not unkindly—"was being born."

"So they rescued you too!"

"Rescued? Kidnapped is more like it."

"You mean you didn't want to go to the Island of the Past?"

Marie-Antoinette shuddered. "I can imagine very few creatures who would. A solitary species, like the North American ground sloth or one of those moles that disappeared without anyone noticing, because no one had ever really seen them in the first place. But macaws are very social beings. An eternity spent on a vast treeless plain? Living in a cave? With nothing except dull-witted dinosaurs and dodos and that dreary old sailor to talk to? No thank you."

Her point made, Marie-Antoinette suddenly flew to the grille and began climbing up it, using her beak along with her claws to make her way up. She must have felt Susan staring at her, because she turned and glanced quizzically at her human companion.

"Yes?"

Susan wasn't sure how to say what she wanted to say. "I can see how being the last of your kind might be a bit, um, lonely. But, I mean, what do you do about . . . ?"

Marie-Antoinette sighed impatiently, then stuck her head through a gap in the lattice. Her voice came faintly from the other side. "About?"

"About . . . you. About all the other extinct species. Do you just forget them?"

The macaw pulled her head back in and looked at Susan severely. "It is one of the peculiarities of your species that it feels it must pass judgment on everything, regardless of the relevance to their own existence. But there is a natural order to things that transcends human concerns. No matter how highly you value yourself, humanity is not the goal of creation, nor its guardian."

Marie-Antoinette's words were certainly food for thought, and Susan was contemplating how to respond when the macaw put her head back through the lattice, and then the hinges of her wings, and then, as suddenly as a popping balloon, the bird slipped through the hole and disappeared.

"Marie-Antoinette!" Susan ran to the lattice. "Get back in here this instant!"

In answer, the macaw only said, "We've come out over the Island of the Past."

"What? How?"

"Well, that's another question entirely, isn't it? One you should probably ask your precious Pierre Marin."

"Of course! I'll find him when we land. I mean, if we land. I mean, um, how do you think we land this thing?"

Susan wasn't sure, but she thought she heard the macaw chuckle. "I don't think you have to worry about that part. You might want to brace yourself though."

"Brace my—*aieeee*!"

For suddenly the radio had started to fall. The descent was so rapid that Susan's feet left the floor, and she found herself twisting about in the cavernous empty space.

"Marie-Antoinette! Help me! Help me!"

"Just relax, Susan," the macaw called, her voice half consoling, half impatient. "Just relax. I'll meet you on the ground."

"Marie-Antoinette, no! Don't go! Help me!"

But it was too late: the blur of red on the other side of the lattice had disappeared. Susan was all alone, and falling.

She hung in the empty space, racking her brain for an idea of what to do next. But there was nothing. She was helpless. She thought of her family. She tried to send her thoughts out like a beacon of love, but it was hard to concentrate on any one image—even her mother and father—with her legs twisting over her head. She was plummeting at an incredible rate.

Then, without preamble, the box exploded all around Susan. She felt the strangest sensation, as if she were a washcloth being twisted out to dry. Down was up and up was down, inside was outside, outside inside. And then there was just . . . bouncing.

Susan opened her eyes, not sure when she'd squeezed them shut. The bright blue sky was overhead, the bright green grass beneath. Both stretched out to infinity. And she was . . .

Bouncing.

Not like a ball, or something rubber and buoyant. Instead she felt like the ground threw her up and away each time she got close. The motion was neither gentle nor smooth, like a trampoline. It felt more like she was being chewed like gum. She rolled and careened up and down and felt a little nautious. But, as far as she could tell, she was okay.

A flash of red caught her eye. A voice that sounded much more stable than any she could muster said, "Are you okay, Susan?"

"M-M-Marie-Antoinette?"

"It's me, Susan? Is anything broken?"

"I—I don't think so." It was hard to concentrate in such constant, stomach-churning motion. "Wh-what's happening?"

"The Island of the Past allows only one member of each species on its surface. You know that, Susan."

Susan didn't like the macaw's tone, which sounded condescending to her ears.

"I'm n-n-not exactly in a p-p-position to think c-c-clearly right now!"

The bird chuckled quietly. "I beg your pardon, Susan. But this *is* Pierre Marin's doing, after all—his injunction, and his presence, presumably, that is causing you to bounce. If it makes you feel better, I would guess that he is experiencing what you are at this very moment."

Susan imagined the pirate wig bouncing off Pierre Marin's nearly hairless skull, and managed a small laugh. "Well, what are we going to—*oof!*—to do now?"

A tone of baffled awe came into the macaw's voice. "I, um, I . . ."

Susan tried to twist in Marie-Antoinette's direction. It was hard: every time she turned her face, her air-flung body twisted in another direction.

"M-M-Marie-Antoinette?"

Susan could've sworn she heard a gulp. "I, um, I think the answer to your question is approaching, Susan."

Susan twisted about. At first all she saw were the low green hills of the Island of the Past. Then, hovering above the hills, she saw the vortex she had presumably just spun out of, stretching endlessly up into the sky. For a moment she thought the vortex was swooping down on her like a tornado, but then she bounced again and an enormous dark shape on the horizon flashed before her eyes. There was something familiar about it, but before she could focus she bounced again, was jerked in another direction. She twisted, caught another glimpse. It looked like a mountain at first—a mountain with legs. A walking mountain—walking toward her.

"Wh-what *is* that?" Susan stuttered.

"It—it would appear to be a . . . a horse. A giant wooden horse."

"A horse?" Susan flailed about, trying to catch another glimpse. "Do you mean the Trojan Horse? The one Charles saw?"

But the macaw didn't say anything. She seemed too stunned to speak.

All the while the huge dark shadow came closer, flickering in and out of Susan's vision as she was buffeted about. It seemed to move slowly, yet its enormous legs covered ground quickly. Susan could see the space between them, more like the sky beneath skyscrapers. All at once the huge beast, which was almost impossible to conceive of as a horse, was beside her. Over her. Enveloping her in its shadow. Its torso was like the bottom of an ocean liner floating above her.

"Marie-Antoinette!"

The macaw's voice came faintly from above; the bird had apparently taken wing. "I think it's okay, Susan." But the macaw sounded anything but calm.

Now a dark shape was descending toward her like a cloud. The horse's head, Susan saw as she tried desperately to bounce out of its way. A hole was opening in the cloud—its mouth, which was at least as big as that of Frejo the whale. Susan had been terrified when she first climbed into the whale's mouth, but it was nothing like this. The horse's head seemed to be as big as Frejo, and it was but the tiniest part of its enormous, enormous body.

A smell of dry wood filled her nostrils. The mouth was closing around her. The air turned soft and brown, like the air in the radio, and there was a tearing sound as the teeth—each as big as a tombstone—ripped through the ground beneath her. And then all at once the bouncing stopped. Susan landed on her bum, hard.

"Ouch!"

The word disappeared into the emptiness inside the horse's head, wafting farther and farther and farther into the great beast's innards. Susan had never heard something sound so empty in her life.

"Hello?"

Again, the swallowing silence. A silence so palpable that there seemed to be an intelligence behind it—a mind that could not, or would not, speak to her. Then Susan heard a faint voice.

"Susan?"

"Marie-Antoinette!" Susan called. She clambered to her feet. The inside of the horse, or at least its head, was a three-dimensional grid of interlocking beams, so that she was enclosed within a network of open-walled cubes, like the biggest jungle gym in the world. "I—I'm in the horse!"

"I know that," Marie-Antoinette called. "I couldn't get in in time."

From high above came two bright patches of light. The eyes, Susan thought.

"Go for the eyes!" she yelled. "I'll meet you there!"

She felt motion now, had to grab on to a beam to keep from falling. She realized the horse must be raising its head. There was a slight creaking of wooden joints, the nostril-tingling smell of ground sawdust. Susan's stomach fluttered as she felt herself rise up and up.

"Susan!" Marie-Antoinette's voice sounded even fainter. "It's moving! It's moving very quickly!"

As if in response, Susan felt a lurching. She knew what that lurching was: the horse had resumed its journey across the plain.

"Go for the eyes!" Susan called again. "Hurry!"

Scrambling, Susan ascended the lattice of beams inside the horse's enormous head, making for the glowing portals far above her. Even though the beams looked as though they were arranged in a symmetrical grid, they were actually quite crooked, each beam canting off at a strange angle, some going on for many feet, while others, unexpectedly, stopped after a few inches. The great beast lurched unevenly as it lumbered across the Island of the Past, making the climb that much more difficult, and several times during her climb toward the eyehole Susan looked up to find herself turned around and facing the wrong direction.

"Marie-Antoinette?" she called. But only a forlorn, deserted silence greeted her. As she looked around the gigantic cranial cavity, the phrase "food for thought" popped into her head again. Before, she had used the words to refer to Marie-Antoinette's speech about extinction, but now she found herself wondering if *she* had become some kind of food for the Trojan Horse. Well, if that were the case, he would find she didn't go down as smoothly as a drink of water. And, gritting her teeth, Susan turned herself around yet again, and kept climbing.

TWENTY-TWO

In the Tower

CHARLES'S FINGERS DANCED OVER THE moon and star, and silent as a gliding hawk, the carpet slipped into the Tower of Babel. It tilted as it descended, and Charles and Iacob had to lean back to keep from falling over. Oddly, though, the mirror books, standing up at the front of the carpet, remained perfectly still, as if they were held in position by a force greater than gravity. With their amulets facing forward and glowing brightly, the books seemed to have turned their backs on the boys, as if they no longer deigned to acknowledge them.

"We have to be careful," Charles said now. "The Wanderer told me the mirror books have desires of their own. We need to listen to them so we know where to go, but that's *all* we should listen to them for."

The carpet reached the bottom of the staircase and leveled off. A corridor stretched ahead, pitched slightly downhill. The light from the amulets pulsed ahead for a good twenty or thirty feet, but beyond that was only darkness.

Iacob peered into the dark corridor. "Ears are not like eyes, Charles. You can't simply close them. And this listening"— Iacob waved a hand over his book—"is a much more subtle kind of hearing."

"I'm just saying we should be careful, that's all. If one of us feels the other is going too far, we should . . . do something."

Iacob turned to Charles and stared at him strangely after he said these words. Glancing down, Charles saw that his hand was on the hilt of the knife Handa had given him when he'd left the Wendat. He snatched it away.

Iacob waited to speak till Charles's eyes met his. "I understand," he said. "We should go."

Charles tapped the stars again, nudging the carpet forward. As they inched down the corridor, Charles was reminded of the long slow beginning of a fun house ride, before the first ghoul jumps out from a corner and makes you scream. He looked around for the edge of a door from which someone might surprise them, but the corridor seemed devoid of any marking. He let his fingers trail over the wall closest to him. It wasn't covered by the shiny tiles that adorned the exterior of the tower, but beneath a thin layer of surface grit the mud bricks were surprisingly hard.

They came to the first corner. Charles eased the carpet to a stop. He and Iacob both looked back at the barely discernible gray patch that marked the exit, then, without speaking, turned forward again. Charles tapped the right arrows and the carpet made a slight scraping noise around the sharp turn, and then they were in the next length of corridor.

Iacob turned to Charles. "Do you think every turn will be like that?" he whispered. "Offering only one direction?"

Charles glanced at the walls again, looking for some kind of sign, although he kind of doubted he'd find anything like the floor guide at a department store. The walls were as blank as ever, but something came to his mind.

"These . . . ziggurats," he said, hesitant to use the word, because he knew the mirror book had put it in his head, "are made of mud bricks, which aren't very strong. So you have to use, like, a ton of them to hold up the building, unlike the steel beams in a skyscraper." Charles stopped when he remembered that Iacob would have no idea what a skyscraper was—although he could tell from the expression on the Greenlander's face that the translation charm had put a rather interesting picture in his head. "Anyway, what I'm saying is, this building is basically a mountain into which a few tunnels have been dug. So chances are there's only one way down. All we have to do is follow it."

"Like a mine!" Iacob said.

"You have mines in Greenland?"

"No. But in my favorite story, Prince Reinulfson must descend into the mines of Karnaka to defeat the troll army and rescue the golden sword."

"I don't know that story," Charles said, somewhat distractedly, because they were coming to another corner.

"Oh, it's a good one!" Iacob said, with almost too much excitement. "Prince Reinulfson's mother, Queen Katalina, has sent her son to live with a shepherd in the mountains because a witch came to her castle disguised as a milkmaid and told her that her husband, Prince Reinulfson's father—King Reinulf— was going to kill and eat their child to make sure he never tried to usurp his throne."

"Yeah, sure," Charles said, piloting the carpet around the corner, which was tighter than the last one. "Maybe you should tell me some other—"

Charles broke off when he caught a glimpse of Iacob's face. He realized his companion wasn't telling the story just to be amusing, but to distract himself from the shadowy depths. The dry desert air was gone now, replaced by a mildewy basement smell, and the mirror books practically hummed with their eagerness to reach their destination. The lights emitted by the books had sharpened, cutting the air like two flashlight beams, and Iacob stared at the golden lines with a half-hypnotized expression on his face.

"Er, you should tell me some other details," Charles said now. "I mean, go on with your story."

Iacob nodded convulsively.

"Right. So, um, Queen Katalina didn't believe the witch at first. But when her first son was born the king took it away when it was seven days old, and ate it. This happened with five more sons, until the queen became with child for the seventh time, and on this occasion she made arrangements to spirit her son away as soon as it was born. She gave him to a trusted maid who took him to her father's cottage deep in the countryside, and told her husband that the baby had died.

"Many years passed. Prince Reinulfson came to young manhood, at which point the shepherd told him the secret of his identity. The prince wanted to go immediately to the castle to kill his father and rescue his mother, but by then the queen had borne six daughters, all of whom the king had eaten, and he had grown too powerful for a mere mortal to confront. The shepherd told the prince that he would need a magic weapon. He said that the trolls of Karnaka lived deep underground in their mines, where they guarded an enormous treasure, the most important item of which was a golden sword that was said to cut through falseness, evil, greed, and cowardice. Prince Reinulfson descended to the very bottom of the cave. The trolls attacked him with their sword, but it was powerless against him because he was pure of heart. He defeated the trolls, and then he used the sword to cut a path straight to

his father's castle. There he found his father in the act of dropping his mother's seventh daughter down his throat. With one
stroke, he sliced the evil king in half and liberated the six
brothers and seven sisters imprisoned in his stomach. Each
brother married a sister, and together they founded a new
kingdom of peace and prosperity for all."

Iacob had spoken slowly and forcefully, as if to draw out his
story, and part of Charles had wondered if he wasn't actually
making it up as he went along. But he was too busy trying to
maneuver the carpet through the increasingly cramped corridor to say anything, and besides, Iacob's voice had been sooth-
ing, and had allowed Charles to free his mind and concentrate
on their path. But now they had come to another corner, and
this time it was clear the carpet wasn't going to make the turn:
the path ahead was too narrow.

Charles turned to Iacob. "We're gonna have to walk the rest
of the way."

The two boys climbed off the carpet. Hesitantly, each took
a book. Charles half expected the book to resist his touch but,
though it vibrated wildly, it seemed, if anything, eager to
come. He was careful to keep the bright beam focused away
from his body, and Iacob's as well. Charles handled his book
gingerly, and he could see Iacob did also. The vibration it gave
off set his fingers tingling, and strange, half-comprehended
images flooded his head. For a minute it seemed to him that
Murray appeared before his eyes—five-year-old Murray, his

face still stippled with chicken pox—but just as suddenly he disappeared. Charles had to fight the urge to stroke the glowing lines of the amulet on his book, as if, like Aladdin's lamp, it would grant him three wishes.

Instead, pressing on the moon, Charles lowered the carpet to the floor. He thought of rolling it up, but since there was no place to hide it in these bare corridors, he figured it was least likely to be seen flat on the ground. Iacob, meanwhile, stared at the ceiling as if contemplating the enormity of weight atop them. A shudder shook his thin frame, and he clutched the book to his chest, as if for warmth, or protection.

"I wish that there was a golden sword at the end of our journey," he said now, "so that with one stroke we could cut a doorway back to our home."

"So do I," Charles said. "So do I."

The two boys set off down the hallway in silence. But after they'd gone a few steps, Charles said, "Can I ask you a question?"

"Of course." Iacob seemed relieved to hear a voice break the oppressive silence.

"Did all those princes really marry their sisters? In your story?"

Iacob blinked in surprise, then laughed slightly. "Of course. It is not uncommon where I come from. Sometimes a brother and sister are the only two people of marrying age—"

"Whoa, that's enough," Charles said, holding up a hand.

"There are some things I don't need to know just yet." And, under his breath, he added, "*Gross.*"

They journeyed on. Soon the corridor became so narrow the two boys had to walk single file. Charles took the lead, even though he felt more exposed to danger. The Wanderer of Days had assigned him this task, after all. Although he was glad Iacob was with him, he knew his companion couldn't really help him. The Greenland boy's face was determined but also confused, and Charles knew that for whatever reason, Iacob wasn't as capable as Charles was of sorting out the confusing thoughts and feelings the mirror book put in your head. And so, clutching the book securely to his chest with one hand and placing the other on the hilt of his knife, Charles led the two boys forward.

The beam from the mirror book stretched ahead in the darkness. The walls were positively damp now, and Charles could feel their slick wetness against one shoulder or the other if he wobbled just a little bit. Step after step the boys marched onwards. Without anything to measure their progress it felt as though they'd gone hundreds, thousands of feet underground. Charles knew that was just imagination running away with him, but still. Where would this corridor end?

Suddenly Charles saw a glint of light ahead. A shapeless golden glow that pulsed slightly, like a heartbeat. Charles didn't know if another person was ahead of them, and he wasn't sure if he should keep going, or stop, or turn and run.

He wanted to ask Iacob what he thought, but if it *was* another person up there he didn't want to warn him of their approach. And so he marched on, staring fixedly at the pulsating light. It seemed to contract as Charles got closer, and the pulsing switched to a steady, slight bounce. Charles couldn't stop staring at it, couldn't stop himself from placing one foot in front of the other and marching toward it, even though he was increasingly certain that the light was bouncing because it was being held by another person far ahead of him, rising up and down in tempo with that person's footsteps as he or she walked toward Charles. Charles knew it was reckless to simply walk up to this person, but he couldn't stop himself. The book in his arms (in both arms, because he'd let go of his knife to hold on to it more securely) was practically humming with its desire to go forward. It seemed to pull him forward like a dog straining at its leash. *Faster, faster*, it said to Charles. *Hurry.*

And now a new shape took form around the circle of light ahead of Charles. A paler glow, also circular, of reflected light. For some reason Charles knew it was a face.

A boy's face.

Featureless as a full moon on a cloudy night, the face stared at Charles as he approached, shining its light at Charles as he shone his light before him. They walked at the same tempo, with the same slight rise and fall. Their heads were at the same height. And suddenly Charles understood.

It was himself he was seeing up ahead, walking toward him.

Charles clutched the mirror book to his chest, even though he really wanted to throw it away. Was this the book's doing? Was this how it worked? Had it made a second Charles who would duplicate every action that he, Charles—the original Charles—made? Would they blur together eventually, until neither knew which was the original, and perhaps fight to the death in order to claim primacy?

Charles could make out the dark circles of glasses ringing its eyes now (slightly lopsided, just like his), the thin mouth set in a firm, determined line. Maybe he shouldn't think of this second Charles as an adversary, but as a helper, a partner even, something—someone—who would help Charles achieve all his goals twice as fast. Someone who could share the burden of Charles's solitary nature. His steps quickened a little without his realization. He was still afraid of meeting his double, but eager too.

The boy's features shimmered into focus: Charles saw tousled hair, disheveled clothing, the moccasins on his feet and the knife at his waist and his crossed arms. Only this boy's arms held nothing. Just empty air and a glowing disk of light where his heart should be. His eyes widened as Charles approached. When Charles stretched out a hand in greeting, he did too. Their fingertips came toward each other.

Charles's hands touched something cold and flat and hard. For a moment, with the boy's hand pressed against his, Charles could believe that a sheet of glass separated him from his twin, but then, when he pulled back his hand and the boy pulled his back at the same time, when he scratched his head and the boy scratched his, and he stopped scratching and waved slightly and the boy stopped and waved back, and then when he gave up and picked his nose and the boy eagerly dug his finger in his own nostril, Charles had to admit that he was looking at himself in a mirror. A wave of disappointment flooded through him. Even though the boy had never existed, Charles still felt as if he'd lost something. He was still alone. And then:

"Charles?"

Charles nearly jumped out of his skin.

"The mirror does not show the books," Iacob continued. "That is strange, no?"

Charles turned back to his companion. In the faint light there wasn't much to separate the two boys: they were about the same height, both skinny, both a little messy, and Iacob's dirty blond hair seemed almost as dark as Charles's. And yet Charles, still feeling the loss of his twin, felt incomparably different and distant from Iacob. He realized again that the task he was doing could only be done by himself.

"Charles?"

Charles shook himself slightly. "I dunno what strange is anymore," he said. "We're underneath the Tower of Babel, being led by a pair of books that deliver messages without being opened. The fact that they don't show up in mirrors is just, well, one more weird thing."

Iacob stared at Charles quizzically for a moment. Then something seemed to catch his eye, and he aimed his light to his left, being careful to tilt the beam over Charles's head so it wouldn't touch his body.

"Charles, look."

Charles turned, and saw immediately what Iacob was referring to: the beams of light from their mirror books shot into a wide open space, so large that the light only nudged at the shadows on the far end. It was a huge room, perhaps a cave of some kind. They stepped inside, and Charles put his hand on the wall. It was smooth and slick, and when he turned the mirror book toward it he saw that it was covered in enameled tile. The light coming from the glowing book was so golden in hue that it was hard to make out the exact shade of the tile, but Charles thought it was blue, just like the ones that covered the exterior of the building.

He and Iacob glanced at each other, but didn't speak. The mirror books' yearning was awful now, a desire so great that it knotted Charles's stomach. It was like being sick and wanting to be better, but not wanting to take the right medicine to feel better. Part of Charles wanted to throw the book away and run, but another part—a part that didn't feel entirely like Charles— held on even tighter.

"It is close," Iacob said, and Charles nodded, even though Iacob was facing the other way. "Is it . . . in this room?"

Charles gripped the book in his hands, tried to focus on what it was saying.

"No," he said finally. "But it will be."

Iacob didn't ask what Charles meant, as if he knew his friend couldn't explain. Instead, by unspoken agreement, Charles turned left and Iacob turned right, and they walked into the huge room. Just a few paces to the left were three steps down, and Charles realized he had been standing on a raised dais of some kind. For some reason he immediately thought of the altar at the front of a church. Were they in some kind of subterranean temple?

Charles looked across the vast space at Iacob's shadowy form. The single room seemed to be nearly as big as Drift House. Occasionally Iacob would wink out of sight. Charles was confused for a moment, until he realized that columns holding up the ceiling were coming in between the two boys. He turned his light toward the center of the room, and could make out a double colonnade outlining a wide central aisle and a pair of bays on either side. Aside from the columns and the dais, there didn't seem to be anything else in the room—at least nothing that the lights revealed. But another sense told Charles that something was coming, and it would be here soon.

If, as Charles reasoned, this was some kind of temple, then the dais would be at the back of the room, meaning he and Iacob were now making their way toward the front. And as he progressed it seemed to him that the air grew fresher. One time he was even sure he felt a breath of breeze—hot and dry, like the desert air outside the tower. Maybe they weren't so far underground after all, if fresh air could get down here? Or maybe the Babylonians had ventilation systems Charles didn't know about. At any rate, Charles breathed in the clean air gratefully, letting it purge the mildewy residue of the damp corridors from his lungs.

Charles flashed his light around the room, looking for some sign that would tell him where to stand, where to open the books. The Wanderer had said he had to do it at the bottom of the jetty, and for all Charles knew a few inches could make the difference between success and failure. Up ahead, he saw another light as he had in the corridor, but he didn't let it fool him this time. He figured it was just the amulet's glow reflecting off the tiled wall, but when he turned the book to one side, the glow remained. Charles saw now that it was broad and diffuse, not at all like the reflection of the concentrated beam given out by his book, but rather like a light coming around a corner. And now it seemed to Charles that he heard—

"Footsteps!"

Iacob's hiss cut through the empty air like a knife. He and Charles rushed toward each other in the center of the room, their lights dancing crazily over the walls of the temple. To Charles they suddenly seemed like beacons, announcing their presence to the whole world.

The footsteps were regular, heavy, multiple, like marching soldiers. Charles trained his beam around the dark room one more time, but couldn't see anything besides the dark shadows of the columns and the unyieldingly flat walls, which offered no place to hide.

"We'll have to go out the way we came in," he whispered. "Put your book inside your shirt to cover the light."

The boys scooted toward the back of the room as quickly and quietly as they could. Charles stuffed his mirror book under the tail of his shirt, but the glow pierced the fabric easily, so gulping slightly, he turned the front cover toward his stomach. The amulet's touch against his skin was simultaneously cold and hot, almost unbearable on one level and yet like nothing at all on another. But Charles didn't let himself get caught up in the strange sensation. He had to get himself and Iacob out of the temple before it was—

Too late.

A second glow suddenly filled the room: a pair of torches seemed to appear from thin air, held aloft by a pair of figures that could have been statues or real humans. Somewhat in front of the two torches, so that their faces were in shadow, stood a second pair, one impossibly tall, the other much, much smaller. Charles felt the mirror book throb in response to this second figure. Beside him, Iacob let out a low moan, and Charles knew he was feeling the same, almost overpowering urge to run up to the dais with his book.

Summoning all his energy, Charles grabbed Iacob by the arm and whirled them in the other direction. By now a liquid orange glow filled the space at the front of the room, outlining a wide trapezoidal doorway. The glow was like the fire at the back of a dragon's throat; from the sound of the thudding footsteps echoing into the cavernous temple, Charles figured that dozens, perhaps hundreds of men must be marching their way. And, judging from the brightness of the glow, each one of them must be carrying a torch.

Charles looked at Iacob. The boy was nothing more than an outline. Not a trace of light came from beneath his shirt, and Charles guessed he must be pressing it tightly against him. For a moment Charles let himself hope that the books would go undiscovered, but at the same time he knew it was not the books' *light* that would give them away. The books' yearning for the dais at the head of the room was so palpable it was like a siren, and Charles couldn't believe that everyone in the room—in the whole of Babel—couldn't hear it.

The marchers began to enter the room now, silent save for their footsteps. They split into two ranks, marched the length of each wall. Charles saw now that there were unlit torches mounted there, and when the marchers had aligned themselves along each wall they turned in unison and used the torches they were carrying to light the ones affixed to the walls. There was a hypnotic sameness to their movements, and it was hard to tell if they were soldiers or congregants. A

short sword was scabbarded at each waist, but the men themselves were unarmored, wearing only pale tunics that left their
legs and one shoulder uncovered.

Charles and Iacob stared at the men, mesmerized. When
the torches on the side walls were lit, the marchers turned
and crossed to the columns and, still in unison, slotted the
torches they carried into metal holders mounted to each column. Then, stepping backward on their quiet, sandaled feet,
one step, two steps, three steps, four, they realigned themselves along the outer walls. They placed their right hands on
the hilts of their swords. They placed their left hands on their
chests.

And then they just stood there.

Not once did any of them so much as glance at Charles or
Iacob. Charles found himself hoping he and Iacob were somehow invisible, although he figured the soldiers were simply too
disciplined to regard two unarmed boys as a threat. Well,
Charles did have his knife. He reached for it, but didn't un-
sheathe it. Even as his fingers closed over the flint, he knew no
blade would protect him here.

He turned to Iacob. "Take your book out."

Iacob blinked in confusion. "What—"

"Do it," Charles said firmly. "*Now.*"

Charles reached into his shirt and came out with the mirror
book. Hesitant but obedient, Iacob followed suit. The books
seemed to turn to face each other of their own accord, and

their twinned amulets glowed so brightly it seemed as if a beam of light connected them. Charles felt the book in his arms yearning, straining toward the dais to his right. Again, he was reminded of a dog on its leash, who smells his master in the dark and strains to run to him. But he refused to look in that direction. Somehow he knew he couldn't give in to the book's urge.

Across from him, Iacob was not so strong. The Greenland boy was turning toward the head of the room as if in a daze.

"Iacob, no!" Charles said, louder than he'd intended. "We have to open them here!"

Iacob turned to him, a look of baffled fear on his face. He held the mirror book at arm's length in front of him. "I do not like this thing, Charles! I do not like what it makes me feel!"

"We have to open them," Charles said insistently, even though the book in his hands was begging to be taken up to the dais. "Right here. On three. One, two—"

"No!" a voice screamed from the front of the room. "Guards, stop them!"

"Three!"

Through sheer force of will, the two boys whipped open the covers of their books. Instinctively Charles squeezed his eyes shut, but there was no need.

Nothing happened.

Well, one thing happened: the awful yearning stopped. Charles felt as if he'd been underwater and suddenly shot into fresh air. He gulped in grateful, deep breaths, even as the book in his arms settled like a fussy baby that's finally fallen asleep.

Charles lifted one eyelid, saw Iacob staring at him quizzically. "Charles?"

A throat cleared at the head of the room. Charles turned, still dumbly holding the open book before him.

The room was hot now, and blazingly bright, and smelled of smoke. On the dais stood the two figures draped in white robes: a man wearing a high hat, holding a length of iron chain that led to a boy, bareheaded, his pale face so smudged with dirt that Charles honestly didn't recognize him at first. But who else could it have been?

"Hello, Charles," his brother said—his five-year-old brother, Murray, said, from a face that was still soft and round, not lean like Mario's, but whose voice had already acquired the latter boy's world-weary tone.

Murray managed a weak but mischievous smile. Pulling slightly on his iron leash, he said, "I bet you're wondering what I'm doing here, huh?"

TWENTY-THREE

Closing the Jetty (part 1)

AFTER SHE HAD BEEN CLIMBING for who knew how long, Susan finally accepted that she was never going to reach the eyehole. Something was conspiring to keep her away from it. Indeed, she was being detoured in the opposite direction, deeper into the horse's—well, its throat, she guessed. Its neck. She called out for Marie-Antoinette one more time, but the only sound that came back to her was the ratchetty sound of wood splintering. The noise came from throughout the horse's head, not just where her hands and feet were landing. Everywhere she looked, dried-up wood fell away to dust that somehow dissolved in the air, and in its place stood rich rounded tensile struts, brownish reddish in color, and warm to the touch, and pulsing.

"Why—you're alive!"

Susan's voice, floating into that vast space, sounded unfamiliar to her ears—grownup, knowledgeable. She wondered if she, too, were changing. She looked at the parts of her body she could see, her arms, her legs, felt her face and chest with her fingers. But the shell of her at least was the same. She looked up again.

"Can you hear me?"

When she had ridden in Frejo to the bottom of the Great Drain last year, she had been able to hear the deep sound of the whale's words even inside his body—a sibilant vibration that had seemed to be inside her even as she was inside the whale. But in the Trojan Horse there was just a . . . feeling. An affirmation that was like the telepathic equivalent of a smile seen through a thick sheet of glass.

"Is Charles okay? Uncle Farley? Iacob?"

Susan blushed at the third name, and even as she felt again the feeling of affirmation, she added, "And Mar—Murray," she corrected, using her little brother's real name.

And now came a feeling Susan could not put words to. Not bad, but not good either. Heavy, like the pressure of water on your eardrums when you have swum too far down and aren't quite sure you can make it back to the surface. But there was a certain clarity to this message, an awe-inspiring if not simply frightening realization that her youngest brother had become something that was somehow beyond her understanding. But what was she to do with such a feeling?

Before Susan could think of the right words with which to express this question, she felt its answer inside her:

Climb. Deeper. Inward.

And now Susan could see that the network of tubes that she was clambering on had coalesced to form a chute leading into the darkness of the horse's enormous torso. That darkness frightened Susan, and she balked at first. She didn't like doing things when the reason why was kept from her. But the horse, or whatever it was, insisted: her only task right now was to climb. As she clambered over the struts, it seemed to her that there was just the tiniest glow emitted by those tubes nearest her—not enough to allow her to see more than a few feet in any direction, but enough to allow her to place her hands and feet safely, as long as she didn't reach too fast or too far ahead.

"Really," she said, although she was pretty sure at this point she didn't have to speak aloud, or even in complete sentences. "You don't have to be so *spooky* about it."

Susan could've sworn she felt a wave of amusement course through her, and she chuckled gratefully. On she clambered, now definitely descending into the depths of the great animal, turning and going down the struts as she would a ladder, one rung after another, down, ever farther down, until she began to wonder if she'd missed a turn somewhere, and were actually descending one of the beast's legs. And just as she thought that, she reached bottom.

She stepped abruptly on the platform, which was soft and slightly springy beneath her feet, as though it were carpeted. In fact it was carpeted, but it was more than that.

It was Charles's carpet.

A shiver ran up and down Susan's spine. But just as quickly there was a reassuring feeling, and Susan knew Charles was okay.

She turned around, looked deep into the endless, dizzying network of tubes. Far in the distance, she could discern a wavering disc of light, as if a search beam were moving somewhere in the depths of the horse's body. Susan started to move toward it, and was almost immediately stopped by the distinct feeling that she was forgetting something.

"You want me to take the carpet?"

Susan wasn't sure what the mental equivalent of "duh" was, but that's what she felt.

She thought of riding on the carpet, but Charles had never volunteered the information about how it worked, and she had been too proud to ask. Instead she rolled the carpet into a tube and picked up one end experimentally, to see how heavy it was. To her surprise, the entire roll levitated off the ground. She had only to catch hold of a bit of a fringe and draw it along with her like a very tame dog.

She turned back toward the light, then stopped short. In the time it had taken her to roll up the carpet, the horse had changed dramatically. In place of the endless network of tubes, a long walled galley had appeared. It was narrow, no more than ten or fifteen feet wide, and a single aisle ran down the center between a set of crude wooden benches that lined either side. Susan had seen drawings of the rowing quarters of the ships the Greeks used in the Trojan War, and she was pretty sure that's what she was looking at, albeit greatly extended—the galley seemed to be hundreds of feet long. As she led the carpet down the aisle, she could almost hear the whine of oars in oarlocks and the groans of slaves leaning into the heavy work of pulling their boat through the waves. Indeed, she could almost feel the boat rocking beneath her feet, although she thought that might be the horse itself, lumbering who knew where across the Island of the Past.

Suddenly something flashed in the corner of her eye. Susan turned, but it was gone already. Gone, but not gone. Flickering shapes seemed to surround Susan, but every time she turned to look at them they melted away. It was as if a second space seemed to coexist with the rowing quarters. This space was also long and narrow, with a center aisle and seats on either side. No matter how hard she tried, Susan couldn't make out anything directly. This second space was brighter than the galley—much brighter. Clear cold light streamed in from windows that ran the length of the space.

That was it! It was an airplane!

And, just like that, the cabin shimmered into view. The wooden benches of the rowing galley were still visible beneath it, barely, and there was yet another layer on top of it as well. And this layer contained—people. Susan kept whipping her head around, kept seeing them, then having them wink out of sight. But in the fraction of an instant that she could see each face, she could make out expressions of what she at first thought was wonder, but then realized was actually fear. A terror so abject it seemed like a revelation. It seemed to Susan that the faces turned away from hers as she glimpsed them, as if *she* were what they feared. She wanted to turn from them too, but even when she closed her eyes and clutched Charles's flying carpet for security she could still see them, still feel their horror and helplessness. And then another feeling came on top of that one.

Be calm. You are safe here.

Susan opened her eyes reluctantly. She stared at the floor to avoid the flickering shapes on either side of her.

"I don't *feel* safe."

It seemed to Susan that the horse actually whispered her name.

Susan.

Susan sniffled slightly, near tears. "Sometimes," she said. "Sometimes it's not enough to *be* safe. There are things you don't want to *feel*. Things you don't want to know about."

She felt the oddest sensation then: pride. Satisfaction, as well.

She let herself look up then. However strangely it had come into being, the cabin seemed to be of normal size, and up ahead she could make out the back of a man's head sitting near the front of the plane. For a moment she let herself hope that it was Pierre Marin—Charles had said the Trojan Horse straddled his house, after all. But even without the negative feeling that came in response to this thought, Susan would have known it wasn't him. Drift House's founder was way too short to be seen over the back of an airplane seat.

Whoever the man was, he didn't wink out when her eyes lit on him, but remained where he was, a solid form, unwavering. All she could see was the back of his head, but she took great comfort in it for some reason. She could see now that his hair was grayer than Pierre Marin's, and instead of being pulled back in a ponytail was instead divided into two strands that hung on either side of his face. His being exuded a feeling of calmness and expectation. Waiting.

"Oh," Susan said aloud, because she suddenly realized he was waiting for her.

She hurried toward the front of the cabin, carpet in tow. She ignored the flickering faces on either side of her, ignored the fear in the air and in the pit of her stomach, and only slowed down when she got close to the man, whose bare left arm, pale brown, wrinkled, stuck out from what appeared to be a frayed leather vest.

Before she could think of what to say, the man turned and smiled at her. He seemed incomprehensibly old. His face was so lined it was like the shell of a walnut, his eyes were so pale they seemed to lack irises. Even the teeth he bared seemed to have been worn down to nubs by untold millennia of use. But the smile itself was warm and . . . and pleased almost, as if he had been waiting for Susan for a long time.

"I see you found Charles's carpet."

Susan was nothing if not honest. "I can't say I found it. I was sort of led to it."

"Many people get lost no matter how well they are led, Susan. You did well. Please," he added then, "have a seat."

Susan took the seat across the aisle, because it was closer to her, and because she didn't mind having a few feet of empty space between her and the man's wizened arm. For some reason she didn't think it would do to touch him. It would be sort of like touching a king, or a ghost. She sat, leaving the carpet hanging in the air between them.

Now that she looked at him more closely, she saw that he was wearing what appeared to be Native American dress, although it was hard to tell if he himself were Native American. He was just too old. He looked at her as well. For a long time, silently, with no expression on his face save for a vague, patient smile. She tried to guess what he was looking for, but couldn't. She was just Susan, after all. Aside from the carpet, there was nothing unusual about her, or on her, at least that she could see. But she got the sense the man wasn't looking for a talisman like the Amulet of Babel, but for a more hidden mark. Something inside her.

The man nodded, and Susan blushed. Had he been reading her mind? But all he said was,

"Do you know where you are, Susan?"

Susan glanced back down the aisle. The terrified faces glimmered in and out of vision, and she squinted to ward them off.

"Um, in a plane?"

The man's smile grew slightly wider. "You say it as if you are not sure. If I said the answer was no, would you be surprised?"

"Well, since I originally got inside a big wooden horse, no, I wouldn't be too surprised."

The old man threw back his head and laughed. "Such an open mind! It is so often the case that when people of your time are confronted by something beyond their experience, they refuse to believe in it. But you see no difference between a real plane and a plane that is a manifestation of your mind. Wonderful, wonderful!"

Susan waited for the man to say more, and when he didn't she elected not to ask. She didn't know much about him, but it seemed pretty clear he would have told her if he'd wanted her to know. And she herself was strangely uncurious. In fact, she was perfectly happy not knowing anything else about this plane, and she decided not to ask any more questions at all. For a girl who'd spent the past several years perfecting her cross-examination techniques, that was a deeply unnatural decision. But Susan figured the old man would say what he was going to say, and not even her most incisive questioning would change that.

The old man sat patiently while these thoughts flitted through her mind, and when she settled in her seat somewhat he nodded at her, as if she had passed another test. His mouth opened, a single word emerged:

"Time."

Susan felt the word wash over her like a wave—like the wave that had swept Drift House out of the temporal world. Which is to say, she felt as though she'd been torn from her foundation, but also that she'd been taken to her true element.

The old man nodded again. "Yes. Time, Susan. Time is like a string. It has a beginning and an end. Only one beginning, and only one end, and only one line leading between them. Like a skein of yarn, no matter how tangled the track of time grows, there is still only one line, and no deviation from it, ever."

Susan thought about this, and then nodded.

"The jetty that Karl Olafson unwittingly opened, and that

carried you to the Island of the Past, is not true time," the old man went on, "but a terrible desire carried in the hearts of men since the dawn of creation. The jetty is a manifestation of the eternal human desire to cheat time, to get to the end without going through the middle. As such, it bores directly for each end, circumventing all the loops and tangles and backtracking and knots of time's natural route, and so bringing things to their end far, far sooner than would otherwise happen."

The old man's words conjured an image in Susan's mind. She saw a maze filled with a million wrong turns and dead ends, only one path leading from the entrance to the exit. But instead of puzzling the way through, a mental bulldozer simply smashed through from one end straight to the other. That must be what the jetty did.

The old man was nodding.

"You understand, don't you? Where the jetty passes through time's true path, it obliterates it."

Susan returned the old man's nod. "Yes, but—" She broke off, for a new set of images was flashing in her head: the scenes she had seen on the drawing room wall, right before the temporal wave had struck.

"You mean the lost cities, don't you? Troy? Pompeii? Babylon? Roanoke? And . . . and Osterbygd?" Susan broke off, had to take a deep breath before she could continue. "But New York was there. At least—the towers were."

The old man nodded. "We are headed there now, Susan."

For a moment Susan's stomach seemed to shrivel up inside her. "It—it's the jetty, isn't it? Not this plane. The jetty destroyed all those cities, and now it's headed for New York. This plane doesn't really exist."

"In your world, Susan, this plane *is* the jetty. Just as it was the horse that tricked the Trojans, the volcano that destroyed Pompeii, the simple failure to adapt that ate away the Vikings of Osterbygd."

"We have to stop it," Susan said, jumping up as if she would run to the cockpit and tell the pilot to turn around. "We have to . . . to stop it."

"Susan." The old man's voice was calm. "You *are* stopping it."

Susan sank down into her chair. For some reason the old man's tone was not reassuring. "But am I stopping it in time?"

The old man looked at her wistfully. "If I were to answer your question temporally, I would say yes. Your parents, your city, will be safe. For now."

Susan repeated his words dully. "For now."

"The time jetty is not merely a force loosed by an ignorant meddler such as Karl Olafson, Susan. The great temporal manifestations and distortions have been in play for thousands of years, ever since your species first began to wonder about the future—which is to say, ever since they began to think. The rush to the end of time is not simply the desire of a few bad men, but rather an aspect of *all* human beings. At certain times it is a small part, but at other times it grows larger. Even the tiniest change, when multiplied by the billions of people who live in your time, can produce enormous fluctuations in the temporal flow. You must learn how to control this desire, or the era of humanity will pass in the twinkling of an eye, and your species, like the dodo and the dinosaurs and all those other extinct species, will end up nothing more than an exhibition on the Island of the Past."

Without any fanfare, the old man leaned over and opened a door in the side of the plane. Susan wasn't sure if the door had been there before, or if it were even real—wasn't there supposed to be a big suck of air when doors opened in flying planes? But all was as calm as before, save that now an expanse of clear blue sky lay before her.

The old man turned back to Susan and tapped the tube of carpet floating between them.

"If you just hold on, you should be able to ride it like a log in the water."

Susan thought she would have been afraid of the thought of flying out the side of a plane. But she was not. Perhaps she was too overwhelmed. Too numbed by sensory data to do more than take each new thing as it came.

"That's it?" she said. "That's all I have to do? Hold on?"

Though colorless, the old man's eyes still managed to twinkle with a bit of mischief. "I'm afraid the real adventure is Charles's this time around, Susan. All you have to do is hold on, with your hands, and with your heart." The old man smiled gently. "And when you see Charles, tell him the Wanderer said hello."

Susan nodded. She was going to see Charles. Charles had . . . met this man. This . . . Wanderer.

"I will."

She stood up and straddled the tube of the carpet. The air outside seemed eerily calm and unmoving. The blue sky beckoned. She tapped the carpet she sat astride.

"Um, giddyup?"

The Wanderer's eyes glowed. "Allow me."

He reached for a spot on the carpet behind Susan. She started to turn—she figured it was a good idea to know where the On button was—but before she could there was a whoosh of air. She fell forward breathlessly, not so much holding on to the carpet as clutching it for dear life with her arms and legs. There was a last lingering sense of amusement, and she knew this had been the Wanderer's—or the Trojan Horse's—parting joke.

The carpet was strong and solid beneath her, and despite the speed she could feel the smoothness of her descent. She wasn't simply falling, she was . . . sliding almost. In a moment she had caught her breath and even managed to sit up. She gripped a bit of fringe and looked down—and gasped.

Manhattan lay beneath her, just off to her right. Her city. Her home, in all its glory and might and multiplicity. Ten thousand square city blocks bristling like a porcupine's quills, surrounded on all sides by glistening water, from the low buildings in the north of the city, Harlem, Washington Heights, to the needle-pointed spires of downtown.

She gasped again. For there, at the southern tip of Manhattan, were two buildings that no longer existed in her time. They gleamed in the sun, identical, unwavering, *real*.

But even as she spotted the pair of towers, a dark cloud formed over them. A huge swirling mass, bigger than the whole island it seemed, blotting out the entirety of the sky, and yet centered directly over the towers. As she watched, a thin line threaded its way out of the center, a harmless string that swelled and swelled and swelled until it was a huge raging tornado ripping out of the sky, reaching straight for buildings.

It was the jetty.

For a moment Susan's heart sank. The Wanderer had lied to her, or he'd been wrong. The jetty was going to smash through Manhattan just as it had smashed through all the other lost cities.

At the very tip of the jetty, she saw a glint as the sun flashed off a bit of metal. Susan squinted, but she already knew what she would see.

A plane. Understanding began to fill her brain.

"No," she whispered. "Please. No."

But the universe ignored her plea. The plane smashed into the first building, engulfing it in flames and smoke and shadow.

"No!" Susan screamed. "You said you would stop it!"

And, as if in answer to her protest, a dark shape suddenly emerged from the cloud above her. It took her a moment to make out what it was: a horse and rider of impossible mountainous dimensions. It was the Trojan Horse, with the Wanderer seated astride it. The horse's tail streamed out behind them like a comet, and a javelin in the Wanderer's hand extended for miles in front.

Horse with rider charged toward the jetty with a gallop like the loudest thunder Susan had ever heard. Just as the tip of the javelin hit the second building and everything—horse, rider, jetty, and building—disappeared in a brilliant corona of light, Susan squeezed her eyes shut. The afterimage of the explosion burned in her eyes, and though she understood that her city was safe, that the jetty's path would stop with the towers, she still couldn't help but wonder: was this *victory*?

It was a long time before she could open her eyes. When she did, she saw that the jetty was gone, and the horse and rider. The towers were gone too, a few last wisps of smoke drifting east over the Atlantic, but the rest of Manhattan still lay below her, glittering, safe. A moment ago her city had seemed so huge and awesome, but Susan saw now that it was tiny and fragile like everything else people make, liable to disappear before you even knew what was happening. She looked down on it like a mother hen—or like an eagle, regarding its minuscule nest from the vastness of the sky.

Her first thought was to try to figure out how to pilot the carpet down there (and without being seen by eight million people) but then she realized that was a moot point. For her city, though safe, was not unchanging. As she watched, it seemed to grow taller beneath her, like sped-up footage of sprouting plants. Taller, ever taller, and thicker, one building crowding against another like bristles in a brush. And then, just as suddenly, they began to shrink, as if they were being pulled back into the ground. Susan realized she was looking into the future, decades, hundreds of years, maybe even thousands. She was seeing the life and death of her city, the growth, the retraction, the inevitable cycle. In the end, in an instant, the city was gone, and only a shimmering green wave of trees and grass covered the island as it must have hundreds of years ago.

But one spire remained. One tower, looking down serenely on the emptied island.

Her tree.

The redwood hung below her, beautiful, majestic, but just as evanescent as everything. In another moment it too was gone, and darkness—the eternal, peaceful, empty darkness of the end of time—descended on the world.

TWENTY-FOUR

Closing the Jetty (part 2)

"CHARLES?"

Charles looked from Murray's face to Iacob's. The Greenland boy was staring at Charles in confusion.

"Did it work? Did we close the jetty?"

The hopeless tone in Iacob's voice suggested he already knew the answer. From the head of the room came a small chuckle. Then:

"Guards. Seize them."

And now something strange happened. A guard took Iacob's arms and pinned them to his sides, and another took Charles's arms and held them tight. But when they were wrenched from their mirror books (which Charles, for one, was ready to get as far from as he could) the open tomes didn't budge. Which is to say, they didn't fall, but hung in the air exactly where they'd been.

Stifled gasps. Charles felt the hands of the guard behind him slacken somewhat. He thought of wrenching free and making a break for it. But where?

Nervous whispers hissed about the room; the guard holding Iacob was looking left and right, as if he wished he were anywhere but there. Before Charles could decide what to do, however, the voice at the head of the room barked, "Silence!"

The twittering stopped; the guard's hands tightened. Charles got the feeling the man behind him was more afraid of the man on the dais than of whatever force held the two books aloft, and he turned now, to take in this man.

The priest—what else could he be?—wore a long white robe edged with rich gold embroidery at the square neckline and the hem. The robe hung over one shoulder, and beneath it Charles could see some kind of undershirt that was also embroidered, in so many iridescent colors it seemed to have been woven from the tail feathers of a peacock. The priest had a long oval face that was medium brown in color, and a bald head that supported a yellow and blue striped hat thingy. Crown? Headdress? Charles wasn't sure what the right word was, but it was very imposing, and beside all this finery Murray looked small and shabby and helpless.

Murray.

When Charles's eyes flickered to his brother, the priest pursed his mouth in a sneer.

"Charles Oakenfeld."

Charles flashed back to the priest's face. The sneer curled up at one side, exposing a single, fanglike tooth.

"Do not be alarmed, Charles. I am no mind reader. Your brother told me your name. But I do not know yours." And he turned to Iacob.

Iacob seemed to screw his mouth shut, which only made the priest laugh.

"Really, my dear child. There is no need to be shy of me. I, for one, offer you my name freely. I am called Nimrod. I am priest and king of the land of Babylon, and soon to be the ruler of time itself." The priest—king?—paused to allow this last to sink in, and then said, "And you are?"

"No friend of yours!" Iacob snarled, and writhed against the man holding him, to no avail.

"Child, child," Nimrod said in a soft voice that sent a chill down Charles's spine. "I am a king. Kings do not have friends. Only allies and enemies. I beseech you," he said, his voice dropping even lower, so that Charles had to strain to hear it. "For your own sake, do not be my enemy."

Charles stirred himself to life. "Why have you done this?"

Nimrod turned to Charles. "Done what, Charles? Brought

you here? Opened the jetty?" He tugged lightly on the chain attached to Murray's neck. "Enlisted the . . . aid of your very unusual brother?"

"Don't believe him, Charles. He didn't do anything. He doesn't know what he's—"

"Silence, boy!" A rough jerk of the chain nearly knocked Murray over.

"He's being used, exactly as your father was," Murray continued defiantly, turning to Iacob. "He stumbled across these devices, just as your father did."

"Silence!" Nimrod jerked the chain again, practically lifting Murray up this time, so that he had to grab the collar to keep from choking. Charles struggled, but couldn't break free from the man who held him.

When both Oakenfeld boys were still, the priest glared down at Murray. "Another outburst from you, and your beloved brother will never see his time again."

Murray stared defiantly up at his captor. "Harm even one hair on Charles's head, and I won't show you how to use the jetty."

"Bah, you think I need you, boy? I have the books now."

"Do you? They seem to have themselves."

Everyone turned and looked at the two floating books. Floating was the wrong word: the books were absolutely, implacably still, and it seemed as if the world floated around them—as if the books were the anchors, and the world a great ship tethered to them by invisible chains.

Beneath his grandly accoutered skull, Nimrod's composure cracked slightly. "Do not stretch my benevolence, child."

"Your benevolence has about as much stretch as this chain," Murray said, fingering the collar at his neck. "You will free Charles and his friend, or I will tell you nothing. The secrets of the future will remain closed to you forever."

"Boy!" Nimrod's shout echoed through the subterranean chamber. But Murray only stared up at him, his features as eerily still as the mirror books.

For a long moment no one moved. Then, finally, Nimrod gave in.

"Very well then. Release the boy's brother and his companion."

The guards seemed only too eager to let go of Charles and Iacob and step back in line.

"You need to walk between the books, Charles," Murray said. "They'll take you back to your time. You too," he added, turning to Iacob. "Step between them, and they'll transport you back to the last place you were."

Charles looked up at his little brother. For the first time he realized Murray was wearing the very clothes he'd worn when he disappeared into the dumbwaiter. What was left of them anyway: his pants were shredded below the knees, his T-shirt in tatters. His shoes were gone and his feet caked in dirt.

Charles cleared his throat. "I'm not leaving without you, Murray."

"Don't be stupid, Charles," Murray said. "Go back to your own time. This doesn't concern you."

"If it didn't concern me, I wouldn't be here," Charles said. "And I'm not going anywhere without you."

"I'll make it easy for you, Charles. I can't go back. Do you understand? I can *never* go home with you. *It's not possible.*"

"But—"

Charles broke off. All at once he understood that Murray knew even less about his condition than the older version Charles had met on the Sea of Time last year, or the one he'd met in Drift House. Those two boys—or one boy at different places in his life—at least knew they could somehow get back to their right place and time. But apparently that knowledge was still in the future for this Murray, and he didn't even have that hope.

Charles glanced at Iacob, who stared back at Charles and nodded. Charles wasn't sure what Iacob's nod meant, but it gave him courage. He turned back to Murray. "I'm staying. With you."

"Charles—"

"No, Murray. It's not right for you to be alone. You're five years old."

"My age is immaterial, Charles," Murray said, sounding like anything but a five-year-old. "And you cannot be with me."

"I'm staying."

"Charles!" Murray stamped his foot. "You're not listening to me. I said it's not possible for you to be with me."

"I'm here now, aren't I?"

The two brothers stared at each other in a curious mixture of love and defiance. Charles had squabbled with his older sister on more occasions than he could count, but this was, to the best of his memory, the first time he'd ever had a serious disagreement with Murray.

Suddenly Murray's face softened, and he regarded Charles as if the ten-year-old were the younger of the two boys.

"Oh, Charles," he said in a hushed, almost reverent voice. "I wish I could tell you all the great things you're going to do." And then his voice hardened. "Make your way to the river."

"Wha—?"

With a jerk, Murray snapped his chain from Nimrod's hands. The priest had been watching the exchange between the two brothers with a fierce and slightly confused look on his face, and his grip had slackened. There was a good five or six feet of loose chain, and before Nimrod or Charles or anyone else in the room quite knew what was happening, Murray—five-year-old Murray Oakenfeld, his pudgy little cheeks puffed out in fierce determination—had swung the chain across Nimrod's face, once, twice, three times, slashing the priest's face open until he stumbled backward and fell to the floor.

"My eyes! My eyes!"

The guards nearest Nimrod approached Murray warily. It was clear they were afraid of more than his spinning chain.

"Charles, behind you!" Murray shouted, and Charles barely had time to twist out of the way before a large form hurtled past him. The guard, unable to check himself, lurched into the space between the two books . . .

. . . and vanished.

Without a sound, save that of his sword clattering to the tiled floor. Even as all the other guards fell back gasping, Iacob pounced on the weapon.

But now Nimrod was standing, propped between two guards. His headdress had been knocked off his shaved skull, and a thick stream of blood ran down the left side of his face. His voice thundered into the room.

"Kill the two half men, but bring the boy alive!"

There was a brief moment of hesitation among the guards, as they all stared at the space where their comrade had just disappeared. Murray took advantage of their fear to charge—straight down the aisle between the two rows of guards, his chain clanking behind him as though he were a runaway dog.

"Get him, you fools!" Nimrod roared.

A dozen guards leapt for Murray's dodging form. Charles had no idea how his little brother would make it. Suddenly a roar exploded to his left. Charles whirled, and saw Iacob lunging forward with his recovered sword. He caught a soldier from behind and plunged his blade into the man's thigh, causing him to scream and tumble to the ground.

Charles fumbled for the knife Handa had given him. He drew the stone blade from its sheath. Compared to the swords, the knife looked tiny, but it was all he had.

A soldier had managed to trip Murray to the floor and clung to his ankle. Murray reeled in his chain and began beating the soldier's face relentlessly, but three more men were closing in. Without giving himself time to think, Charles ran forward and drove the knife into the meat of the soldier's right shoulder. The man screamed and rolled away from Murray.

Charles stared into his brother's face. "Murray—"

"Remember, Charles," Murray cut him off. He stood poised before the two books. "The river. Now close your eyes, and hold on to your glasses."

Charles obeyed instinctively.

"Iacob," he called, screwing his eyes shut and taking firm hold of his lopsided glasses. "Close your eyes!"

The chain clanked as Murray leapt for the space between the two floating books. Nimrod's voice screamed from the far end of the room.

"Don't let him esc—"

The priest-king's voice was drowned out by an explosion, and Charles's eyelids flashed pink and purple and finally searing white, as a wave of energy knocked him to the floor. He rolled over one body, another, felt the sharp tip of a sword nearly pierce his ribs, and twisted out of the way.

As his body came to a rest and the echoes of the explosion faded, the sound of moaning filled the room. Charles blinked his eyes open warily, wiped a film of dust from his lenses. Soldiers lay tossed about the room like rag dolls, some forlornly still, others with their hands on their eyes. Cries of "I'm blind, I'm blind" told Charles exactly what had happened.

Charles whipped his head toward the mirror books. The first thing he saw was that the two tiled pillars closest to them had shattered, and a large section of ceiling had collapsed. So much dust shrouded the air that Charles couldn't tell if the mirror books were still there or not. But then he saw a thick beam of light pulsing through the cloud, and as some of the dust settled he saw that the beam emanated from one of the mirror books. It still floated in the air, but it was no longer stable. Instead, it spun slowly, almost lazily, and from its open pages came that thick beam of light. Of the second book, no trace remained.

And now Charles smelled burning. How could a room of mud bricks and tile be on fire? He whipped his head around for the source, and saw that where the beam of light passed over the walls it left a black smoking track behind.

"Charles!"

Iacob's dust-shrouded head emerged from beneath a pile of writhing, blinded soldiers.

"We must run!"

But Charles ignored him. Instead of turning for the exit, he ran straight for the book. And now a second voice called out.

"Demon! I will kill you myself!"

Charles whirled, and saw Nimrod rise from the wreckage at the head of the room. Aside from the cuts on the left side of his face, he appeared unharmed, and he held a sword in each hand.

"Charles, duck!"

Charles turned and fell to the floor, just as the burning beam of light swept through the space where he'd been. He heard its sizzling passage, then a kind of muffled *whump* as something—another pillar?—exploded beneath the beam's heat.

"Charles, come on!" Iacob was suddenly beside him. "That ray is destroying the pillars that hold up the ceiling."

Charles pushed Iacob's hand away. "I have to find something!"

"Charles, the ceiling could fall down. Maybe the whole building!"

Charles froze. The whole building? Collapse? It suddenly occurred to him that that's what had happened to the historical Tower of Babel. Had he come to the very moment the tower was destroyed?

But Charles didn't allow himself to dwell on that possibility. He squinted at the mirror book, trying to see if it still bore the seal on its cover. But as far as he could tell, it was bare.

"We have to run, Charles. Before it's too late."

Over Iacob's shoulder, Nimrod was fighting his way toward the boys. The flashing beam of light slowed him, and he seemed to be limping as well, but his progress was inexorable.

Charles looked back at Iacob. "I'm sorry. I have to find something. For my brother. You go on ahead if you need to."

"Charles, your brother . . . exploded." Suddenly Iacob's eyes went wide. "It's the amulet, isn't it?"

Charles didn't answer, just fell on the pile of rubble beneath the book. Up close, its heat was like an open oven, and Charles had to take off his glasses because the sweat and dust rendered them virtual blindfolds. Half blind, choking on dust, he sifted through the debris.

Iacob knelt beside Charles. "Charles, you cannot do this! Look what the amulet did to my father!"

"Murray *needs* it. And besides, don't you think it's better he has it than someone like your father?"

"Demon!" Nimrod's voice roared behind them. "Prepare to meet the end of *your* time!"

"*Charles.*" Iacob's voice was pleading.

Charles's fingers continued to sift through the dust. "Don't you see, Iacob? If we leave without taking the amulet, then Nimrod will find it. For all we know, all this could happen *again*. And Murray won't misuse the amulet. He just needs it to get home. I *have* to get it for him."

There was an excruciating silence while Iacob considered Charles's words, and then he put a hand on Charles's shoulder.

"Keep looking. I'll deal with him."

The Greenland boy stood up and began pelting the priest with broken pieces of brick and tile. His aim seemed pretty good, judging from Nimrod's curses. Meanwhile, the debris was so thick that Charles knew it was a one in a million chance he'd find what he was looking for. He found Murray's pants, his shirt, the collar and the iron chain that had been around his neck. Despite the gravity of the situation, he giggled at the thought of his brother materializing naked somewhere. . . .

"Charles, hurry! Nimrod is almost here!"

If he could just see a little better! But the dust was everywhere. Charles threw bits of brick left and right, but this only made the dust worse. He let out a grunt of frustration.

"Charles!" Iacob screamed. "Come *on*!"

All at once calmness flooded Charles's being. He took a deep breath, his shirt over his mouth to filter the dust, and closed his eyes. Then he thrust his fingers into the pile. In his mind, his hand was a mole, perfectly capable of sensing everything in the darkness. His fingers dug down, left, curled over a chunk of something.

"Charles!" Metal clanged against metal now. "Charles, he's here!"

Something almost infinitesimally small ("Don't say 'infinitesimal,' Charles, it's *affected*") brushed against the side of

Charles's hand. He twisted his wrist, snagged it, pulled his hand from the dust. Only then did he open his eyes.

There, in his palm, sat a tiny blob of gold. The seven lines were gone, and it had shrunk considerably—it was heart shaped now, just like the locket Murray wore around his neck—but for that very reason Charles knew it was the right thing. He squeezed his fingers tight around it and felt the faintest of tingles, as the amulet called out for Murray across the farthest reaches of space and time. Charles realized it was his brother the amulet had been calling for—had been leading him to— the whole time. Somehow the amulet belonged to Murray, just as it belonged to the mirror book.

Another clang. An *oof*. Charles turned to see Iacob on his back a few feet away, Nimrod standing above him with both swords raised.

"Where is the demon?" Nimrod screamed. "As you value your life, tell me now!"

Without thinking, Charles grabbed a handful of gritty dust with his free hand and threw it at Nimrod's one good eye. Charles's aim was true. Nimrod's face exploded in a cloud of dust and he dropped one of his swords (narrowly missing Iacob, who rolled out of the way just in time). Charles's fingers had already closed around a chunk of brick the size of a large dictionary, and he hurled it at Nimrod's chest. The priest stumbled backward but managed to stay on his feet. He was blinking his eye rapidly, and Charles couldn't tell if he could see or not.

Charles looked around for something else to throw, but before he could grab something there was a sound. Later on, Charles would say it sounded like a light saber in *Star Wars*, but at the time Charles only knew he had to duck. He hurled himself on top of Iacob, who was struggling to stand.

The beam of light emitted by the one remaining mirror book sliced through the air—the air, and Nimrod as well, cleaving arms, chest, and head from legs and stomach, which fell to the ground like birds shot from the sky. With a terrible muteness, the priest's mouth opened and closed, but there was no air to give voice to his last words. With a final twitch, he was still.

Charles dropped the amulet in his pocket and grabbed a sword. "Let's go."

Iacob blinked the dust from his eyes. "Now? I was just starting to like it here."

The Greenland boy was cut off by another explosion of dust. Yet another pillar had shattered under the book's rays. A moment later, one more pillar went, and then a chunk of ceiling fell to the floor.

"Well, if you put it *that* way," Iacob said, "let's go."

Crouching, the two boys half ran, half crawled their way toward the dais and the exit behind it, only to discover that the doorway that led to the hall—and the flying carpet—had collapsed.

"We'll have to go for the front door," Charles said.

"But your carpet," Iacob said. "How will we—"

"We'll figure that out later," Charles said, as still another pillar exploded.

The boys ran the length of the room. Twice they had to throw themselves to the floor to avoid getting lasered by the beam of light. One time Charles landed right on top of a soldier, who turned his burned face toward Charles and looked at him blindly.

"We have done wrong!" the soldier croaked. "We have brought the wrath of God upon us!"

Iacob grabbed Charles and pulled him up. They ran the rest of the way to the door and staggered through it, only to find themselves plunged into sudden darkness.

"Ch-Charles?"

Charles turned to Iacob, whose face was barely visible in the dim light emanating from the dust-clogged room behind them.

"It's okay, Iacob. I think I know the way."

And he did know the way, now. The darkness almost made it easier for him to see the images he'd encountered in the mirror book in the tree above Drift House. Taking Iacob's hand, he led him up the ramped hallway without tripping or faltering. It was a long walk, and Charles could feel Iacob's fear in the darkness, but Charles knew he wouldn't get lost now.

And then they were there. They turned a corner, and a twinkling yellow portal lay at the far end of one last corridor.

Iacob turned to Charles. "The things of your world are miraculous. Miraculous and terrifying."

Charles shook his head. "They're not of my world."

Iacob's teeth caught the distant light, but Charles couldn't see if he was smiling or frowning.

"No, Charles, they're of both our worlds. This"—Iacob waved his hand in the direction of the destruction they'd just escaped—"this is where we come from, isn't it? My father, and Father Poulsen for that matter, sound very much like Nimrod to me, no matter how many centuries separate them." Iacob shook his head. "Your brother said something about the river. Do you know the way there as well?"

Charles shrugged. "There's only one way to find out."

It hadn't occurred to Charles to wonder why there was light at the end of the corridor. As a boy of the twenty-first century, he took illuminated nights for granted; but as they drew closer to the exit he saw that the light was unsteady and shifting about. Not merely flickering like a flame, but dancing, jumping, surging in great waves. Either there was an enormous number of people with torches running around outside the exit, or the city of Babylon was on fire.

"Charles?" Iacob's voice indicated he, too, had guessed at the scale and confusion of the fire outside.

"I don't know," Charles said to Iacob's unasked question. "But we'd better be careful."

He held his sword in one hand, Handa's knife in the other, and Iacob brandished his sword in return. There were grim smiles on the boys' faces, suggesting both their determination and their sense of the slight ridiculousness of two and a half small blades against an entire burning city.

They crept the rest of the way out. The tunnel opened into a narrow courtyard that ringed the tower, whose enormous bulk hung like a weight on their backs. The courtyard contained only palm trees and flowerbeds bisected by narrow stone channels filled with slow-moving water, but on the far side of the wall a great orange light pushed up into the night sky. A low blanket of smoke stretched as far as the eye could see in every direction, eerily luminescent from the light of the burning city. The smoke shrouded the tower, making it impossible to see its apex, or—if it still existed—the vortex of the time jetty. As Charles looked up at the sky, he prayed that the jetty *was* closed. But if they had succeeded, how would he and Iacob get home?

Iacob took hold of Charles's arms to start them moving. "We should hurry, before whatever is out there"—he gestured at the fiery glow beyond the courtyard's walls—"comes in here."

Charles nodded, and lifted his dragging feet. He could hear angry shouts, terrified screams, clangs and clashing and the general ruckus of mayhem.

"It sounds like . . . like a war," Charles said, hesitating because he didn't really know what war sounded like.

"It *feels* like war," Iacob said. "It is a strange time," he continued as they picked their way from shadow to shadow. "The people possess so little, and yet they build structures as miraculous as this one."

They came, finally, to the corner of the tower. Iacob had poked his head around the edge, and a look of dumbfounded awe took him over.

Cautiously, Charles looked around the corner. And now he wondered what had so shocked Iacob, for there were two choices: the immense and incredibly steep staircase on the side of the tower, that did in fact seem to ascend to heaven, or the wide open gates of the courtyard, through which could be seen the spectacle of the burning city.

It was the second scene that held Charles's attention, for even as he looked at the dancing flames and the figures running back and forth—some in terror, some in pursuit—he suddenly realized he and Iacob had to get through them to make it to the river.

"It *is* war," Iacob whispered. "But how did it break out so suddenly? The city was peaceful when we arrived."

Charles didn't answer. He was studying the expanse of courtyard and the wide gateway and the tangle of smoke and flame-filled streets beyond. Something closer caught his eye: a sparkle of reflected firelight off the water sloughing through a nearby stone trough. He pointed to it excitedly.

"These channels must run to the river," he told Iacob. "We just have to follow them."

"But they lead to the wall," Iacob said.

"We can pick up the trail outside. We just have to get through that." Charles pointed to the chaos beyond the gates.

"Quick then," Iacob said. "Before it gets any worse."

Crouching behind a raised flowerbed, the boys made their way toward the gateway. The running figures—some carrying infants, or baskets piled with food, or lances—shielded their faces when they ran past the opening, as if they were afraid of looking directly at the building that loomed over their city, or what was left of it.

"They're terrified of the tower," Charles said. "The Bible says God punished the people of Babel for building it. Do you think that's what's happening now?"

"I think we do not have the luxury of contemplating such questions right now," Iacob said. "Let us first save ourselves, and worry about answers later."

Charles nodded. "There." He pointed at a line of squat buildings crowding the temple walls. He surveyed the wide, empty space between the gates. "We can use those shacks for cover, but we're going to have to run for it."

"Okay," Iacob said. "On three. One—"

"Two—"

"Three!"

The boys dashed from the cover of the flowerbed and onto the wide road that led through the gates. Charles felt the temperature go up as they neared the entrance, but even more palpably he felt the shadow of the enormous tower at his back, and so he raced toward the flames. For what seemed like an eternity the boys were running across the wide open avenue, just like all the other people running through the streets beyond the gate. Every second Charles expected to hear a soldier shout, or feel the blade of a lance pierce his body. And then, with a dive, he was behind the row of buildings, Iacob tumbling on him a moment later.

The boys looked at each other with mutual grins on their faces.

"Wow," Charles said. And then, parroting Charles, Iacob said:

"I *know*. Wow."

The boys trotted swiftly behind the row of buildings, which were little more than stalls. Judging from the sacks of things—grain and beads and clay jars—they were on the edge of a market square. Charles contemplated taking something as an artifact back to the twenty-first century (assuming he made it back, of course), but as his fingers trailed over a tiny clay bottle stoppered with wax, he felt the foreignness of it, and rejected the plan even before he'd acted on it. These things would have to make it to his time the old-fashioned way:

minute by minute, year by year, over the next twenty-five centuries. Even if all that was left by then was dust.

They came to the end of the stalls and faced the next open
space. Charles spotted a low palm whose fronds offered thick
shadow at its base.

"There," he said.

They didn't count this time, just glanced to either side
and ran.

To either side—but not directly in front of them. Charles
hadn't taken two steps when he collided with a man who
seemed to have appeared out of nowhere. He wasn't much
taller than Charles, though he was thick in the shoulders and
waist, and Charles bounced backward, nearly tripping over
Iacob coming up behind.

The Babylonian man stared at the two boys wildly. His
beard and hair had bits of hay and dust stuck in them, and
there was a gash on his left cheek dripping blood. More blood
welling from that arm, which hung limply at his side. And then
his mouth opened and a few garbled words came out, and he
ran off.

Charles and Iacob dashed for the cover of the palm. When
they were safely shielded, Charles said, "The translation charm
didn't work on him. Why?"

Iacob knew nothing of the translation charm, but he remembered something else. "According to Father Poulsen,
when God destroyed the tower—"

"All the languages changed!" Charles finished. "Is this . . . are we really at the destruction of the Tower of Babel?"

For one moment, Iacob's face went far away, as if he were listening to something Charles couldn't hear. And then he turned to Charles.

"I think—I think we caused it."

"You mean . . . the mirror books? But they were just supposed to close the jetty."

"I think the tower and the jetty are—were—the same thing."

Of course! The symbol on the amulet, and the fact that the books had drawn them to the very bottom of the tower. It all made sense. What didn't make sense was the idea that Charles and Iacob had brought about the tower's destruction—that they had done what the Bible said was God's work. It—it was just too much to contemplate.

He pulled a palm frond down and looked at the city. Men and women, soldiers and civilians ran through the burning maze of streets. To Charles's modern eyes, they seemed like players in a video game, some of them guessing correctly and escaping, others guessing wrong and running into swords, or flames. Behind and above all this was the tower, and Charles could see the first enemy soldiers scaling the immense staircase now, pushing over statues and urns filled with flowers and burning oil as they made their way to the smoke-shrouded top of the building, where Charles knew they would tear it apart, brick by brick if they had to.

He turned back to Iacob. "This is going to get worse before it gets better. We've got to get to the river."

Iacob nodded, pointed. "There's the canal. Let's go for that house, there."

The boys dashed, half crouched, from bush to house, house to hole, hole to ruined wall. Charles didn't look at any of the faces they passed, nor did they look at him. He noted that everyone seemed to be alone, each man, woman, and child fending for himself or herself, each against his neighbor or enemy, and he was grateful for Iacob's companionship. For his part, the Greenland boy was even more single-minded, pointing out this or that bit of cover without speaking, looking at Charles only to see if they were headed in the right direction.

The canal they were following disappeared underground at some point. But by then the ground had a distinct downhill slant to it, and Charles simply piloted them down the slope. After what seemed like a thousand fifty- and hundred-yard dashes from one skimpy bit of shelter to the next, the boys rounded a long row of connected buildings whose roofs burned in a single blaze and saw that the maze of streets more or less stopped. Palm trees grew thick here, and in between them were shacks and tents, many trampled or smoldering. But over the tang of smoke Charles could smell the cool wetness of a large body of water.

The boys picked their way carefully through the shanties. Every corner was blind, and even on the straightaways it was impossible to see more than five or ten feet ahead. Once they rounded a corner and sent an enormous pig squealing, and Iacob flung out his arm in a protective gesture, like a father slamming on the brakes and reaching reflexively to protect his child in the passenger seat. The two boys stood panting, their hearts racing, as the fat pink creature disappeared into the shadows, and almost as soon as they started again they jumped a second time, because a piglet went squealing after its mother, followed a moment later by its twin.

Iacob fell against a trunk, a small laugh escaping his mouth. "If that is the worst thing that happens to us, I will consider myself truly fortunate."

But Charles wasn't paying attention. He cocked his head. "Do you hear that?"

"Hear . . . ?"

"Music," Charles said.

"Music. Charles, there is a war being fought. I do not think anyone is playing—" But then Iacob broke off, for it was clear he heard it too.

It was a jazzy sort of number, dominated by brass horns and strings that were thousands of years away from being invented, and these were joined by a woman's staticky voice, half speaking, half singing.

> *All of me . . .*
> *Why not take all of me?*

Charles grabbed Iacob's hand. "It's the radio!"

"You mean . . . the box . . . with Susan!"

"It has to be!" And, without waiting to see if Iacob followed, Charles dashed toward the sound. Now the tents and shacks seemed to spring up just to get in his way, and Charles jumped and flailed and ran with all his might.

"Susan! Susan, we're here!"

"Charles!" Iacob hissed behind him. "Be quiet. You don't know—"

"Susan!" Charles screamed over his friend's warnings. "Susan, wait! We're coming!"

Then the shanties were gone and Charles crashed down a steep slope toward a wide, flat bar of water. The river was dark and light at the same time, reflective and hollow and, as far as Charles could see, empty of everything save for the mirrored flames of the burning city at his back.

> *All of me . . .*
> *Why not take all of me?*

He raced down the pebbly, scrubby slope, Iacob hard at his heels.

"Susan! Susan, where are you?"

All of me . . .

"Susan!" Iacob was calling now. "Susan, are you there?"

Why not take take all of me . . .

The boys skidded to a halt in the mud at the river's edge. The empty river lapped at Charles's moccasins, Iacob's bare feet.

Baby, take all of me!

Charles looked upriver, Iacob looked down. They looked back at each other. Charles felt a growing fear building in his stomach.

"Charles!" Iacob pointed over his shoulder.

Charles whirled around. A shadow lay on the water, so small it could have been a whiff of smoke or a reflected cloud. But it kept its shape as slowly, patiently, it inched toward them, and now Charles heard a man's voice—a living man's voice—join the woman's recorded tones:

All of me . . .
Why not take all of me?

Charles could see the shape of the boat now, a man's back,

the delicate spiderlines of oars dipping into the water on left and right. Moonlight bounced off a bald head. A few strands of hair flitted in the lightest of breezes. Charles wanted to run then, but he felt as if roots had grown from the bottoms of his feet and held him in place.

"Charles!" Iacob's voice came from just a few feet away, but Charles couldn't turn his head away from the approaching rower. He thought of the myths he had read in school about the man who rowed people from the land of the living to the land of the dead. Of all the people. Him? Here? *How?*

Iacob took hold of Charles's forearm. "Charles, who is this?"

"It—" Charles didn't know how to answer. "It's not Susan."

And still the boat rowed straight for them, the rower never once turning to check his course. Just plying his oars and singing softly in a voice that sounded young and old at the same time.

All—of—me—

Without a sound, the prow of the little rowboat came to shore, neatly seaming the space between Charles and Iacob. The gangly figure in the center of the craft stowed first one oar in the bottom of the boat, then the other, and then he leaned forward and, with a gnarled hand, turned off the small tombstone radio that sat in the boat's stern. Only then did he turn his grizzled, lined visage to Charles. His teeth—which had once seemed so stained in daylight—glinted bright and white in the reflected fires of Babel.

In his pocket, Charles felt the miniaturized amulet buzzing with all its might.

Mr. Zenubian smiled. "Recognize me now, Charles?"

TWENTY-FIVE

Row the Boat

SUSAN WASN'T SURE HOW LONG she rode the carpet. Seconds, hours? Days? Time had never seemed so irrelevant. Darkness had fallen. Not a creepy darkness, but a great emptiness. Looking at it made Susan tired, and she laid her head down and slept.

A whiff of smoke jolted her awake. She sat up and looked down, expecting to see the burning towers of her own city, but instead saw the light of a thousand fires twinkling over a broad plain. A broken shape on the horizon blotted out the night, and from it came the biggest fire of all, and a column of smoke as large as a mountain range. Susan stared at the broken tower for a long time, until the faint sound of singing came to her ears.

All of me . . .
Why not take all of me?

The voices were male, a warbling adult bass and one or two boyish tenors, and they all sang terribly, terribly off-key.

All of me . . .
Why not take all of me?

She recognized Charles's squeak (she would know her brother's voice anywhere) and she could guess that the second boy's voice belonged to Iacob. As the carpet soared down over a wide flat river she added her voice to theirs.

Baby, take a-all of meee!

"Susan!" Charles's voice called out, still half singing.
"Charles! Iacob!"
And then the tall figure plying the oars of the boat turned around. A wicked grin split Mr. Zenubian's lined cheeks.
"Hello, Susan. Glad you could drop in."
As if programmed, the rolled-up carpet aligned itself over the length of the boat and settled into it. The carpet was so long and the boat so short that it had to lie diagonally, and even then a good foot or so hung over the stern, and the boat itself settled so deeply into the water that the top of the craft

was only a few inches above the surface. But once she had landed Susan risked capsizing the entire craft to throw her arms around her brother, and then again around Iacob. Charles returned her grasp immediately, and, after a moment, so did Iacob. Only then did Susan turn to face the man who sat in the bow, steadily pulling at the oars to steer the overburdened boat toward the center of the wide river.

"Hello, Susan," he said a second time. "Surprised to see me?"

Susan turned around, looked between Charles and Iacob to the small tombstone radio that sat in the right-hand (was it starboard?) side of the stern. Then, again, she turned to face the rower. Steeling her voice, she said,

"Mr. Zenubian. It's very nice to meet you again."

At this, Drift House's former caretaker threw back his head and laughed so hard the boat wobbled from side to side, and one of the oars slipped from his grasp and Susan had to snatch it before it floated away.

"Now see here!" she said, brandishing the oar like a bat. "You'll get us stranded if you behave that way!"

Mr. Zenubian's laughter redoubled, and he dropped the other oar. Charles lunged for it.

"Mr. Zenubian!" Susan said. "You needn't be so self-righteous. Just because you've managed to stay one step ahead of us—"

"Susan," Mr. Zenubian managed to sputter. "After everything you've seen and done, are you *still* so literal-minded?"

"*I'm* not literal-minded! That's Charles!"

"*What?*" Charles said from behind her. "We came twenty-one centuries to save you, and *this* is the first thing you have to say to me?"

Susan whirled on Charles. "*You* came to save *me*? *I've* come to save *you*."

A fresh bout of laughter at the front of the boat cut off the children's squabble.

"Oh, how I've missed this," Mr. Zenubian cackled. "Promise me you'll never change."

Susan looked at Mr. Zenubian, who regarded her with a mischievous smile, and then she turned to Charles, whose smile mirrored Mr. Zenubian's. Even Iacob seemed amused by the proceedings, although he looked a little scared too.

Susan squinted at her younger brother. "You know something."

Charles fought an unsuccessful battle to keep a smile off his face. "I think you should be looking the other way for answers."

Susan turned. Mr. Zenubian stared at her. She searched the caretaker for some clue as to what their big secret was, but all she saw was his familiar uniform, still as dirty—and smelly—as she remembered. His stringy hair hung down his lined, unsavory face, and his long lanky arms plied the oars again. The entire spectacle was maddeningly *un*revealing, and made all the more so by the fog that was beginning to swirl over the river, mixing with the smoke into a curious amalgam that was simultaneously wet and dry, cold and hot.

Still, there was something . . . In the eyes? The set of the jaw? Something familiar. Some seed of knowledge that she felt would grow if planted in the right soil. But it just wouldn't come, and the fog was getting thicker all the time, making it that much harder to see.

"Ugh! I give up!"

The answer came from a most unexpected source.

"It's Murray!" Iacob sang out.

Susan whirled and looked at the Greenland boy. He stared at her with a pleased grin on his face, and what with Charles and Mr. Zenubian—Murray? really?—she felt so surrounded by self-satisfied boys that she didn't quite absorb the full impact of Iacob's words.

She turned back to the figure in the front of the boat, who still plied the oars, pulling the boat into the thickening fog. The lights of the burning city were a faint glow now, the shouts and clangs as distant as a TV heard through an apartment wall.

"Is it—?" But before she could finish her question, she saw that it was true. "Murray," she said in a hushed tone of voice. "Um. Wow. *Murray*." And then, waving her hand in front of her nose, she said, "You need a bath!"

When the laughter had died down, Charles said, "We only just found out too."

"He didn't tell us," Iacob threw in. "Charles figured it out."

The fog had grown so thick that Susan could barely make out Charles's grin. "I just had more clues than you," he said modestly. He dug a hand into his pocket, and something glinted in the faint light. Looking past Susan to this strange new version of Murray, he said, "This is yours."

Susan gasped—Charles had Murray's locket. "How did you—?"

Charles chuckled quietly. "It's a long story. I'll tell you later." He held out his hand to Murray. "Don't you want it?"

Susan turned back to Murray, who seemed strangely uninterested in the sight of the locket. "I'll get it from you later. It's important that I keep rowing right now, or we might end up in Timbuktu. Or even Timbuk-three."

A small grin cracked the side of Murray's gnarled face, and Charles couldn't tell if he was serious or joking. He stared at his brother for a moment, then, almost reluctantly, put the amulet back in his pocket.

"Am I correct in assuming you're taking us onto the Sea of Time?"

"You are as correct as your grammar, Charles," Murray said. "I'll have you back to Drift House before daylight."

Now Susan turned back to the front of the boat.

"Is it," she began. "I mean, can I . . . ? Do we . . . ?" She sighed in exasperation. "Will you tell us what's going on? Or at least what happened?"

Murray smiled and, though it was a kind smile, Susan was hard-pressed to find any trace of her brother in it. She saw a bit of Mario—the new, sardonic part of his personality that had developed after he became a Returner—but none of the little innocent boy she had known.

Murray pulled on his oars slowly, patiently. Charles recognized this movement from his own journey with Tankort, but to Susan each of her strange new brother's strokes seemed to last an eternity, and it was all she could do not to stamp her foot in the bottom of the shallow craft. Finally Murray sighed.

"This is the kind of story that usually begins 'Once upon a time,'" he began, "but that beginning would be inappropriate here, because this story in fact begins in the time before time, or at least time as we know it. Not even the Wanderer of Days knows where the mirror book came from, let alone its twin. Some say the Atlanteans made it, and others claim it hails from the New World, from a tribe whose name has long since been lost. Thousands of years ago the Wanderer was able to remove the amulet from its cover, but he knew that eventually the two pieces would find their way back to each other—that the jetty would be opened, and the temporal universe be permanently destroyed. But with your help, that catastrophe has been prevented."

"But why would anyone make an object that could only do harm?" Susan said. "What could they possibly gain from it?"

Murray shook his head. "The Wanderer told me once that he didn't think anyone made the mirror book. It was his belief that it came into existence at the same time humanity did. That it is nothing more than an expression of the dark side of human nature, the side that has always yearned after destruction and death."

"Well, you've got the amulet now," Susan said. "So that's it, right? No more threats to time?"

"Not exactly," Murray said.

"Not exactly?" Susan echoed.

"If the Wanderer's theory is correct—that the mirror book is nothing more than a manifestation of human desire—then the same threat still exists, at least in theory."

"I don't understand," Susan said. "Are you saying the threat isn't really the mirror book? That it's—people?"

Murray nodded. "Human beings are the only sentient beings left, Susan. As such they control time's flow completely. As you saw, the time jetty took form in our world in many different ways, all of them reflecting the human psyche: it can be the war that destroyed Babel, or the bombs that obliterated Hiroshima and Nagasaki, or the environmental destruction that led to the downfall of the Easter Islanders. Even when the jetty takes a natural form, as with the earthquake that sank Atlantis, its effect is only felt because of human choices: an earthquake can only kill you if you choose to live on a fault line."

Iacob cleared his throat. "Is that why Osterbygd failed? Because of the jetty?"

"A failure to change can be every bit as dangerous as change itself. Often more so."

The fog was blowing away now, Susan suddenly noticed, and the breeze was decidedly chilly. Glimpses of cold gray water were visible.

"But how do we stop this?" Iacob said. "Is it because there are so many people now? Do they have to die?"

Susan and Charles looked sharply at Iacob. He had said this last so dispassionately, as if he were merely being practical.

"Nothing so dramatic," Murray said, his voice as flat as Iacob's. "It is not so much the number of people that is the problem, but the fact that they all want the same thing."

"But," Susan said, "it seems to me that people want different things. That's why there are so many wars."

"Maybe there are so many wars because everyone wants war."

"No one *wants* war! Wars are terrible!"

"Then why do we keep fighting them?" Murray said. He held up his hand before Susan or anyone else could answer. "I must leave you with that question to answer on your own. We're here."

And it was true. The last of the fog was whipping away in a

fierce, cold breeze. And there, bobbing on the water, was the familiar shape of Drift House. Murray pulled at the oars with more visible effort now, and sometimes little lips of water splashed over the side of the dinghy.

"This last part," he said breathlessly, "might be a bit *hairy*."

The boat dipped and rose in the waves, and the three children held on to whatever they could hold on to. Murray said they didn't need the radio anymore, so Charles turned it off and took it in his lap for safekeeping. Murray's breath whistled through his nose, and Susan stared at his long thin arms plying the oars, his stringy hair hanging wetly down his gnarled cheeks. On the Sea of Time Murray was sage and strange, but in the real world he was merely *old*. Her brother. Murray. Old. It was a little sad, but mostly it was weird.

"I don't . . . always . . . look . . . like this," Murray panted, stealing a smile at Susan. "I thought it . . . would be . . . a good disguise."

Susan laughed. "All I can say is, *phew*."

Eventually, somehow, they made it. One of the Greenlanders spotted them, so Uncle Farley and Iussi were there to help them aboard, and in a moment Murray and the three children were sipping hot soup in the drawing room—whose walls, they all saw, showed a return to Greenland in their immediate future. Uncle Farley used the radio to set a course, and then sat down with them to get the news. "You children always seem to have all the adventure, while I sit here and keep house."

But Murray surprised them all by excusing himself. Though it was early, he said the rowing had tired him out. He took the amulet from Charles, dropping it casually in his pocket, then headed to one of the spare bedrooms on the second floor. Just before he went upstairs, he winked at his older brother and said, "I think you've earned the right to a room of your own."

TWENTY-SIX

The End of Osterbygd

THE NEXT MORNING, WHEN SUSAN came down for breakfast, she heard low voices coming from the music room. It turned out to be Murray and Iacob. Their heads were bent close to each other, and the Greenland boy had a look of intense concentration on his face, as though he were trying to remember a chemical formula for a test. He looked up with a startled— and, Susan thought, slightly guilty—expression when she entered the room.

"Susan," Murray said. "Good morning."

"I hope I'm not interrupting."

Murray shook his head. "No, no, we were just waiting for everyone to wake up. Coffee?"

"I don't drink coffee," Susan said.

Murray grinned. "You will," he said, "before you know it."

Iacob had walked to the window and pulled the curtain aside. Susan saw the coast of Greenland stretched out before them. It seemed familiar, as if it were a place she'd been to many times before. She was able to pick out the sharp roof of the church from the line of houses where Iussi and Gunnar and the remaining colonists lived.

Iacob turned back to the room. "I think I would like to try some coffee," the Greenland boy said quietly. "It will be my first taste of . . . the future. But hopefully not my last."

Within a few hours everything was hustle and bustle. In Susan and Charles's absence, the Greenlanders had worked out a deal with Karl Olafson's men on Leifsbudir, and the latter's boats were tied to the stern of Drift House. All morning and afternoon the long dark ships rowed back and forth between the house and Osterbygd, bringing a dozen boatloads of colonists with them. Still, it took Susan a moment to realize what was going on. When she did, though, she pulled her uncle aside.

"Uncle Farley! Are they . . . leaving?"

Her uncle nodded. "I've agreed to take them to Iceland."

"But . . . but isn't that changing history?"

"History tells us the Greenland colony disappeared at the end of the fifteenth century. No one knows exactly how or why." Her uncle shrugged. "Well, now we do."

As the Greenlanders filed on board, they seemed too awed to be frightened. Most of them retreated to the third floor, or hid out in the solarium (the colonists had insisted on bringing their livestock, a small herd of sheep who immediately set to work decimating Drift House's tropical plant collection). A few of the younger colonists walked through the house looking with fascination at this or that. To make everything just a little more confusing, the translation charms stopped working right in the middle of the transport operation: after three days in the real world, the Sea of Time water had fully deintensified. Murray spoke just enough Old Norse to direct the colonists, but that was all.

Susan, especially, felt the loss of their ability to communicate acutely. It seemed to her that Iacob was taking the abandonment of Greenland just a little too easily, and she wanted to know what had happened to change his mind about leaving. She felt sure it had something to do with the conversation she'd caught him having with Murray, but there was no way to ask him about it. Whenever they crossed paths, they could only smile and shrug and laugh weakly.

Last on board was Father Poulsen. No translation device was needed to render the epithets and spittle that flew from his gray-bearded mouth. He waved his cross at paintings and statues and side tables, yelling maniacally, until Iussi and Gunnar half guided, half dragged him up the stairs to the third floor. Occasionally his voice could be heard during the overnight voyage to Iceland, shrieking at this or that imagined sign of the devil.

They offloaded the colonists about a dozen miles from the modern city of Reykjavik. Last on, first off: Father Poulsen stormed down the stairs as soon as they started herding the animals into the first boat.

"The *phragmipedium schlimii* and *laelia purpurata* are beyond salvage," President Wilson muttered, watching as the scrawny sheep milled down the front hall.

"There, there, President Wilson, we can always order more plants," Uncle Farley said. "I'm more concerned about my—ah!" He rushed to chase a sheep away from an embroidered table runner. "Seventeenth-century Chinese silk," he said as if the animal might understand him. "Shoo, shoo!"

Last off were Iussi, Gunnar, and Iacob. It was a strange goodbye, since no one could really understand anyone. Murray did his best to translate, but all he came up with was "Thank you," and "Be well," and, again, "Thank you."

"Thank you, Charles," Iacob said, his eyes half crossed in concentration. "You . . . are . . . strong." They shook hands.

"Thank you, Iacob," Charles said back to him. "You are strong too."

Iacob looked to Murray. "Strongtu?"

Murray smiled, stuttered a few words.

"Ah!" Iacob said, nodding. "Strong!" He pointed at Charles. "You . . . me . . . strong!"

He turned to Susan.

"Susan," he said. "Thank you."

Susan opened her mouth but nothing came out. She felt as if she knew less English than the Greenland boy. Surprising herself, she grabbed Iacob and pulled him close in a tight hug, then suddenly pushed him away. She had felt something press against her chest.

"Iacob," she said, reaching for his neck, "did Murray give—"

Iacob stepped back, glancing at Murray nervously.

"Susan," Murray said. She looked at her much older brother. He shook his head.

Susan sighed. She *wanted* to ask. But the look on Murray's face was so severe that she didn't dare. She turned back to Iacob.

"Goodbye," she said, in the most level voice she could muster.

Iacob nodded. "We . . . meet . . . again?" There was a question in his voice. Susan wasn't sure if he was wondering whether they would ever see each other again, or if he was merely wondering if he'd gotten the words right.

She smiled weakly. "Maybe."

Iacob glanced at Murray, then back at Susan. He shook his head vehemently, took her hands in his. "We meet *again*," he said emphatically. This time it was Susan who glanced at Murray, who shrugged, a small grin playing on his face.

"Maybe."

And then they were gone. The crew of Drift House watched to see that the boat landed safely ashore, and then Uncle Farley turned them to open water. When they were out of sight of land, Uncle Farley pressed a few buttons on the little radio, and a moment later Susan and Charles felt the rolling subside considerably, and the light turned yellow and warm. They were back on the Sea of Time. They stayed only long enough to discharge Murray, who settled himself in the punt Mario had with him when he first showed up. No one asked him where he was going or when he would be back.

Before he went he hugged Susan and Charles. His embrace was warm but strange—grownup, slightly distant. Charles had met one of his mother's aunts on a trip to London, and the hug she had given him felt like Murray's: affectionate, but a little businesslike. As Susan said, "He might as well have shaken our hands."

"Maybe it's better though," Charles said as the strange figure rowed out into the Sea of Time. "At least he doesn't seem to miss us so much."

"Yes," Susan said. "I guess there's that." She turned to her brother. "He gave Iacob the locket, you know."

Charles blinked his eyes in surprise. "The—*amulet*? Why would he do that? He needs it to get back to us."

Uncle Farley put a hand on his niece and nephew's shoulders. "I think the locket is only a piece of it, and perhaps not even the most important piece. I think there are things he has to do first. He will come back when he wants. When it's the right time."

A few days ago one or the other of the Oakenfeld children might have protested. What could be more important than family? But they had seen so much in such a short time, had come to realize how full and rich the world was, how much more than any one person, any one family. Still, Charles felt there was nowhere he'd rather be at that moment than with his sister and uncle. He only wished his brother—his little brother, the brother he knew—was there with them.

Apparently, Susan felt the same.

"Uncle Farley," she said, "I think it's time we went home, don't you? A slice of pie," she said with a small grin. "Then home."

"A capital suggestion," Uncle Farley said, rubbing his stomach. "And who knows what adventures are still in store for us. It's only the beginning of the summer, after all."

But Susan surprised him. "No," she said. "I want to go *home*." She looked at her uncle and her brother. "I think I've seen enough, at least for now."

At his sister's words, Charles thought of Tankort and all the other Wendat. He had looked them up in a book in Uncle Farley's library and discovered that they had in fact perished in the French and Indian War—that even though a truce was declared, the Iroquois had tracked them down and killed all but a tiny party, who legend said had taken to their canoes and disappeared into the waves. He nodded.

"Yeah," he said. "Me too." He turned to Uncle Farley. "Let's go home."

EPILOGUE

1492: The Captain and the Cabin Boy

HE SAILED UNDER THE SPANISH flag. Ferdinand and Isabella, who paid for his journey, and were to use the profits of his discovery to drive the last of the Jews and Moors from a newly unified Spain, knew him as Colón. In his own language he was known as Colombo, but English speakers, who were also to benefit greatly from his voyages, remember him as Columbus. Cristóbal, Cristoforo, or Christopher: he is the man credited with discovering the new world, even though he arrived five hundred years after Erik the Red settled his family at Brattahlid, Greenland, and fifteen or thirty thousand years after the first Eurasians walked across the frozen waters of the Bering Strait, and didn't stop walking until they had settled every square foot of the new continents, from the Aleuts to Tierra del Fuego, from Ellesmere to Piura, from the Golden Gate to Hispaniola. History remembers also that the great captain wasn't looking for new lands, but rather a new route to India. But in this too the history books do not quite have the story correct.

"Land!"

The cry from the crow's nest of the *Santa Maria* doesn't wake the dozing captain in his berth belowdecks. He has been at sea for forty days. Water and food rationing have been in effect for the past two weeks, and days earlier, the *Pinta* deserted in the middle of the night. The nimble *Niña* ranges far afield from its lumbering command ship, as if it too is eager to abandon this fool's quest. By now it has become clear there is no route to India, only water and water and more endless, empty water. Some have even heard whisperings that India was never the goal. That the captain is looking for something . . . new.

The only thing that keeps them from mutiny is the fact that they do not have enough food to return to a known port.

Now a dozen weary sailors make their way to the bow. They do not trust the cabin boy high on the mast. In the first place, he is not Spanish or Italian, but hails from some barbaric northern land. And, as well, he spends an inordinate amount of time with the captain, despite the fact that he is the lowest-ranking member of the crew. For the past four days, however, he has

been up in the crow's nest, insisting they will reach their destination soon, and most of them believe the hot sun and lack of
adequate food and water have addled his wits, until his eyes
have made up the thing they want to see. But because there is
nothing else to do, they too shade their eyes with their hands,
and squint across water that has been empty for so long most
doubt they will ever see land again.

It's true the water looks different. Bluer than the dark
green depths that have surrounded them for more than a
month. And Cook insisted he saw a bird two days ago. Half the
crew disbelieved him, the other half thought it had been an
albatross, an omen not of land but of death.

Suddenly someone points. There, in the distance!

Could it be? The thinnest green line separates sky and sea,
which are nearly the same color. Someone calls for the glass.
More sailors run to the stern. Could it really be . . . land?

The captain hears the sailors' tread creaking on the planks
above his stateroom. He pulls a pillow over his head. He
knows he should restore order, but he too has come to doubt
the reality of the dream he is chasing. How could he have let a
strange boy convince him that a new world lay on the western
edge of the Atlantic, let alone convince him that *he* could find
it, that his name would become the most famous in sailing history, save perhaps that of Odysseus?

The captain met his informant six years ago on a trip to the
Norwegian colony of Iceland, when the young Italian had

been little more than a cabin boy himself. The boy, still a teenager, had come up to him as if he already knew of the desire for discovery that lay in the Italian mariner's heart. Without preamble, the Icelander launched into stories of limitless lands to the west. Of cities to rival Rome and Cordoba, rivers that could drink the Nile and Danube, of plants and animals that were sweeter, stronger, stranger than anything previously known. In fact, many of the men in the Reykjavik taverns talked of western lands, although their descriptions sounded far less hospitable than the boy made them out to be. But the boy had one thing they did not: a tiny golden locket of a craftsmanship more delicate than anything else in all of Iceland. It was possible that the boy had stolen it from one of the European ships that occasionally docked in Reykjavik, but the boy insisted it came from the new world. As proof of its distinctiveness, he allowed the young Italian to look inside the locket. There were the most remarkable miniatures he had ever seen. A boy and a girl, the former wearing spectacles with strange, thick rims, the latter short-haired and staring at him with the most assertive eyes he'd ever seen on a female. Hills lay in the background, empty sky stretched overhead. The young Italian had never heard of a painting so small, so realistic, let alone seen one. He had asked if the new world the boy spoke of was filled with objects as remarkable as this one.

The boy's smile was mysterious and full of promise.

"It will be."

Now there is a knock on the captain's stateroom. The door creaks open, and the captain pulls the pillow off his head to see his cabin boy leaning into the room. His hair—pale brown, unlike the dark-haired Italians and Spaniards who make up the rest of the crew—is pulled back into a ponytail, and his skin is bronzed from the sun, which has grown relentless in recent days.

"Eh? What is it, boy?" Still half asleep, the captain blanks on the cabin boy's name. It is an odd word—the captain is quite sure the boy made it up when he left Iceland. "Quoin," he says now, not sitting up. "What is it?"

"Captain," Quoin says, "we're here."

Charles's Glossary of Affected Words

baluster: No two ways about it, "baluster" is just a fancy word without much use, since all it refers to is a post—in this case, the post of the railing that runs around the poop deck.

congregant: A congregant is a member of a congregation. A congregation is the collective name for the members of any organization, but nowadays it is almost always used to refer to the members of a church—which is how Charles is using it too.

coniferous, deciduous, chlorophyll: Charles, being a bit of a science geek (well, more than a bit, really) knows that "coniferous" and "deciduous" refer to the two different kinds of trees. Coniferous trees are evergreens—i.e., the ones with needles that stay green all year long. Deciduous trees have leaves that fall to the ground each autumn. If you live in the city, as I do, I doubt that means much to you, but if you live in the suburbs or the country, then you've probably helped your parents rake fallen leaves into a huge pile and then jumped in them, which is fun as long as the leaves are dry and springy, but a little gross if they're wet and slimy. Oh, and chlorophyll is the stuff that makes leaves green, and that also helps plants turn sunlight into energy through a process called photosynthesis. I don't know how that works, myself. Charles probably does, but since it doesn't really have much to do with the story—and since this glossary entry has gone on plenty long enough—I think we'll skip it for now.

evanescent: "Evanescent" is a very pretty word (if I do say so myself) that has a very specific meaning: it refers to something that is seen in the very act of disappearing. I suppose I could've just written "fading away" or something like that, but as I said, "evanescent" is such a pretty word . . .

faggot: A faggot refers to sticks that have been tied together to make them easier to carry. See, that's easier to say, isn't it?

fealty: Someone or something, either Karl Olaf or Charles's translation charm, was working a bit too hard here, because "fealty" just means "loyalty." It specifically means "loyalty to your king," which is what Karl Olaf likes to think he is, so I guess it was Karl Olaf who was reaching for the fancy word, not the translation charm.

hubris: See, the danger of acting like a smarty-pants is that someone who's even smarter than you will come along and make you realize that no one likes to be talked down to—which is what President Wilson is doing to Charles when he accuses him of having hubris. "Hubris" means "excessive or obnoxious pride"—as in the kind of pride that goeth before a fall—and President Wilson could've just said "excessive pride," but then he wouldn't have shown Charles that he still knew a few things Charles didn't.

infinitesimal: A big word with a small definition. No, really: it means "small." If you want to get technical, it means "really crazy small," but in general it just means "small."

men-at-arms: Soldiers. Get it? Men with arms (not the kind that grow out of your shoulders, but, like, weapons). That's all: soldiers.

Nordseta: The Nordseta was an annual hunt the Greenland

Vikings, who lived on the southern tip of the island, used to take up the northwest coast each year. They would hunt things like polar bears and arctic foxes and gyrfalcons and other things that have white fur or plumage, such things being prized commodities in their society, and also back in Europe. ("Nord" is the old Norse word for "north," if that helps.)

rune: A rune is a character in one of the alphabets used by various civilizations a long time ago—from, say, the third century all the way to the thirteenth. They look kind of like pictures, but to the people who used them, they looked like letters—or, more accurately, words, since a rune usually referred to a specific thing, and not just a sound, like the letters A, B, C, etc.

sentient: You mostly hear people use the word "sentient" when they're speculating about whether there might be life on other planets, and whether that life is like humans—namely, able to think. Which is what "sentient" means. It's how we distinguish ourselves from animals, who—as far as we know, anyway—aren't able to think, although I myself think President Wilson might have a thing or two to say about that.

subliminal: Oh, Charles. He really shouldn't tease Susan for the way she talks when he uses words like "subliminal," huh?

"Subliminal" means, literally, "below the threshold of conscious perception," which is so complicated it requires a definition in and of itself. Basically what it means is that there are some things your regular senses—sight, hearing, smell, etc.—can't pick up consciously, but some other part of your brain that you're not really aware of *can*, the idea being that this information is stored somewhere, and you just have to figure out how to find it. If only the brain came with Google. Who knows what we'd find in those subliminal archives?

umiaq: First Norse; now Qaanaaq. You've probably heard of (or even seen) a kayak, which is a small boat invented by the various peoples who lived in the North American Arctic. The umiaq is another boat, only it's much bigger, and not covered like a kayak. In fact, it's a lot like a big canoe. Except they called it an umiaq.

vitrify: To vitrify something means to turn it into glass, usually by making it really, really, *really* hot. (No, you can't stick something in your oven and turn it into glass: it'll just catch fire, so DON'T DO IT!) If you've ever taken a pottery class, you've vitrified clay when you put it in the kiln and fired it, but some things in nature also get that hot, like sand when it's struck by lightning, or the lava that comes out of volcanoes. Hot. Really, really hot.

winsome: Although it looks like a typo (win some, lose some?) "winsome" actually means "to be charming," in the way that children are said to be charming. Do you ever think of yourself as charming, let alone winsome? I doubt it—this is clearly one of those words coined by adults who don't remember what it's like to be a kid.

ziggurat: A ziggurat is a pyramid, but a very specific kind of pyramid. When you hear the word "pyramid," you probably think of the famous ones in Egypt that have nice smooth triangular sides. But a ziggurat is built in a series of levels, or terraces, each of which is smaller than the one below, so that the silhouette looks a bit like a staircase. The Mayan pyramids were often built in ziggurat form, as were many temples throughout the Middle East.

DALE PECK

is the author of *Drift House: The First Voyage* and several highly acclaimed books for adults, including *What We Lost* and *Hatchet Jobs*. Currently at work on a book for teens, Dale lives in New York City.

Learn more about Dale
and the Drift House voyages at
www.drifthouse.com